THE GOOD
MESSENGER

THE GOOD MESSENGER

A NOVEL BY
JOHN SIMMONS

Urbane
PUBLICATIONS

urbanepublications.com

First published in Great Britain in 2018 by Urbane Publications Ltd
Suite 3, Brown Europe House, 33/34 Gleaming Wood Drive,
Chatham, Kent ME5 8RZ
Copyright © John Simmons, 2018

A CIP catalogue record for this book is available from the British Library.

ISBN 978-1-911583-88-2
MOBI 978-1-911583-89-9

Design and Typeset by Julie Martin
Cover by David Carroll & Co

Printed and bound by 4edge UK

Urbane
PUBLICATIONS

urbanepublications.com

History is not the past.
It is the present.
We carry our history with us.

James Baldwin, *I am not your negro*

The past is a foreign country: they do things
differently there.

LP Hartley, *The Go-Between*

Pure memory remains as elusive as a bar of wet soap.

John Le Carré, *The Pigeon Tunnel*

What's past is prologue.

William Shakespeare, *The Tempest*

For my grandparents:

Harry Branch 1886–1917
and Jessie Branch 1887–1972

1917

PROLOGUE

Even the gods needed a messenger. Ask Hermes, he'll tell you it's a divine calling. Messenger, courier. The poor sap who runs the lines between officers who have no offices. A runner, legman, stringer. Just for liaison, they said, not dangerous.

That was me with the battle order. I was nippy even in the mud of the trench, even in those big boots when the shells were kicking in. Private Tree was famous for just avoiding trouble. Over the top you go, boys, I'll stay here with the Captain.

The sniper's bullet took the Captain out, before he had time to read that scrap of paper. Was he following orders when he slid down the steep side of the trench, like a boy in a playground game, and crumpled at my feet? There was a bloody red hole where his nose had been, and I stood there holding out the message in my hand. The paper was splattered with mud and blood, his eyes could never have read it.

•

Iris didn't want to read the message. She dreaded having to pass it on to those who would have a deeper love than hers for this fallen soldier.

Of course she knew the news anyway. She could tell it from the postman's craggy face. It was clear he had delivered this message before to different women with different names but the same spelling of death.

'Thank you," she murmured. The postman touched the peak of his cap and retreated from the outburst that would come from deeper within. Not from her, though. She held herself together.

"Mother." That was the most difficult part, she had never grown accustomed to calling this distant woman by such an assumed name. *My husband,* she might go on to say. No. *Your son is dead.*

She was surprised at the calmness of the reception. Like the silence after a shell-burst, just a ringing in the ears.

•

When this bloody war is over, what shall we do? I was relying on Teddy to come back and lead the bank in better times. His desk with the blotting pad on the polished wood surface, and with the telegram on top of that, gave no answer at first.

Then it suggested a letter, which he wrote in blue ink with his fountain pen. Just a few lines that would convey the layers of a father's grief behind the soft despair of his upper lip. He stiffened enough to ring the bell for the messenger boy and Tommy slid quietly into the room. He was only 14 but would rather have carried a rifle to battle than a letter to a posh house.

Tommy's time would come but Teddy's had gone. "I'm very sorry," he said to the grieving father. His boss was buttoning his coat over his suit, knowing that for the sake of appearances, as well as mourning, he could be permitted to take the afternoon off.

"Is there a message, sir?"

He shook his head, not trusting his words to the exposure of speech. He rested a trembling hand on Tommy's head with a touch that seemed paternal even as he slipped the letter into his jacket.

•

Unable to face the scene in prospect at home, seeing only the certainty of blackness there, he met the gaze of the girl leaning in the Soho doorway. Her smile offered the temptation of a present kind of comfort, if not understanding. Who would understand the mind of a father in his fifties who has just suffered bereavement? She would not, but face to face she would look into his eyes as if there were no shame or blame in corporal relief. There was no need to talk so he cried a little, from pain or pleasure, she would never know for certain.

Afterwards, buttoning himself up again, he took out two 10 shilling notes. He asked the girl to deliver a different kind of note to his home address. He took the letter from his pocket, and wrote 'IRIS, 23 Langham Gardens, Chelsea' on the envelope in his best tombstone lettering.

He made for the river that was already thickening like tar in the gathering gloom of November. He would slip quietly down the steps into water that was not at this stage quite icy enough to change his mind.

•

Edna looked in the mirror that was propped up behind the washbasin. She wanted to apply some fresh lipstick before heading home. Then she remembered the letter she had been paid to deliver.

Shall I just post it? Her conscience wouldn't allow that as she had been paid in advance for this service, and she felt the obligation of the man's request. She checked the address – it would take her out of her way, but it felt like a duty to discharge. After all, she had been paid handsomely by the man whose tears had aroused her pity or perhaps her gratitude.

She took the bus and got off near the river, with Battersea on the opposite bank. A tugboat sounded a sad note in the background, pulling its tarpaulin-covered cargo towards the sea. Edna turned into the street and stopped outside the large house, checking the number, then looked at the three storeys, the white stucco and the double-fronted door in some wonder, some resentment. She noticed that the curtains were black as if in mourning, allowing little light to seep out from the inside. *Do what you came for.* She walked up the steps to post the envelope through the letterbox but the door opened inwards before she could do that. With the hallway light behind her it was hard to see the woman's face but Edna heard disapproval radiating from the servant's voice: "I'll take that."

The door closed and she walked away into the drizzle that had just begun. She decided to walk home even though she would get soaked. She had anger to walk off; perhaps the rain would wash it away.

PART ONE

1912

1

SATURDAY

good good good goodgoodgood. Picking up steam and speed. *Be a good boy.* His mother's words chuffed along in his ears as the train forged through the fields and woods of the Kent countryside. *Be a good boy be a good boy be a good boy.* The train whistle seemed to affirm his determination to do his best. *Yes. Yes.*

The boy pulled his cap tighter down on his head, leaving no hair visible, and he stood up as the train rattled into the station. It was Tommy Shepherd's first trip away by himself, and he wanted his mother to be proud of him. There would be reports sent home, for sure: *Tommy tried hard, he did his best.* He hoped for nothing more, dreaded anything less.

The steam was puffing from the locomotive's chimney and swirling like tobacco smoke down the length of the platform. Behind the platform, beyond the white fence, past the sign saying LUCKHURST, the wood was dense with heavy-leaved trees. The wood looked impenetrable and Tommy's heart felt weighed down by the fear he had felt last year when seeing the sea for the first time. The sheer immensity of what was unknown to him, how would he ever know? The guard blew his whistle, waved his flag, and the train started to pull away in a billowing cloud of steam, away from Luckhurst and on to the next halt down the line.

At the age of nine he could be forgiven for nervousness at the prospect of strangers. *Be a good boy.* His mother's voice in his head urged him down the platform to the exit gate.

"You must be the boy," said a man all in grey; grey suit, grey hat with a peak.

Tommy looked at him, wondering if he would be allowed to dislike this man or would that be going against the 'good manners' placed upon him as an expectation. Because first impressions were that this man disliked him, so why should he not return that immediate antipathy?

"What's your name, son?" the man asked. "I mean, what do they call yer?"

Tommy could not be comforted by a roughness of accent so like his own even if that was the man's intention. Oh, he was conscious of his own voice but how was he supposed to know better? He did not really understand why, but he did know that he would be expected to talk as nicely as he could to these strangers. He knew because his mother had told him so. But this stranger seemed no better than him and this was puzzling.

"Well? Cat got your tongue?" the grey man persisted.

"What's it t' you?" the boy spat out. A flush of irritated surprise crossed the man's features, raising his mother's words to the surface of the boy's consciousness again. "Me name's Tommy."

"Well, Tommy, you're gonna have to watch yourself. Mrs H'll never put up with rudeness. Just foller me and you'd best keep quiet."

Suits me, thought Tommy, struggling with the size of his suitcase and the deadening weight of expectations. Fortunately he did not have to walk far, just the few yards to the black motor car parked alongside the station.

"Get in! Give us that." The man stowed Tommy's case in the luggage space next to the driver's seat.

"In this?" Tommy's eyebrows were raised high.

Understanding crossed his face like a breeze passing through summer leaves, and left a smile trailing behind. A sound like "Cor" escaped his lips.

•

When Tommy had settled into the back seat, the man turned the starting handle at the front of the car. The engine roared and then subsided into a smooth ticking; the driver slid into the front seat and turned his head. "All right, lad. We'd better get on, let's be pals, you and me, we're too alike not to. You can call me Rodgers."

Tommy just smiled, smelling the leather of the seats. It was the first time he'd stepped inside a motor car and he wanted to enjoy the ride. So he kept quiet as the car moved forward and turned right into a lane with hedgerows on either side that soon gave way to trees dense with shadow. But at this moment Rodgers interested him more.

"How'd you get to be a driver?" To make himself heard above the noise of the engine, Tommy stood up to position himself just behind Rodgers' shoulder.

"It's easy. Anyway, I'm the *chauffeur*."

"What's a *showfer*?" Tommy was a good reader, his mother had always encouraged him, but he only knew words properly when he had seen them written down. *Is it spelt like that?*

"It's a Frenchie word. Means a driver."

"So why use it? Ain't the English good enough?"

"Ah, there's a question, Tommy."

"And what's the answer?"

"I don't know. But the English is generally the best."

This is what Tommy's schooling had taught him. *The English are best.* One of those facts you learnt like the alphabet and sums and all the pink areas on the map of the world. *Knowledge is good – just learn what you need to know.*

School might try to persuade that life is simple, that simple is good, that choices are few, but the drive leading to the house suggested that there might be more to life than he had imagined. This house had more windows than he could count, so there were still things to learn.

•

When the car stopped, he stepped out without waiting for Rodgers to open the door. He walked up the steps towards the portly man in a suit at the top. Tommy recognised him as Mr George Hardinge from a photograph his mother had shown him. She had impressed upon him that he was the man responsible for this visit, he was the one above all for whom he had to be good.

"Thomas, welcome to Hardinge Hall. You are very welcome." He was trying hard but it was obvious that he was not at ease with children, or not with this child.

"Thank you very much, sir. I am pleased to be here." Tommy had practised his first words in his best voice, but had not expected to be called 'Thomas'. No one called him Thomas even if his mother had once told him it was his full name: Thomas George Shepherd.

"Good, good. As I say you are most welcome, Thomas."

"People call me Tommy, sir." Tommy understood enough of adult ways to stop an unwanted habit forming; like making clear to his mother that he would not eat cabbage so there was no point putting it onto his plate.

George Hardinge looked dubious but said "As you wish", and motioned to Rodgers to bring the case up the stairs. "Come in and meet everyone – Tommy." He spoke the name with an air if not of distaste then at least of disappointment.

Following Mr Hardinge, Tommy walked through into the hallway that was dominated by a huge stone staircase. His eyes opened wide at the scale of everything. Paintings of men in old-fashioned clothes hung on the walls, looking at him sternly, and Tommy decided to outstare them, if not now then at some point soon.

This was no time for staring at pictures; there were people standing as if ready for a photographic portrait. Going through one of the double doors, Tommy found himself in company and needing to remind himself of his mother's expectations. He remembered the need for politeness as he was introduced to Mrs Hardinge ("my wife"), Edward ("my son"), Muriel ("my daughter"), another young woman "and this is Iris". It was baffling – so many names, some of them difficult to say, all lined up in a row. A stiffly starched row standing for a boy in clothes worn to softness by frequent use.

"Thomas prefers to be called Tommy," announced Mr Hardinge, feeling the need.

"Good for you, Tommy," said the young man who was the son introduced as Edward. "You must call me Teddy, much better than stuffy old Edward."

"Edward is not stuffy, Edward," said Mrs Hardinge. "It is a name fit for a king so I hardly think you should reject it."

Tommy was relieved that the squabbling over names reduced the formality of the situation. Though Mrs Hardinge, he sensed instinctively, was not one whose formality would ever be reduced below a certain level.

"How do you do?" she held a hand out towards the boy. He had once seen a photograph in a discarded newspaper, a scene in black and white of people who looked like this, so he took his lead from the memory. He held the hand and kissed it.

"Very well, thank you, m'am. How are you?"

There was laughter. As ever, laughter lowers tension, at

least for those who laugh, if not for the laughed-at. George and Teddy thought this was good fun. Mrs Hardinge thought otherwise.

"You should simply reply – How do you do. It is not a question." She looked away from the boy towards her husband as if not wishing to see more. "There is much for us to teach here, George, much for him to learn."

"Indeed. But a little something to eat will not harm the learning. Come, Thomas, we have tea and cakes. I hope you like cake."

He judged that a nod would be permitted, for he was losing his trust in words. They might easily betray him here. The china plate with its blue picture of a garden, and the fork placed upon it, threatened further betrayals. He was rescued by the young man, Edward who would be Teddy, taking him and his plate to the table with cakes laid out upon it. "I think you would like this one," suggested Teddy. "It's filled with strawberry jam and you look like a jam boy to me."

Teddy showed Tommy to a chair and brought him a piece of cake on the plate with the fork.

"Eat up," said Teddy. "Then we'll get you settled in."

Tommy looked at the cake. He was hungry as he had long ago eaten the sandwich provided by his mother, almost as soon as the train had pulled out of Charing Cross station. The cake looked tempting so he picked it up and bit into it.

"Is that good?" asked Teddy.

Tommy mumbled agreement with his mouth full.

"Does he know manners?" Mrs Hardinge muttered to herself and the room at large. "No, of course not."

No manners. Tommy bristled at the unfairness of the accusation, and determined to prove that it was not true. But he had no idea how to go about that.

"It's all right, eat up. I'll show you the ropes," said Teddy. "We want to make sure you have a good time."

What is a good time? Tommy thought it might involve not being where he was. He hated being the centre of attention and, sensing this, Teddy started encouraging his sister and the young woman to get themselves served.

"Come on, Muriel, Iris. What will you have?"

The maid, who seemed to have no name, brought tea and cake to the others. Tommy sank back into the relative obscurity of his chair but he could still overhear conversations from other parts of the room.

"Why are we doing this, George?" asked Mrs Hardinge.

"It's our duty, Catherine. Perhaps our Christian duty. The boy's poor and deserving."

"He's a ragamuffin. The ragamuffin child of your office cleaner."

"Which means I must set an example. He can be brought on. We can make him into a good boy because he deserves our favour."

"Why? You have never explained – why this boy? There are many needy children of the poor."

George adjusted the collar that he wore even on this summer day of domestic leisure. It allowed him to display the beard that gave him a more regal air, even to wave his hand dismissively as he had seen the king do.

"His mother has given the firm good service. For more than ten years. It's a simple act of charity."

"Charity? Do you dress your case with a Christian word?"

"Love, if you prefer. Though you rarely express that word."

Mrs Hardinge lifted a piece of cake on her fork. Then lowered it to sip her tea instead.

"The boy will be bored," she said. "Idle minds make mischief."

"We will make sure that he is occupied. We will feed his mind as well as his stomach, and that will be a good deed for us all to share."

Tommy focused on the last mouthful of his cake, keeping his eyes away from adult attention. But not his ears.

"Time to show you your room, Tommy. Rodgers has taken up your suitcase so let's go and take a look."

Tommy got to his feet, surreptitiously wiping his hands on the flannel of his short trousers. As he followed Teddy out of the room, people made noises that tried to be friendly. "The library later," called out George Hardinge to his son.

•

Tommy's bedroom was on the first floor. It was bigger than the flat where he lived with his mother in Covent Garden. He felt intimidated not excited by the difference. It was difficult to concentrate on what Teddy was telling him about the wardrobe, the bed with the white sheets, the chamber pot underneath, the desk, the jug of hot water in the washing bowl, the lavatory opposite.

"I'll leave you to sort yourself out, Tommy. This is your room so no one else will come in – unless you ask. And the maid will tidy up and clean, of course."

I must keep the room tidy then, thought Tommy.

"I wager your mother would like to receive a letter from you too. Just to say you have arrived. There's paper and an envelope on the desk, and we can post it for you. We don't want her worrying, do we?"

Teddy left him to himself, saying that he would come back in an hour to take him to 'the old man' in the library. It was all very puzzling. Tommy looked out of the window at the lawn that seemed impossibly green – it had been unusually wet that August. Then he sat at the desk to write his letter home to his mother, finding it hard to find the right words or even enough words. The task was made no easier by the scratchy pen that he had to dip into the inkpot. His words were spattered inkily onto the page but he managed to write the address on the envelope more legibly.

He needed to wash the ink stains from his fingertips so he poured warm water from the jug into the washing bowl, working up a lather with the soap. It seemed a way of putting his other life aside, at least for now, becoming used to the surroundings of the room that was his private area of this grand house.

•

At 5 o'clock Teddy came to take him down to the library where George Hardinge was waiting for him. After a few pleasantries enquiring about his room, which Tommy answered with reluctant monosyllables, their conversation moved to a more serious level. The older man inevitably had to lead but he spoke slowly, as if the conversation was difficult for him.

"Tommy, I am pleased that you are here. Very pleased. Your mother is, she has always been, a good woman and I recognise that. I wish to help her. By which I mean I wish to help you. Is that understood?"

Tommy nodded, though he did not really understand. He wondered if he was about to be told off. *What for?*

"Good. I wish to take a personal interest in you. In your development. You can become better, you can rise above this, the role that life might seem to have assigned you. With a little help. My help, of course."

Hardinge paused, staring at Tommy who was staring at his own feet.

"It's a matter of education. Education matters most of all. But the accomplishment that unlocks education is reading. And writing. Because the two must, must feed, feed each other. This is why I wished to see you in this room, the library."

He spread his arms, displaying the room around him with its shelves of books, before continuing.

"Do you read, Tommy? Good. And you can write, you know all your letters obviously because you wrote to your mother?" Tommy nodded at moments that seemed appropriate. "Then I have a suggestion to make. Actually it's more than a suggestion. I *insist* you must read and write while you are here."

"What if I don't want to?"

"You will disappoint me. More importantly you will disappoint your mother."

Tommy felt he had been manoeuvred into a position against his wishes. Though he could hardly find an objection. His mother, reading, writing, these were things he loved; but was he being asked for books to fill a gap where his mother should be? He was missing her already.

"This room, the contents of this room, are at your disposal during your time here. I would wish you to take advantage of this opportunity. I am going to give you something that will enable you to do that. I wish only to do you good."

Tommy's heart sank because he suspected that their views of the world might be far apart. It struck him that the most simple of things – the most common words, for example – might conceal the most complicated, confusing ideas. *Good. Who says? What's good for you might not be good for me.*

"First, though, I wish you to indulge yourself in books. Do you have books at home, Tommy? I think not. But books are necessary for a civilised life. I know you can read, and the more you read, the better you will become. Books are the fountain of knowledge, the source of our morality. We must all read to improve ourselves."

George Hardinge paused to study the blank face of the boy standing in front of him. Tommy licked his dry lips, his tongue sliding from one side to the other of his mouth.

"I think you understand. I believe you are a good boy, a clever boy. So we must make you even more so. See here – on these shelves – books of many kinds. You must feel free to explore them. Many of them you will not understand – yet – but in time…I have hopes for you. For the time being, though, I have selected a few books – books that I believe you will benefit from reading, and I have placed them on this table. I wish you to take a look, browse through them, take your time – then choose two that you will read while you are here with us. So come, here are the books."

Tommy slid off the chair where he had perched a little uncomfortably. There was no escaping; he felt his mother watching. On the table were half a dozen books. They all looked thick and heavy. The few books in his school were all slim and battered; these books felt and smelt new. He looked at the outsides, picking each one up like an ancient object, afraid that he might damage them. He read the titles on the cover bindings: *Great Expectations, The Water-babies, The Boys' Book of Science, Everlasting Things.* They look difficult. *The History of the World for Children.* Perhaps. *The Wind in the Willows.*

"It's very hard, sir," he decided to say. "Which ones do you think are good?"

"It's not for me to choose. It's for you. Open up one or two, start to read."

He opened the nearest book, the one that looked smallest. *The Wind in the Willows* by Kenneth Grahame, he read. He wished there might have been pictures but he began reading and the scene sounded a little familiar, a little exciting: "They reached the carriage-drive of Toad Hall to find, as the Badger had anticipated, a shiny new motor car, of great size, painted a bright red (Toad's favourite colour), standing in front of the house." He was not sure of every word but he understood the general meaning, and it connected with his own arrival at this place earlier that day.

"Is this Toad Hall?" he asked. "This house, I mean. Is that why you have this book?"

"No, Tommy, I have it because it is a good book. And also, perhaps, because I know Mr Grahame a little. The clever man who wrote it, I have met him once or twice."

"And you liked him, so you got his book."

"Not quite like that. But you are not completely wrong. I think though that you would enjoy that book. Take that and choose one more."

Tommy had a good feeling about the book he had chosen so he was not that keen to choose another. He picked up the *History of the World* because it was underneath *The Wind in the Willows*.

"Good," said Mr Hardinge, "you have chosen. You may take the books out of the library to read wherever you wish. The drawing room, the parlour, or read here in the library, of course. In your bedroom, if you wish. But I will ask you about the books, to find out how you are taking to them. I'm sure you will learn a lot, not least many new words. Here, by the way, is a dictionary, in which you may look up words that you do not understand."

Tommy nodded. He had no idea what a dictionary was. He simply wanted to escape. Adult conversation was hard and he did actually want to read some of this book about Toad Hall.

"One more thing before you go." He pointed at the books Tommy was holding. "*That* is reading. We also want you to improve your writing. Do you write much?" A shake of the head. "Well, you must. A letter home to your mother at least once every three days. And this – this is something I have for you. Or two things really, though they are both the same."

George Hardinge walked around the desk and pulled open the drawer. He took out two notebooks, identical in size, one with a black cloth cover, the other green. Each had gold blocked lettering on the cover spelling out HARDINGE HALL. Each had a small pencil tucked into the spine.

"These are for you, Tommy. You may take these home with you when you return to your mother. It will be good for her to see what progress you will have made in your time here. This one – this black one – I suggest should be for you to keep a diary. You see it is lined. Write down what you do each day. Keep it to yourself, show no one except your mother. So put nothing in it that you would not wish her to see. Just as I hope you will say nothing that you would not wish her to hear. Understood?"

"Good. This second notebook is for you to use in a different way. It will be a good way for you to get to know all the members of the household a little better. Take the green notebook, ask one person a day, let us say, and they can write something to you in your own notebook. Something – perhaps a word or two of advice – something that will be of value to you, something to remember afterwards."

Tommy found it strange to be told about 'afterwards'. It lifted his spirits a little to have confirmed that his stay was definitely seen as limited in time. Two weeks had seemed a long time away from his mother, but here already it was within reach.

"Thank you, sir," he said, sensing that he had found the

moment to make his exit – at least for a short time. He backed out of the room, carrying the two books and the notebooks. Inside his bedroom, he opened the green notebook and read the inscription on the first page, hand-written in black ink:

To Thomas George Shepherd

God watches over you. Do not give Him cause for disappointment. Behave well so that your parents may be proud of you.

May this notebook become a lifelong source of edification and recollection.

Your friend and patron
George T.E. Hardinge

2

SUNDAY

Tommy had never experienced insomnia before. So it took him by surprise to wake up and open his eyes to a darkness so dense that he found it frightening. Darkness and silence, like hands clamped over his eyes and ears. At home, in his own bed, he was always reassured by faint gleams of light and the low sounds of a city showing it was alive. Here, alone in a strange room in the countryside, there was no light, no sound, no sleep.

He concentrated and he found that by looking and listening he could make out shapes around him that must be furniture and he could hear sounds that might be the house itself creaking in its sleep. The concentration made him more wakeful, and the more wakeful he became the more his eyes and ears adjusted. He heard sounds outside that must be animals in the surrounding woods. Was that screech an owl? Was that barking a dog? He slipped out of bed and parted the curtains at the nearby window. He had never seen such a bright moon, never seen such stars.

Back in bed he lay under the sheet, remembering. He had survived his first day, not always comfortably, but at least it was done. Downstairs the grandfather clock in the hallway chimed twice. He had no wish for the night to pass quickly because daytime would return him to this world where he was alone with strangers. He remembered the dinner and its torment of cutlery. What were all those different knives, forks and spoons for? So many of them – yet they made it harder to eat, particularly under the gaze of Mrs Hardinge.

These strangers were strange. He did not like them. He feared he would never satisfy Mr Hardinge's expectations of him, and that it would be impossible to win Mrs Hardinge's acceptance. Teddy was possibly a friend, if only for the duration of this stay – at least he attempted to be nice. Teddy's younger sister Muriel was a problem because he found it hard to say her name, and she was at an age when disdain for children had to be expressed – at that cusp between childhood and near-adulthood. The other girl was the greatest unknown. Iris seemed as reluctant to be there as he was but he did not know why. Perhaps she might be his ally? But why would he need an ally? Why should he think in such war-like terms?

He became aware of the objects in the room taking more definite forms. The wardrobe was still very dark but he knew it would also be dark in daylight, towering and heavy and varnished to a brown that was almost black. It looked so forbidding that he had decided not to use it, not even to open it in case he released something frightening inside. He had placed his few clothes in the drawers of the sideboard that Teddy had called a chiffonier.

He drew the curtains with a succession of short tugs that gradually let in the dim daylight filtering through grey clouds. His window had a view across the wide lawn that was bounded by the trees on the left and the driveway on the right. He realised that the creature in the half-light on the lawn was a rabbit and he smiled because he had never seen a wild rabbit before. He wanted to see a rabbit close up, perhaps to stroke it.

Aware of the dawn chorus of birds that seemed to be greeting him, he remembered his favourite hymn that they sang in school and he hummed 'Morning has broken' to himself, as if for courage. He found himself attracted by all that he saw and heard, emboldened to put on his clothes, tie his shoe laces and find his way down the stairs into the world outside.

As he walked down the broad staircase, he was startled to a halt by the sudden chiming of the grandfather clock. He stopped, listened, it struck five times. He carried on into the silence that followed, then stood on tip toes to open the main door to the outside.

"Hello, Tommy," said Mrs Rodgers the cook, on her way to the outside kitchen door. "You're up bright 'n early."

"Thought I'd have a walk," he said.

"Well, don't go far. I'm just startin' breakfast."

He wanted to see a rabbit but all he now saw on the lawn were scattered piles of earth, as if dug up and abandoned. Later he would learn to associate these with the mole in the book he was reading. The moon of night-time had disappeared, hidden behind the veil of clouds that had been drawn across the sky, grey light with uniform clouds and a dewy drizzle in the air. As if there were a tide in the sky, light grew brighter, a gentle wave rising. As he walked across the grass, the air became less damp and his eyes gazed on the hint of a golden glow that was feeling its way into the lowest clouds beyond the wood, above the trees, guiding him, it seemed, towards the sanctuary of a garden refuge, in silence, for the birds no longer had a song that he was aware of.

On the edge of the wood was a cottage with white walls. A cottage but quite a substantial house, at least in his eyes. Curious, he pushed open the wooden gate and stepped through into the garden. The garden was dense with plants and flowers, very few of which Tommy could identify, apart from the roses. There were no gardens where he lived, and the public parks were dominated by trees and rough grass and shrubs that did not flower. He was not accustomed to the scent of flowers; these flowers whose names were yet to be revealed as hollyhocks, salvias, pansies, anemones, marigolds, lavender, poppies. The flowers tumbled over each other and wafted a perfume stronger than he had ever smelled before. The aroma was heady, the scent of flowers heavy in the still air, as he sat down on the wooden bench under a drowsy canopy of wisteria, flanked by rose bushes. Within seconds he fell asleep.

He was hardly aware of being lifted by Rodgers and carried inside the cottage, up the stairs to a bedroom where he was laid on the bed, falling deep into sleep. When he woke up he saw Rodgers sitting on a chair at his bedside, watching over him.

"All right, young feller?" he asked. "You was tired." Rodgers' mouth broke into a half-smile at the corners.

Tommy rubbed the sleep and the dream from his eyes, the dream that had held him in such fleeting contentment but was now forgotten.

·

Tommy realised he had to make up for behaviour that was seen as not quite right. He had drawn too much attention to himself and that had never been his intention; for his own comfort he needed to return to a state of relative invisibility. There had been too much consternation at his return, carried through the doors by Rodgers.

"He'll do, sir. Just needs a breakfast."

So Tommy was sat down with a big plate of sausages, bacon, eggs and fried bread. It was true, he was hungry, and he was left alone to eat the food without judging eyes. Afterwards he was told that they would be attending church so he was not to wander off again.

Eventually they gathered in the driveway. They lined up in an order that everyone seemed to know, with Mr and Mrs Hardinge at one end, flanked by the family with Tommy attached, then the servants in descending seniority with Albert the gardener's apprentice at the rear. Then they set off on foot in procession, keeping close to the road that wound through the woods.

Like schoolchildren they walked in pairs. Tommy was with Muriel who had nothing to say to him, and that suited him well enough. It meant he could eavesdrop on Teddy and Iris who were in front of him. Not that they had much to say to each other, though Teddy tried hard, but Tommy could hardly blame her for a lack of interest in the weather. It was a day of middling heat, with a sky half-filled with clouds, and only the lightest of breezes.

"Perhaps it will rain later."

"Perhaps."

"We will see."

Oh God, said Tommy to himself, as his mother might have. Then realised this might not be the right thought as they entered the village and the church spire came into view, with the bells pealing and summoning them closer. To reach the church they had to pass by the front of The Badger's Arms, the pub by the village green. A young woman, with a cloth in her hand to wipe the wooden bench, called out to them.

"Drop in for a drink afterwards."

The man in the pub doorway looked sharply at her, hissed her name "Rosie" as if she had transgressed. This look was matched by Mrs Hardinge when Teddy called out: "You will both be welcome at church. Why don't you come?" The procession of the Hardinge family crossed the green and filed into the church, where the family occupied the front pews.

Tommy's previous visits to church had always been with the school. Once a week his class would be taken to the service at St Thomas's, and in school assembly the children would close their eyes to pray and respond *Amen*, then sing a hymn while Mrs Pauley hammered away at the piano keys. He quite liked it but it meant little to him. It was simply part of school, and not a subject he and his mother shared in conversations, as they did with reading, writing and arithmetic.

Here, sitting in the front pew, his eyes wandered around the church, taking in the altar with its high gold cross, the pulpit, the stained glass windows through which light streamed in many colours onto the stone pillars. He looked over his shoulders at the congregation, the people of Luckhurst village in their Sunday best suits and dresses, looking no more comfortable than he felt. To his surprise he saw the young woman from the pub, long fair hair now pinned back, finding a place on the pew behind. She was by herself and she smiled at him, causing him to look quickly away. Next to him, Teddy opened up the hymn book, whispering to him "This will be first".

> *All things bright and beautiful*
> *All creatures great and small.*
> *All things wise and wonderful*
> *The Lord God made them all.*

Tommy knew the hymn so his mouth could form the words, even if no one would hear his voice. He preferred listening to others singing and Teddy had a confident voice that carried the tune. It seemed he was the leader of this choir, ready to lead the way at the prompting notes of the organ.

After that, the service became more and more puzzling, and Tommy's thoughts slipped in and out of the maze of meaning formed by the spoken words. The vicar's voice was soporific and Tommy, still short of sleep, found his eyelids drooping till shaken awake by *Amen* and the singing of a second, unfamiliar hymn and words intoned *in the name of the Father, Son and Holy Ghost* his bare knees feeling the rough fabric of the cushion as he knelt under the exhortation *love ye your enemies and do good* listening to what seemed a story whose meaning could not be fathomed *a certain rich man which had a steward* looking round for enlightenment *will anyone explain* this though the priest's eyes sought to lock with those on the front pew but Tommy himself cast his eyes down *spare them, O God, which confess to their faults* to be *righteous* if that is right *to the glory of thy holy name.*

It was time to file out, down the aisle of the church, Mr and Mrs Hardinge leading the way. Tommy felt befuddled, bemused yet strangely exhilarated by the service. He had been struggling to understand many of the words spoken but this left him wishing to understand better. He suspected that the language was a way of creating mystery, of saying you cannot know everything. *Good.* He wanted to know more, to taste the wafer in his mouth and know what these words on his tongue might mean.

"Well, that was jolly, wasn't it?" said Rosie as she followed him out of the dark porch into the strangely bright grey light that filtered through the clouds gathering overhead. Was this addressed to him, was he meant to reply? Rosie had already moved on, beaming a warm smile at the family that Mrs Hardinge attempted to freeze with a stare, but Rosie had swept past, with a swish of her long dress, heading towards The Badger's Arms where her father was standing in the doorway, waiting for the influx from church.

"Insufferable," Mrs Hardinge muttered, though Tommy thought the church's message was about teaching you to deal with suffering.

"Tommy," said Mr Hardinge, "wait here for me. I will walk

with you through the woods back to the house. I must speak with the vicar while the others walk home."

The others seemed to know this arrangement for they had set off and were already in the lane that led to the house. A shadow crossed the ground where the clouds passed the sun. Tommy felt his spirits sink at the prospect of a conversation from which there would be no polite escape.

He stood outside the church, reading the board that displayed the list of services at 'the parish church of St Luke' and the vicar's name 'Rev. Geoffrey Jones'. Much of it was a foreign language to him. He wondered about Eucharist, even Evensong. But his musings were simply to pass the time, and soon he became aware that the clouds had continued to roll in a black mass across the sky. Heavy drops of rain began to fall, like pebbles thrown from above. He had no choice but to retreat inside the shelter of the church. The hollowness of the empty church made him tread silently, not wanting to disturb nor to be noticed by whoever might still be here.

He heard voices from somewhere out of sight. For a brief moment of terror he imagined that this might be the voice of God. It had never occurred before that God might speak to him. But then he realised with disappointment and some anxiety that the voice was Mr Hardinge's, a father no doubt but not God the father. Tommy stayed behind the stone column, able to hear but not to see the two men in dialogue.

"That parable. Tell me, Reverend. You seemed to be addressing it to me."

"Not at all. To everyone."

"Not to quibble. I took it as for me." There was a silence before Mr Hardinge resumed. "You must explain it. Are you calling me a bad steward – or a bad master?"

"Neither. The parable makes no judgements like that. But

it does ask us to think – what do we do? and what do we do with money? Remember 'we cannot do anything that is good without thee'. Money is not ours. It belongs to God. You must think how to use it wisely, as God would wish. Seek his guidance in prayer."

"You think me wealthier than I am. I feel impoverished."

"You are wealthy. In earthly matters. But wealth will buy you no favours in heaven. Yet we live with mammon, we have choices in the way we live."

"So, what should my choice be? To give away my wealth?"

"No. To do good with it."

Puzzled by the silence, Tommy dared to peek around the column where he saw the two men kneeling in prayer. It was his chance to sneak away as quietly as he could. Outside, the summer shower had passed as suddenly as it had arrived. The gravel gleamed wet and there was a green freshness in the air. When Mr Hardinge emerged it seemed as if Tommy had stayed as immobile as one of the gravestones that stood upright on the grass.

"You must be feeling hungry," said Mr Hardinge, as jolly as he had ever been. "Come, I want to show you the way home through the woods."

They walked past the lane then turned left into the trees that bordered the road into the village. Tommy followed in the footsteps of Mr Hardinge, pushing aside branches, trampling the low scrub. "Muddy. But magnificent. This can be your territory, Thomas, or at least your playground. You must feel free to treat this wood as your own – Tommy, I should have said. Force of habit. You have always been Thomas in my mind. Your mother called you that to me." Tommy was relieved that he was not required to join this monologue that the adult was passing off as conversation. "Wonderful trees.

This oak. Horse chestnuts. Beeches. Trees are good for boys to climb, so they say. Boys must be boys. And see here, here is the stream. Certainly not a river, though we have had a great deal of rain. You might see fish, find other animals. I wanted you to see the possibilities of life. God knows, it's hard to see them sometimes. Perhaps harder in the crowded streets of London." Tommy had to walk fast to keep up with the pace of the man who seemed hardly aware of his presence. "You see, it is not far. We shall arrive not long after the others. Food will be on the table soon. But I wanted to show you this wood. It is for you, at least while you are here." The trees were thinning as they drew into sight of the big house and Tommy could see Iris in her white dress, sitting at a table under a parasol. "Time to eat, Iris. Now we have all worked up an appetite."

Dinners, suppers, breakfasts, any mealtimes, were already turning into trials for Tommy. It was not just the need for unfamiliar manners and sometimes unfamiliar food but the agony of conversation. What to say? How to answer? *Not with your mouth full*, he knew that much already, Mrs Hardinge had been insistent. He concentrated on his food, particularly the roast beef and potatoes that he liked, hoping that such concentration would absolve him from the need to be part of any dialogue. But he could listen, and he found some of the conversations surprising. Adults were not, after all, that grown-up, and some of them were hardly any more comfortable than he was. Who could be comfortable in the unsmiling presence of Mrs Hardinge? Not Iris, it seemed. She sat tongue-tied while everyone listened to the painful scrape of her fork on the china plate, a sound that provided no answer to the question.

"Well, no doubt we will find out in your own good time," said Mrs Hardinge in a tone that was almost kind. The question had been about intentions, and Iris was unsure what was intended by the word. She worried that the purpose was to expose her, that the motive might be cruelty, her eyes like those of the squirrel in the woods that Mr Hardinge's stick had swished at earlier. Iris excused herself and retired to her room.

It seemed that Tommy wore a cloak of invisibility, at least in the eyes of the family. He kept his eyes lowered and ate his food as quietly as he could; that way he was unnoticed and the conversation carried on as if he were not there. Perhaps they believed he did not see or hear or feel in the same way that they did. If he did not react, he could stay within his own world and not have to venture into theirs.

"Does he want pudding?" Mrs Hardinge momentarily noticed him but his nod allowed the table conversation to continue. A fly on the wall, a squirrel up the tree, a bird on the branch. Tommy found that he liked this unseen vantage point, it offered him a possibility of secret knowledge, and that might amount to something more useful in time. Besides, what value was there in being part of these conversations? They were pointless and, he sensed, not really honest.

"Mother, I can't ever love her, she doesn't even like me."

"Edward, she is not so foolish as not to like you. She may not love you, but love is never essential."

Teddy flushed with anger. "It matters to me."

"Of course, of course," his father soothed. "There is an advantage in the match. You know that. We simply ask you to try. Give the poor girl a hearing at least — if she'll get up the courage to say anything, that is. I grant she is not easy, she has no natural grace. She is reluctant to connect with your interests. We have yet to discover hers. But, I say again, there is an advantage to your family. The Fakenhams are well-to-do. And I find her rather pretty, to tell the truth."

His wife gave a tut of what might have been agreement or

disbelief; exasperation at the very least, because she hated to have her will thwarted.

"You must do as your father wills," she said evenly, with a look that said 'the matter is closed'. She dipped her spoon into the ice cream sundae that had been set before her, a treat she had allowed as one of her few new enthusiasms. She looked around the table with a hint of contentment, taking in the sight of her husband absorbed in his own thoughts, her son suppressing rebellious feelings, her daughter smiling mischievously to herself. And the young boy licking his spoon.

"We will teach you manners too. We will teach you to speak better while you're here too, Thomas. We will make sure you say 'something' not 'somefink'. Little things but they matter if you are going to get on."

There ended that day's lesson. Tommy went up the stairs to his bedroom with the memory of Mrs Hardinge's mimicry in his ears, her gloating smile before his eyes. It was afternoon and muggy with warmth and rain with a bluebottle buzzing in the background through the many rooms; and the household settled down to doze through the afternoon, all content to escape the wakefulness of being startled into the company of others, sinking into the comfort of white cotton pillows and private reveries.

3

MONDAY

Next day, refreshed by an unexpectedly long sleep, Tommy went down the stairs to breakfast. He had rushed to get ready, feeling a little ashamed to be woken by the chambermaid Susan with the words "Come on, you are a sleepy head". He found everyone else already deep into the ritual of bacon and eggs, tea and toast. Tommy settled down at the far end of the table, hoping for continuing invisibility.

"You must have slept well," Mrs Hardinge accused him down the vista of linen and cutlery.

He gave a nod and stared at the food on his plate. That morning he struggled to get through it. It was not the food. The food was what he liked: sausages, bacon, fried egg, fried bread. If he could just concentrate on eating, he would be fine. But it was torture to be brought into the conversations that limped painfully up and down the table. It was no better that he was seldom included. This meant that he could listen to the others talking and squirm a little inside for the humiliation spread with the appearance of politeness onto the plate of Iris, spooned like sugar into her teacup so that she had to smile and affect acquiescence, if not gratitude.

"It is a lovely day for a walk, Edward. Iris would be interested to see more of the grounds," said Mr Hardinge.

"Not sure I can, father. I have to show Tommy the woods. Otherwise he'll be bored."

"Iris might be bored, too."

"Iris," said Mrs Hardinge. "Are you able to amuse yourself?"

"That is not the point. Iris is our guest and here to spend time with Teddy."

"I suspect she can manage without me."

"No. You are obliged to."

"What about poor Tommy?"

"That is a good point. I will stay here today and spend time with Tommy."

"George, how can you? It is a day for the office in London."

"I will telephone to say I am staying here. This duty is more important."

He went out to the hall where the telephone, an object unfamiliar to Tommy, stood to attention on a polished mahogany table. He listened with curiosity and wonder to Mr Hardinge's voice booming into the mouthpiece and, apparently, being heard by someone thirty miles away in London.

"There, that is settled. I told them to bring forward the quarterly audit. Wanted to make sure they are busy."

Coming back into the room, he ignored the look of disdain on Mrs Hardinge's face and turned to Tommy.

"So, you and I, we have some exploring to do. Go and get ready, and I will meet you at the front entrance in fifteen minutes."

Tommy was ready on time, boots on and knapsack on his back, having been beckoned down into the kitchen by Rodgers for instructions. *Everyone tellin' me what to do, how to do it.* He found it hard to understand why. Why was Mr Hardinge spending time with him? It was as if he felt guilty and needed to make up. *Was it one of those thoughts to keep down, out of sight?*

"No idea, Tommy," said Rodgers. "But make the most of it. He seems to have taken a shine to you."

"Let's start with the walled garden, then we can go through

into the west wood," said Mr Hardinge in the doorway. He was still dressed for a day at the office, in his dark-grey suit and white shirt with Ascot collar and tie, but had simply swapped his usual top hat for a felt country hat with a feather in its black band. This seemed a ridiculous outfit to Tommy but he knew better than to laugh, even when Mr Hardinge completed the outfit with wellington boots.

"You never know. Woods can be muddy. Now, what do you have in your knapsack, Tommy?"

"Mrs Rodgers made me a sandwich in case I get hungry. And a water flask."

"Good. But is that all?" A nod. "Then I think you should go and get your books. A book to read and a book to write in. That will see you through the day and through life."

When Tommy returned, properly equipped with a fuller knapsack, they set off, turning right down the gravel path. The walled garden was a surprise because he had not expected to find people at work, yet here were four men digging, raking, cutting, hoeing. As Mr Hardinge and Tommy walked down the path through the vegetable beds, the men stood up and nodded a polite greeting, though their grins seemed a little sly to Tommy as he looked back. The names of vegetables were being reeled off as they walked: onions, runner beans, cabbage, carrots, beetroot, peas, then strawberries, raspberries, gooseberries. "It's like harvest festival. Reverend Jones would be pleased."

They walked through to the gate at the far end, where Mr Hardinge stopped with a proprietorial air. "Take a look. All things bright and beautiful." Tommy stood still and looked around at the vegetable beds inside the red brick walls, then looked up at the sky that seemed so much bigger than he was used to. There were sprinklings of puffy white clouds in a wide blue sky. "We might even turn you into a country boy."

Through the gate the dense wood started within a few paces. This wood, as they made their way slowly through it, pushing aside bushes and brambles that intruded onto the path, seemed wilder and darker than the wood they had entered the previous day. "I thought you should see this wood, Tommy. It is a proper wood, we hardly tend it. But it grows as nature intended. Without our attention. What a thicket of words, without meaning to do that."

Tommy liked Mr Hardinge rather better in the woods than in the house. They seemed to liberate him, loosen his speech until he hardly seemed aware of what he was saying. The advantage for Tommy was that there was no pressure to respond; he could simply listen, or simply ignore what was being said, and it did not matter if he said nothing. *Saying nothing suits me.* As they walked, they made slow progress because the wood was dense and the path had peetered out. The leaves were thick on the trees, the sunlight could barely penetrate, making it dark inside the wood, turning the filtered light green.

"Ash," said Mr Hardinge, patting the trunk. "Noble tree. Sweet chestnut there, and a beech, see the catkins. An oak, how will you recognise it, see the shape of the leaves, then notice the acorns, you only see acorns on an oak. A lime – not like the fruit – but a grand tree this, look at it and the boughs that create places to sit in – but only once you've climbed up to them. Easy for a nimble boy like you, of course. You have permission to climb trees."

Tommy took notice of that; he would like to climb these trees. In London the plane trees were not for climbing. Suddenly the prospect of spending time in this place seemed more attractive.

"Now take a look at this. This is the one thing I've done to this wood."

Before them was a low rectangular building made entirely of wood. "I call this the hide. It's a wonderful place to watch nature. If you stand inside there and keep quiet, the animals don't realise that you are around. You can watch birds of every kind. You can see squirrels, stoats, deer, foxes, though we don't like *them*, even badgers sometimes."

"Badgers? Can I see a badger?"

"You have to be lucky. Are you interested in badgers? Because of Mr Badger in the book?"

Tommy felt as if a secret had been discovered. He had been reading the book; he had been enjoying the book.

"So, do you like *Wind in the Willows*? You can always sit inside here to read it and take a look every so often to spot a badger – or a vole – water rat or a mole." Mr Hardinge seemed to find this funny enough to laugh.

"You can also write in your notebook here. Write down everything you see. Who comes and goes. Mr Badger and his friends. These woods are your playground, you will find them more interesting than being cooped up in the house all day. Boys need to be free. Is that all right?"

Tommy nodded. *Stay out of sight.* He took that as his instruction; he was happy to follow it. He preferred the prospect of wild animals in the woods to some of the fierce humans in the house. He remembered how Muriel had stuck out her tongue at him this morning when no one else was looking.

"So, how are you getting on, Tommy? Do you think you will like it here?" He nodded again. "That's good. We want you to be happy. Is there anything you are not happy with? I want to know you better – to see if I can continue to support you."

Tommy was more puzzled than ever. An early experience of being patronised can make a mark for life. But he said nothing.

"So, tell me, is your room comfortable? Do you like the food?"

"Very well, sir. Thank you." Politeness was a challenge but he realised it might have an advantage, so he felt emboldened by the morning they had spent together, surprised even that he felt he might like this man, perhaps only for fleeting moments. He hesitated but spoke. "I wonder. I like Rodgers. Is it all right if I ask him things?"

"But of course. He's a good-hearted fellow, I'm glad you like him, that speaks well of you."

"Perhaps he could tell me some things to do. He knows the woods all around."

"Tomorrow I'll get Rodgers to set you up for the day. Point you to places to explore. Teddy must spend time with Iris."

"Why? Why is that?"

"Can you keep a secret? We hope Teddy will marry Iris. It will make a good match."

Not much of a secret, Tommy thought, and said. "But Teddy doesn't like her."

"Oh? How do you know?"

"He says so. He said it to you yesterday when we was having supper."

"Ah. Yes. We should be more discreet. But you should not believe everything you overhear. Things overheard are often not meant to be heard – they might not be the truth."

"I don't mean to hear things. But I can't help it at breakfast, or when we're all sittin' at table."

"True. But you must learn to judge what is good for you to hear, and what not. Difficult, I know."

"Can I have breakfast in the kitchen tomorrow? Then I can talk to Rodgers about what I can do in the day." Tommy reckoned he would enjoy his food more if he were just with Rodgers.

Mr Hardinge seemed surprised by the request. But he was unable to think of a reason to turn it down. "If you wish. I will speak to Rodgers."

•

Tommy was adamant that he wanted to play in the woods, that he was happy to be by himself. He had his sandwich and a book to read. Having stressed his keenness to read, he felt he was winning the argument. Soon he felt a shiver of anxiety as he watched the forest closing behind the man's back, but then a thrill of excitement that he was on his own.

He looked around the hide. It was as plain as a man-made room can be: the walls were wood, there was one wooden chair and a blanket for colder weather, a door with a metal latch and a horizontal viewing window along one wall. If Tommy sat on the chair next to the window he would have enough light to read, if he wanted. He did not want to, not at that moment. He wanted to wander the woods, to explore what he now thought of as his domain.

The undergrowth was tangled and difficult to walk through so the tree in his path almost seemed to invite him to climb upon it, to go upwards above the vegetation that was so dense at ground level. He found the climbing easy; it was not a big tree but he was surprised how different the view was from above. It was a surprising view of the world. He imagined himself as a squirrel, this fork in the branches as his nest. Settling into it as if into an armchair, he took out his book to read, passing an hour in a parallel world as a mole coming in from the snow, relieved to be rescued by the intimidating but kindly badger.

He had finished his sandwich, made with a slice of beef from yesterday's joint. He thought that his mother would be pleased to see how well he was living. A sudden shadow of homesickness needed to be swept away like the crumbs from his sandwich; he packed his knapsack and slid down the tree to the ground.

Progress was slow through the woods and he had to keep pulling up his socks to avoid being scratched by thorns and nettles. The sight of the village ahead, houses peeking through the trees, was welcome. There was the church with its tall spire, and just a hundred yards past it he saw the pub. Relieved to see such places, strangely familiar after such a short acquaintance, he broke into a run along the road.

"What you doin' then?" asked the girl at the pub.

"Minding me own business," he replied.

"Cheeky thing! Ain't they taught yer manners yet?"

He wondered whether he should stick his tongue out at her. Muriel might have goaded him on. But then the need for politeness reasserted itself – for self-preservation if not for higher motives. There was something about the girl, her commonness, that provoked him towards a rudeness he rarely expressed at home. He was puzzled by this, by her.

"What's your name?" she asked.

"Who wants to know?" She looked at him as if disappointed, as if to say 'I thought you was better than that'. "Sorry," he said. "It's Tommy. What's yours?"

"Rosie, of course. You knew that, didn't yer? Sit down, it's a quiet day, no customers."

So Tommy sat down on the bench outside the pub, underneath the purple flowers of wisteria. Rosie brought him a glass of lemonade and sat next to him as if she might have something to say. If so she was interrupted by the approaching noise of an engine. They looked left along the road to see the motorcycle approaching with its empty sidecar, rattling along next to it.

"My, they're catchin' on like wildfire. Wonder what it's like to ride in one?"

Tommy nodded, not realising how brightly his eyes shone at the prospect, even as he spoke words to himself that sounded like "Poop – poop". Rosie tousled his hair, something he hated, restoring his attention as the motorcycle disappeared through the village.

"Right then," she said. "So, tell us a bit. Why you stayin' at the big house? You don't seem like no posh boy."

"I'm not. It just happened."

"Like a fairy tale, eh? So tell me, what's he like, that Teddy?"

"Mr Edward to you."

"You said you wasn't posh."

"He's nice enough. Don't really know him."

"I'd like t' know 'im. Seems a good man," she chuckled to herself. "Tell yer what, give this to him, secret like." She had the handkerchief ready in her hand, as if she had planned this moment. As she placed it in Tommy's hand he could smell the *eau de cologne*. He wrinkled his nose in distaste. "I want you to give that to 'im but not let anyone else know. All right?"

He supposed it must be, he could hardly refuse as she'd given him the lemonade to drink. "And you're not to use that hankie. You got one of yer own? Good. You should use it."

He opened his knapsack to put the handkerchief inside and out of sight, though he suspected the handkerchief would be easier to smell than see. Prompted by Rosie's question, as if to reassure her of his understanding, he blew his nose on his own square of white cotton. He lifted up the book he had been reading: seeing the green notebook underneath gave him an idea.

"Don't ask me why, but I've got this book. I'm supposed to get people to write in it." He held it out to Rosie to open up, its green leather cover displaying the gold letters of Hardinge Hall. There was only the one message from George Hardinge in it, on the opening page. "Will you write something in it for me?"

"Lord, there's a strange thing to be asked. But why not? you help me, I'll help you, and we'll be friends." She smiled at him and drew out the pencil. "What sort of thing, though?"

"Something I'm supposed to remember, to do me good? You have to think of it yourself."

Rosie shook her head, wondering what she might write. She chose a blank page towards the middle of the book, not wishing to follow too closely behind the pious opening message. Then she painstakingly wrote the words in small capital letters to make them easier to read: *"KEEP YOUR NOSE CLEAN AND YOUR THOUHTS TO YOURSELF. BE A GOOD MESSENGER. ROSIE."*

Tommy felt he had achieved something he had not expected. Perhaps there was a point to this business of collecting messages – it was interesting to see what people had to say to him. He remembered to thank Rosie while tying up his knapsack, ready to head back through the east woods to the house.

"Don't forget now," Rosie called after him. "And not a word to no one."

•

Tommy had intended to stay in the woods longer but he was conscious that he had a mission to fulfil. The scented handkerchief was worrying him. Would the scent wear off, as it did from his mother's clothes, and if it wore off, would that matter? The east woods were not as dense as the west ones, and he could see glimpses of the house every so often. He found a tree that seemed to invite him to climb it. It had a knobbly trunk that almost formed steps leading upward to the first low boughs, and dense foliage above the lowest bough. He climbed a little higher until he found a comfortable place, settling into this new-found experience, with only the buzzing of insects to disturb him. He read another chapter of his book, in which he found his own feelings of homesickness growing stronger as he identified with mole's feelings at finding his old home. A tear trickled down his cheek.

There was nothing for it but to go back to the house and discharge his duty as soon as he could. He went into the drawing room, hoping to find Teddy, but disappointed to see only Muriel.

"What are you doing here, silly boy?" she asked.

"Nothing," he replied.

"You're a nasty boy," she said to him. "And I wish you weren't here."

He shrugged. *Not much I can do about that.*

"I don't see why Father should take you off to the woods, as if you are special. Why does he give more attention to you than me? It's not fair."

He knew that another shrug would not help, but he could not help it, he shrugged.

"Oh why do you keep doing that? Go away, will you? I don't want to see you."

Tommy backed out of the room and ran up the stairs.

"You're in a hurry," said Teddy at the top of the stairs. "Slow down, we don't want an accident."

On his mission of secrecy, Tommy put his index finger vertically across his lips, and then beckoned Teddy down the corridor. He opened the door to his bedroom, and waved to Teddy to enter.

"I say, this is all very mysterious. What's eating you?" asked Teddy.

Tommy opened up his knapsack and drew out the scented handkerchief, handing it to Teddy with the words "It's from Rosie". Teddy was surprised. He looked down at the white fabric, and raised it towards his face as if testing its authenticity as well as its scent. He slipped it guiltily into his jacket pocket.

"Damned cheek of the girl. When you see her again, say I want to return it to her."

•

Later on he sat at dinner being questioned by Mr Hardinge about his day in the woods.

"So what did you do to occupy yourself, Tommy?"

"Not much."

"Not much sounds too little. Tell me more."

"I read a bit. And I climbed trees."

"Good. Did you enjoy yourself? And did you meet anyone in the woods?"

When he shook his head it seemed an honest answer, at least in his own justifying mind. His meeting with Rosie had not been in the woods. Instinct told him that it would be best not to talk about that meeting, a feeling confirmed by Teddy's smile. Secrets shared could be the making of a friendship; at least he hoped so.

But even if the conversation moved on, he could not escape the regular torment that came with cutlery. Relaxing a little, he forgot himself and stuck his fork into a potato with his right hand.

"That's not what we do?" It was the voice of his chief tormentor, Mrs Hardinge. The uncertainty surrounding etiquette might never go away, even when he knew the word. For now he felt its shadow hanging over him, and quickly put the fork down onto the plate. He squirmed at the clatter the metal made against the china plate. His only consolation was a quiet smile from Iris who sat opposite him.

They even knew about all this in *The Wind in the Willows*. He had just read something like this – perhaps he could learn manners from Ratty as he sensed Mole was doing? But it was the only sentence in the book that he had disliked so far, when Badger thought table manners 'belonged to the things that didn't really matter' only to be contradicted by a voice that now sounded in his head like Mrs Hardinge. 'We know of course that he was wrong, and took too narrow a view, because they do matter, very much, though it would take too long to explain why.'

He picked up the fork in his left hand and cut the potato with his right hand.

Mrs Hardinge pursed her lips, feeling vindicated but unwilling to give approval.

4

TUESDAY

Rodgers placed a couple of sausages on Tommy's plate. In his grey chauffeur's uniform he seemed overdressed for the kitchen, but he wore the uniform well. Tommy was sitting at the side table that was topped with white enamel, chipped here and there to show black patches underneath. It was the first morning of the new arrangement – breakfast in the kitchen – and Tommy felt his tongue loosen as well as his spirits.

"They're good 'uns," said Tommy.

"Course they are. Can't beat our sausages."

"Can you give us another?"

"Goodness, Tommy. You pack your food away, right enough."

As Tommy cut into his third sausage, he felt he should make conversation. "How is Mrs Rodgers?"

Rodgers smiled, looking quizzically at Tommy. "She's just over there. Looks fine to me."

Tommy looked at Mrs Rodgers who was peeling potatoes. Rodgers said: "It's good of you to inquire."

Why? wondered Tommy. *Out of this thing they call 'politeness'? Or because it's a way to keep out of trouble?*

"So what shall I do today? Did Mr Hardinge tell you?"

"He left early, I drove him to the station. Didn't say anything to me, no."

"So what shall I do?"

"Up to you. But if you go to the woods, you could wait a bit till it brightens."

Tommy was enjoying this breakfast without pressure. No Mrs Hardinge to tick him off. He wondered about asking for another sausage.

"I'll go later. If the rain stops. I want to find the river."

"River? Nothing but a stream. Still...nice enough for a boy to explore."

Tommy had his green notebook with him. He reasoned that it would be easier to ask Rodgers to write in it than any of the others, so he asked with an unusual amount of deference.

"Oh Lord, what a thing to do. This takes thinking about."

While Rodgers was thinking Tommy got his other book out to read. Struggling to find his place, he came upon the description of Badger's kitchen that now seemed surprisingly familiar. A week earlier it would have been beyond his experience. Now it seemed like a record of his surroundings. "Rows of spotless plates winked from the shelves of the dresser at the far end of the room, and from the rafters overhead hung hams, bundles of dried herbs, nets of onions, and baskets of eggs."

"There," said Rodgers, "that will have to do. I'm not one for writing but I know that they'll read it so needs must."

It was true that the words had been scraped out with a painstaking effort. Each letter seemed traced into shape, with no attempt at the joined-up writing that Tommy had been learning at school. This made it easier for him to read: *'There's things in the woods as you might not wish to see. Mind how you go there & in life.'* J Rodgers

•

Returning to the main part of the house, Tommy was careful to be quiet. He had no particular wish to be spotted and drawn into a conversation so he walked with soft treads through the hallway to the foot of the stairs. As he did so he heard voices coming from the dining room, unmistakably the voices of Mrs Hardinge and her son.

"If you are not in London – learning banking as your father puts it, as if there is anything much to learn – you have to do your duty here."

"My duty? You mean Iris?"

"I mean your intended. She is an eligible young woman. You know there are family advantages to the proposed arrangement. That is your duty."

"You are my mother. Are you urging duty upon me before any feelings? I would rather marry the commonest girl in the village than be forced to marry someone I don't have feelings for."

"Feelings will develop. Enough to satisfy your baser instincts at least."

"I cannot."

"You will. You must. Fakenham's is the best establishment in Tunbridge Wells. It will be beneficial to unite our families."

"But I do not love her. Nor does she love me."

"She might not be to your exact taste but what does that matter? It has nothing to do with it. You never liked cabbage but you have to eat it. Because we know it is good for you."

The grandfather clock started chiming, and it chimed eleven times, heralding the descent of Iris down the stairs and setting off the barking of the dog who had been sleeping on the landing. Tommy was grateful that she laid a calming hand on the agitated labrador, grateful that the noise must have covered the sound of the conversation in the dining room. Tommy clattered noisily up the stairs to his room, avoiding Iris's eyes and the panting dog.

•

Many hours later, after being cooped up by the drizzle till late afternoon, Tommy was itching to get out of the house. He was itching, literally, as he had been bitten by insects the previous day and now he found it hard not to scratch at the bites. He splashed cold water on them as the prelude to going outside. Insects would not deter him from spending time in the woods.

In front of him greylight drifted like a drizzly mist. It seemed that you might touch it but it slipped through your fingers. Behind him he saw a black cloud lowering in the sky above the house. It was an eery light, as if created by the moon rather than the sun lurking with uncertain intentions behind the clouds. *You won't catch me.* Tommy ran into the woods to find the stream that Rodgers had told him about.

"Will I see a water rat in the woods?" Tommy had asked.

"Rats? No. No rats. You might find fish in the stream. A vole perhaps. Dragonflies. Even a frog."

This sounded enough of a list to explore. So Tommy had listened to Rodgers' instructions on how to find the stream. And if it rained, the water might just swell the stream that Rodgers had called 'nothing much' into a river.

The rooks were cawing with their harsh raw calls high at the top of the trees. No dawn chorus of birds welcoming the renewed world. Their signals were to defend their territory against all-comers at all costs. A message that the young boy could pick up and reinforce with his own recent reading. These voices were not benign species. All creatures had to be on guard against all other creatures.

Tommy liked it on the riverbank. As Rodgers had told him he made for the railway line, finding the stream cutting across the path that led to the tracks. His imagination had been fed by his reading and now he imagined every sound as emanating from a water rat mucking about in a little boat. *If only I could see him.* Tommy screwed up his eyes to encourage the vision to appear. As he opened his eyes wider again, the sun flashed shafts of light through the branches that overhung the water.

He ate an apple, throwing away the core behind him into the foliage that covered the ground. When he looked for it later ants were swarming over it, sending a shudder through him. He was not yet comfortable with the thought of sharing these woods with so many creatures he disliked. There were not many ants, beetles, slugs or bugs in *The Wind in the Willows* but these woods were full of them and the very thought made him feel itchy. Getting to his feet he brushed his clothes and skin with his hands, banishing any unwanted intruders, then thought he would run to escape their invisible reach.

He had always liked to run. And here in the woods when he ran he seemed to go faster than ever as he flashed by tree after tree. Just like Billy Tree. Billy had gone to Tommy's school and his legend as a runner fast as the wind had lived on long after he had left the school. He imagined that he was racing Billy Tree and that he was winning.

Tommy ran to the edge of the wood, across the rough road that led to the house, then entered the west woods. Everything was so much darker here, the leaves overhead so much denser and the ground underfoot so much more overgrown. There was a wildness that he liked, imagining that he was the good Robin Hood stalking the bad Sheriff's men. There was no point in running, or even trying to run here. The brambles caught at his woollen socks.

Unexpectedly, because he had no map, no plan in his head, he found himself back at the hide where Mr Hardinge had brought him yesterday. He pushed at the wooden door, closing it behind him when he realised that the window allowed in enough light to see. It was a fine place to read, to lose himself in the world of the book, to share the fears and dreams of these animal heroes, eventually to sleep, with the light fading, unable to fight off the drowsiness that laid a soothing hand over his eyes.

When he woke, he was unnerved by the darkness of dusk. *What's the time?* He had no idea but he felt an immediate panic that the sky seen through the black leaves outside the window was a deep blue in which stars were beginning to twinkle. The vividness of his recent dream made him panic. In his dream he had been running through woods pursued by stoats and weasels. The faster he ran the faster they chased him until their sudden closeness had forced him out of the dream.

He had no idea how much time had passed but knew that it must be too long, that he should have returned to the house several hours ago. He quickly ran through excuses to tell but none of them would do if he did not find his way out of the woods first. Although he was sheltered if he stayed here he reasoned that Mole had found refuge by being brave, so he must also be brave and escape the wood. His fear of being missed at the house, the attention he would draw to himself if that were so, overcame his fear of the darkness of the woods.

He had no certainty that he was heading in the right direction. If there was a path he could not see it in the blackness that now made it hard to see further than a few feet ahead. The woods were full of noises that he tried to put out of his mind, but the buzzing of insects in his ears could not be ignored. Stumbling through thick undergrowth, he tripped over many times, stinging nettles adding to his discomfort. There was small relief when the moon slipped through the scudding grey clouds and shone a white light through the trees.

Tommy stopped, stood still, allowing his eyes to penetrate the surrounding shadows, but his eyes filled with tears. He had not meant to cause trouble but that was now his main concern.

He imagined Rodgers searching the house, the gardens, stepping into the woods but retreating because he could not see. *What would he do? what shall I do? press on.*

He stepped forward in the dark, taking as big a step as he could, finding firm ground before bringing his other foot forward. Two steps, three, more, touching the rough bark of a tree, feeling his way around the tree. Having no sense of time, but sensing that minutes were hours, then feeling the sudden relief at the sight of a light ahead. In his excitement he went tumbling again into a bank of ferns that left him dripping wet.

Now he was out of the woods and on a road that was lit by the moon and the glow from houses ahead. He had never felt such a joyful sense of relief. The light from the windows of a house were beckoning him forward, promising safety and comfort. As he drew closer he recognised the house as the village pub, The Badger's Arms, and he cast aside all embarrassment or fear to push open the door. Entering he was suddenly engulfed in noise and light. People were deep into their evening's drinking, their faces gleaming in the glow of oil lamps.

"What you doin', lad? You can't come in 'ere."

The first man to see him did not speak unkindly but it was not the welcome that Tommy now craved. He burst into tears.

"Poor little mite," said a familiar voice. "But it's a good question. What are you doing here?"

He could say nothing but allowed himself to be taken into the soft fabric of Rosie's skirts. With heaving shoulders he sobbed while Rosie stroked his hair.

"Come on," she said. "Let's go through to the snug."

He was comfortable enough on his own in the snug with a cup of tea and a piece of cake. Rosie brought a blanket in to wrap around him, noticing that his legs were covered in bites and scratches. Her sympathy sent her outside again, returning soon with a handful of dock leaves that she wrapped around his legs.

"Any better?" she asked. She tried to get Tommy to talk about what had happened but he was still working out what he would say to people at the house. He knew it would be better not to have more than one story. He confined himself to saying "I got lost".

"Tell me then, did you give my hankie as I asked you?"

Tommy nodded.

"And? And what did he say?"

"He said you had a cheek."

"Really. And why is that?" No more than a shrug in response. "Well, he should tell me so himself."

Rosie went through into the pub, leaving Tommy worried that he had upset her. He had no wish to be ungrateful for kindness.

"We've sent someone up to the house to say you're here. I expect they'll send Jack with the car to collect you – he'll be here soon."

"Thank you," he said, on his best behaviour.

"There's something you can do for me to say Thank-you," Rosie said. "I want you to give this to Teddy. But only when he's on his own. You know what it's like – you don't like to be embarrassed, do yer?"

She gave Tommy a piece of paper that was folded over several times until it was tiny. He slipped it through the blanket into his pocket and smiled at her to say he would deliver it. Soon after, Rodgers came through the door. It was good to see him, even though his face was unsmiling.

"You've got some explaining to do, young man. And it's past Closing Time. Come on, let's get you home."

5

WEDNESDAY

Next day Tommy woke up with a feeling of foreboding, not knowing how he would be treated, expecting to be punished but not knowing how. He decided to stay in bed as long as he could, simply to delay the inevitable harshness of words or worse. Already he suspected that life held no greater punishment in store than words directed to do harm: or even innocuous words that cause a bad effect. His worst fear was that Mr Hardinge would have been summoned, and that his mother would be informed. Was it hope or fear that he might be sent home?

He did not expect, when his door was opened, that Mrs Hardinge would be the one to walk through it. He straightaway sat up in bed.

"I see you are alive," she said. "At least we are spared that trouble."

He started to get out of bed, pulling his borrowed nightshirt over his legs.

"No, stay there. I think we need to confine you to bed today. There are always consequences to actions and you must learn lessons. I will get Mrs Rodgers to bring you some toast and then later a broth." She spoke these words like an officer to her adjutant – in this case one of the junior servants, a young girl who gave the impression that she would rather not be there.

"Winnie will give you a bath. I'm sure that will be needed. Give your clothes to Winnie who will ask Mrs Larkin to wash them. I don't know why your mother sent you with so few clothes, but you need to change them more often. If necessary we will furnish you with some of Edward's old clothes that we have saved."

Tommy wondered about protesting but he thought he was getting off lightly. So he kept quiet, imagining that would be an acceptable response. Mrs Hardinge looked satisfied and she swept out, leaving Winnie to follow her instructions. Tommy stayed in bed as Winnie dashed in and out of the room, drawing the water for a bath. It was the first time Tommy had been in a bath with taps; he might have enjoyed splashing around if he had not been constrained by his and Winnie's mutual embarrassment. She was a girl not much older than himself.

He returned to his bedroom wrapped in a rough white towel, then changed into the clean nightshirt that had been laid out on his bed. Winnie came back with a bottle of pink liquid and cotton wool, then dabbed the calamine lotion on his bites. The lotion's coolness was a relief. His now unnaturally pallid legs, blanched by calamine, with some patches applied to his face, gave him all the appearance of sickliness.

After yesterday's escapades he was happy to forgo the outside world, particularly as he was discovering there was a much larger world inside his own head. He was in bed reading, enjoying his punishment rather more than would have pleased Mrs Hardinge. She might never appreciate the possibility of intellectual pleasures, and she certainly never encouraged them in her own children. If this undermined her husband's inclinations, that brought some satisfaction in itself.

Teddy entered the room, peering around the door cautiously so as not to wake him. Seeing Tommy sitting up with his book in hand, he came further inside.

"Well, you created a bit of a stink," said Teddy. "We all were fearing the worst."

Tommy was puzzled. Did he smell? What could be worse?

"So it's a day in your punishment cell," said Teddy lightly. "It's not too bad. I'll put in a word for you later and see if we can get you up. It's boring just staying in bed reading."

"No, it's not. I like it." Tommy was determined not to feel punished.

"If you say so. Is there anything I can get you?"

Tommy shook his head. Then he remembered that there was something he had to give Teddy. He reached into the drawer of the bedside table and took out the folded piece of paper that Rosie had given him.

"What's this?" Teddy asked, opening it out.

"Rosie gave it to me. To give to you."

"It's nothing," said Teddy, folding the paper again. "But thank you. Church business."

Tommy suspected that Rosie's business had little to do with the church. The pinkness in Teddy's face suggested that it might mean something outside religious instruction.

"Anyway, I'd best be on my way. Things to do. But what's this?" He picked up the blanket that Tommy had thrown onto a chair last night. "Not one of ours."

"It's Rosie's. She gave it to me to keep warm last night after I got lost."

"Really? That was good of her. I think I ought to return it. It will only be polite."

The demands of politeness were becoming no clearer to Tommy but he watched Teddy leave the room with the blanket tucked under his arm. As his footsteps went down the stairs, Tommy remembered that he had meant to ask Teddy to write in his green book.

•

Later, when Iris visited, the question was in his mind so he asked it. Iris looked surprised and delayed for more thinking time. "I don't know what I should write."

"You don't have to write much. Just so I can say it's done."

"Let me see," Iris held out her hand. She opened the book and read Mr Hardinge's words standing guard at the opening. Flicking through she read the message from Rodgers and smiled; then the one from Rosie and frowned.

"Who is this?" she asked.

"Just the girl in the pub. The one that looked after me."

Iris nodded, murmuring distractedly: "How very kind of her."

She sat there, gazing out of the window at the front lawn fringed by woods, deep in thought. Tommy looked at her in turn. She was like someone staring through the window of the hide in the woods, intent on spotting movement among the trees.

"Ah well," she sighed eventually, as if defeated by what she had seen or failed to see. "I will think about this and write something in your book another day."

Tommy was engrossed in *The Wind in the Willows*. When a bowl of broth was brought on a tray, he was reluctant to stop reading. He had no inclinations to escape through the window like Toad. He was laughing and crying and sighing inside as the characters became real inside his head. When Toad slid down the rope to the outside world he was torn between annoyance at his naughtiness and joyfulness at his daring. But poor Rat and Mole, told off by Mr Badger. At Mrs Rodgers' urging he set aside the book to sip the reality of a thin broth with a slice of unbuttered bread, as prescribed by Mrs Hardinge.

Left alone again, he read the next chapter. He found it puzzling. Mole and Rat had managed to find the missing young otter, but there was something deeply mysterious in the supernatural help they had been given. Who or what was this god-like creature with curved horns? What were pan-pipes, why was their sound so beguiling? It was puzzling but there was something in it that made him feel his world had been opened to an expanded sense of wonder. He read it again, seeming to recognise some of the scenes from the woods where he had been. This second time he understood it no better but he loved it even more. For the first time he was reading with pleasure not for the story that was being told but for the sense that so much was being revealed that words could not properly express.

And this mystery was not concerning, it brought no fear, just the word *awe* that he now knew for the first time, for the awe evoked by the natural world. As he read again the words whispered to him like the breeze stirring the reeds at the riverbank, like the birds chirping and the pipes playing a melody that was always on the brink of passing out of hearing while the boat slipped quietly through the water towards the horizon where the moon shone its reflection onto the liquid surface and he felt the mildest sense of motion as if drifting without effort but as if in pursuit of something would always remain out of reach until the golden glow ahead beckoned him onwards towards the comfort of familiar company as soon as...

Sometimes you wake from a dream to a feeling of shock, as if shaken out of slumber before time. And sometimes you wake feeling at least for those first few contented moments that you remain in the warm embrace of this other world that has seemed even more real than the world you live in. Tommy rubbed his eyes, reluctant even in that action to wipe away the memory of the mystery that still lingered within touching distance.

He raised the book that had slipped to the side and read the chapter's last words: *"With a smile of happiness on his face, and something of a listening look still lingering there, the weary Rat was fast asleep."*

•

That afternoon he read on more slowly, dropping in and out of sleep. Toad was locked up in prison and about to escape disguised as a washerwoman. Tommy found it funny but he had been spoiled by the magic of the previous chapter. There were two worlds and he no longer felt quite sure which one suited him better. It was a relief when Teddy came into the room to say that he could now get out of bed, as long as he was feeling better.

"I never felt ill."

"Well, the day is nearly done and it looks like you've slept any illness away."

Now that he bounced out of bed, as if to demonstrate his recovery to Teddy, he realised that he was light-headed.

"Are you giddy?" asked Teddy. "Perhaps you *are* ill."

Tommy shook his head and looked for his clothes. "Here," said Teddy. "Mother found these for you. They're old ones of mine while yours are being washed and dried."

Tommy would rather not have worn these clothes. He knew they would not fit him, knew that he did not like the look of them. If they were old they seemed newer than his own clothes but of a style from another time altogether. His friends in the street at home would laugh at him dressed like this in rust-coloured knee breeches trousers and what seemed to him more like a blouse than a shirt. *At least they won't see me.* Despite his misgivings he allowed Teddy to fit the braces to the breeches, adjusting them to keep the waist high. He pulled at the elastic of the braces, enjoying the twang as he let go. The strange trousers did at least cover his ghostly-pale, calamine-white legs.

Soon it was dinner-time and Tommy almost wished he was back in his own room. But he was hungry and released from his convalescent diet.

"I am glad we did not send for the doctor," said Mrs Hardinge. "You see, he is perfectly well."

"He's a strong boy," said Teddy. "At least he will be if he eats all his food."

"Well, eat. But remember your manners."

Tommy was pleased to be given permission to concentrate simply on the pork chop and potatoes on his plate, allowing the slow conversation to move around him at the table.

"Where did you two go today?" asked Mrs Hardinge of Teddy and Iris.

"I just went for a walk in the woods," said Teddy.

"With Iris?"

"No. I couldn't find her at the time."

"I went for a walk into the village," said Iris. "It's a pretty enough place."

"Were you there? I didn't see you."

"Perhaps you did not look out for me."

"Perhaps you did not, Edward. You surprise me that you are not more considerate." After a pause to digest her potato and the effect of her words, she continued. "Well, you are lacking in many qualities. But I am sure Iris will forgive you if you simply do your duty."

Teddy sighed. Addressing him like this in front of Iris was a new line of attack. "What duty did you have in mind for me now, mother? Not that it will interest Iris at all."

Mrs Hardinge chewed at a sinewy piece of meat, not quite able to swallow it. As it finally disappeared, the words were released. "There are, as you know family duties. But also, if we are being frank, duties that keep us from idleness. You show little inclination to be usefully employed in your father's business. You were intended – setting aside other intentions – to spend at least a day or two a week at the bank in London."

"I'm bored by banking. I'd rather father set me up in something more congenial."

"Congenial. What counts as congenial in your eyes?"

"I might join the army."

"You must not. They will send you off to war."

"To defend my country."

"To be killed."

"But there is no war."

"To be killed in a foreign country we do not know or even like."

Everyone had stopped eating. It reminded Tommy of those times in the playground when two boys squared up to each other, eyes locked. Iris stared down at her plate, the food hardly touched. Mother and son looked at each other, not able to say a word, while Muriel looked on, as usual with nothing to contribute. Tommy also said nothing and kept his fork poised above a potato that still looked golden and tempting to him, if only he could find a way to eat it without drawing attention to himself.

Aware that his fork hung in the air like a baton to quietness, Mrs Hardinge asked: "Thomas, would it be an act of kindness to say you can eat your food in the kitchen with Mr and Mrs Rodgers for company?"

There was a deep silence. He knew it was up to him to break it but it was agony to do so. He felt four pairs of eyes looking at him, and he wanted to shrivel out of sight.

"I thought so." Mrs Hardinge looked at each of the others in turn.

"I wouldn' mind," finally came to Tommy's lips.

"Well done," she smiled at Tommy, then addressed her next remark to the rest of the table. "At least he seems to know his place. It is a start."

She rang the bell that sat on the tablecloth in front of her. The sound seemed cheerful and spiteful at the same time. Tommy was pleased to be shown out, his dinner plate carried before him to the kitchen, while he hitched up the uncomfortable trousers.

6

THURSDAY

"There will be high tea on Saturday. Mr Hardinge has decreed."
Mrs Hardinge emitted a sharp sound that might have been
open irritation or disguised indigestion. She dabbed the napkin
against her lips, indicating an end to her breakfast. "So it will
be done."

Why is tea going to be high? Will we go upstairs? Tommy
dared not ask. A display of ignorance might fan Mrs Hardinge's
temper. It was bad enough that he had been summoned from
the kitchen to receive his orders for the day when he had hoped
to be left to his own devices.

"Thomas, despite your fall from grace we have forgiven
you. You will be allowed to go out again today. Are you sorry
for what you did?" The boy nodded downwards to the carpet.
"Truly sorry?"

The serving maid, following a gesture from Mrs Hardinge,
started to clear the breakfast table. Tommy wished he might be
swept away too, to save further embarrassment.

"Good. We will trust you." She stared at the maid who was
clattering the cutlery against the crockery. "Quieter, Susan, you
must learn a little restraint."

Trusted to do what?

"It is a fine day. So this is what I propose. Edward, you will
walk Iris around the gardens. It will be instructive for you. I
suspect Iris will display a greater knowledge of the plants than
you possess yourself. Good. While you are doing that, Thomas
will walk the dog in the woods. You know Nellie, do you not,

Thomas? She is a well-behaved creature. Labradors have a good nature, unlike many human beings. Do you like Nellie?"

"That's me mum's name," blurted Tommy, a little confused by this coincidence.

"My mother's," corrected Mrs Hardinge.

Really? Your mum too? Don't say it. He kept the sly thought to himself behind an inward smile.

"While you're enjoying yourself with the dog, I'll be busy writing invitations. Mr Hardinge wishes to invite people to high tea on Saturday so you will meet some of our local acquaintances."

•

Tommy was nervous about the dog. There was no dog at home so he was not used to being in charge of one.

"You'll be alright," Rodgers reassured him. "Here, come and stroke Nellie." He did so nervously. "Don't be timid with her. She'll sense it. Best be firm."

Rodgers bent down and whispered instructions to the dog. "Does she understand?" asked Tommy.

"Course she does. She'll want to understand you too. Come an' talk to her."

Perhaps animals do understand after all. Like Mole and Ratty. They talk.

"That's the way," said Rodgers. "See, she likes you." Tommy's face was next to Nellie's. It was true, the dog seemed comfortable in Tommy's company. "I'll come with you to the lawn, then you can head off into the east woods."

Nellie walked obediently between them as they crossed the lawn. At the gates of the cottage, Rodgers patted Tommy and the dog on the head. "Off you go," he said.

At first Nellie did exactly as Tommy wished. His wishes were simple: *don't run away*. But as they moved deeper into the woods, the dog got more and more interested in her surroundings, and less and less aware of Tommy. She spotted an animal and started barking with excitement. The squirrel scurried up the nearest tree and disappeared around the other side of the trunk, while Nellie barked furiously "Stop it, Nellie," Tommy pleaded, "squirrels are nice."

If the squirrel could escape up the tree, it was harder for rabbits to get away safely. Nellie chased after rabbits in a frenzied state. She stopped, her tongue lolling out of her mouth, then she raced away again in pursuit of anything that moved in the woods. Tommy ran as fast as he could after the dog but it was an unequal contest. The dog was quickly out of sight, with Tommy trailing behind, realising that he did not know where to follow. He listened, sometimes hearing the sound of barking in the distance, but every time the noise faded away, leaving Tommy not knowing where he should go. He sat down on a fallen tree trunk, tears again pricking at his eyes, tormented by a new sense of failure.

"Tommy!" he heard someone calling him and he called back immediately. "Here!" Soon he was relieved to see Teddy tramping through the undergrowth towards the tree where he was sitting.

"Are you alright? Lost Nellie?"

Tommy could not bring himself to the confession in words but a tear trickled down his cheek in answer.

"Don't worry, she'll turn up. Happens all the time. Expect she'll be waiting for us when we get home."

Teddy sat down next to him on the tree trunk. He lit a cigarette and blew smoke up towards the canopy of leaves.

"My mother is difficult," Teddy said, as if the thought might not have occurred to the boy. "We all have to live with it. She should not have asked you to be in charge of Nellie. At least not yet. I thought you might struggle."

"It wasn't Nellie's fault."

"Of course it wasn't. She knows her way. Nothing to worry about. I've masses of time."

"I thought you was walkin' with Iris."

"I was. But there are only so many flowers a man can look at. And not many words that you can say. I'm not good at gabbing. She wanted me to find you anyway."

"Really? Why's that?"

"I think she likes you. Probably more than she likes me. But we can't help that."

Tommy observed Teddy as he smoked, sitting there with a distracted look in his eyes. He thought about the other girl.

"Do you like Rosie?"

"Rosie? Oh, that girl. I gave her back the blanket. We had a little talk, enjoyed it actually." A smile crossed his face; in his mind he seemed pleased to see her. "Anyway, we'd best be going. Better make sure that Nellie has found her way home. Like Little Bo-Peep and her sheep."

They walked through a dense area of bushes. Deep in the undergrowth there was a mass of fur streaked with blood. Teddy stepped over the body of a fox that had been savaged by another animal. Tommy backed away, deterred by the gore and by the flies attracted to the carcase.

"Good riddance," Teddy said with some venom.

"What's a riddance?" asked Tommy.

Teddy looked puzzled. "It just means I'm glad it happened. One less fox to worry about."

"Why do you worry about foxes?"

Tommy, for once, wanted to keep a conversation going in case a pause led them back to uncomfortable subjects.

Tommy himself, seeing this evidence, felt more inclined to worry for the foxes. Teddy seemed to care less for animals than he did – and Teddy might not regard water rats, moles, badgers, as his friends in the same way that he did. It seemed that, in the animal world, only dogs were friends to this man with the twitching cane.

"Foxes are vicious creatures and they eat our chickens," he said.

"Who do you think killed the fox?"

"Might have been a badger." Tommy was shocked and not sure whether to believe Teddy. "You'd better watch out for badgers too."

They pressed on, Tommy casting glances back over his shoulder until the carcase of the fox with its black cloud of flies disappeared from view. Now the sun's rays were golden and straight as they pierced the leaves, dappling the leaf mould under foot, leading them into a small clearing. From here they could see the side elevation of Hardinge Hall through the trees ahead. Cheered by the sight, knowing that he was not lost again, Tommy began to run with sheer relief and Teddy joined him in the race, both of them tossing out words like apples flung behind them. *Run. Faster. First one there.*

"There she is!" Teddy called out, spotting Nellie at the top of the grass embankment. Nellie began barking to greet them. Tommy could see Iris running towards them as fast as her long dress would allow. It was the first time he could remember seeing Iris and Teddy laugh in each other's company, and he thought that laughter made Iris seem so much prettier than Rosie.

•

Mrs Hardinge had finished writing the invitations to high tea.

She was just putting the stationery away in the roll-top desk in the study.

"After lunch, I have an errand for you to perform. You will need Rodgers, so go and bring him here. He knows what is needed."

Rodgers did know. He was already in his grey chauffeur's uniform, so he walked from the kitchen with Tommy.

"Take the car," Mrs Hardinge said "and deliver these to the addresses on the envelope. I'm sure you can read my handwriting but just check."

There were half a dozen letters she had placed on a silver plate and Tommy confirmed that he could read the addresses. The names were not names he was used to, all surrounded by abbreviations before and after the main names. He passed them to Rodgers to do the same.

"Be off with you, then. Make sure you hand them personally to someone in each house."

The garage was at the back of the house. It was an old barn smelling of oil and petrol, with the second car taking pride of place but surrounded by items of garden equipment, tools and tins, bicycles and appliances needing repair.

"Too many things need doing," said Rodgers, looking around, "and not enough time to do it. Never mind, this is more fun. We can enjoy our little drive."

Tommy was allowed to sit in the front seat next to Rodgers this time. It would make it easier to do the deliveries, and they could talk more easily above the noise of the engine. It seemed Rodgers was more in a mood for talking than usual, responding to questions that had built up in Tommy's head.

"What does high tea mean?"

"It's a tea for posh people. And believe it or not, you are the reason for havin' it."

"Why me?"

"I think Mr H wants t' show off how good he is to his friends. So you'll be on parade, like a little soldier but without the uniform."

Not knowing what to make of this, Tommy looked left as they drove down the lane away from Hardinge Hall, then turned into Luckhurst village. Rodgers tooted the horn, less for safety than for show: he wanted people to look at the car and its driver. The passenger too felt a small surge of pride that he was part of this scene, like one of the acts in a visiting circus. *Wish mum could see me.* High above the roadway, he felt superior as he never had before. Rodgers pressed the horn again as they passed the pub and Tommy saw, perhaps imagined, a hand waving from inside.

"Yes, Mrs Rodgers is going to be busy baking. Bread and cakes and scones. But she likes that."

"Will there be sausages?"

"I don't think so, no, not for high tea. It's a bit like a picnic but inside. Though if the weather's nice, might be outside. Angel cake, ginger cake, Victoria sponge, meringues. Scones and crumpets, with butter and jam. Sandwiches, lots of them, cress, cold tongue, ham and beef, cucumber. Long French bread, I like that though I don't much care for France. Pickled gherkins, they're my favourites. Ginger beer and lemonade. And tea, of course, different kinds of tea. Me and Mrs Rodgers and Winnie and the girls will have a bit of a feast of what's set aside. But you, my lad, you'll be in there scoffin' as much as you like."

Tommy pulled a bit of a face, raising his cheeks and eyebrows. The food might prove too much for him if he had to digest it with the chatter of adults.

"Here we are, here's our first delivery. It's Mrs Millicent, a nice enough old lady, one of Mrs H's friends – not that there's that many. Just go up the path and ring the bell – expect the maid will answer. Then hand over the letter and come back."

So he did. And so he did at other houses, most of them large but none as large as Hardinge Hall. The vicarage, with the letter to Rev. G. Jones. Sir James Booth. Mr Ronald Whiteman OBE & Mrs Ethel Whiteman. Gen. H. Carstairs.

One letter remained, to an address outside Luckhurst. "The Chorleys live further out, just back from the canal. We'll have to stop the car and walk along the towpath. Better be'ave, he runs the Conservative Association, Mr H likes to butter 'im up."

They got out of the car, but Rodgers was reluctant to leave it unattended, so he pointed the way for Tommy to go. The path ran alongside the canal until a lane led off to an imposing country house.

"You, boy! What are you doing? Up to mischief, I'll wager." A man with a large moustache, waxed and upturned as if echoing the wing collars of his shirt, strode towards Tommy wielding a walking stick as a warning rather than a support. "Who are you?"

"Mrs Hardinge sent me with this," and Tommy held out the envelope. "For Mr and Mrs Chorley."

The man took the envelope and calmed down as he opened it. Having read it, he grunted "Say Yes. No time to write." With his arms, one hand holding the stick, he shooed Tommy off the premises. The boy was pleased to be gone, particularly when he reached the towpath just as a narrow boat was passing, pulled by a barge-horse, trudging heavy-hooved down the narrow path. Tommy enjoyed walking at the horse's side until he came to the stile near where the motorcar was parked with Rodgers sitting on the running board.

"All done? That was quick."

"He said Yes. But not nicely."

"That fits. Get in."

There were very few cars on the road and people in fields and gardens stopped their work to stare at the sight of this car with its young passenger. They passed more horse-drawn carriages and carts than motorcars. Mission accomplished, they were home in time for a not very high tea.

As he made towards the stairs up to his room, Iris was coming down, and they were met by Mrs Hardinge.

"Ah, the postman has been. You both have letters."

Tommy and Iris seemed surprised and pleased by the delivery. Iris took Tommy's arm and led him into the drawing room so that they could open and read their letters at the same time. They sat at opposite ends of the green velvet sofa in this sickly-green room, reading in silence. Tommy soon finished, there was not much to read; his mother was not a skilled correspondent. She hoped this found him as well as it left her.

"Your mother, Tommy? I hope she's well, what does she say?" asked Iris.

"Not much. Who's yours from?"

"It's from my pa. He has things to say. Apparently I have to try harder and there is no chance of me escaping from here at any time soon. Not till duties have been discharged."

Iris sounded bitter, even to Tommy's untrained ears. "I expect you will," said Tommy. "Strikes me you're very good at it."

Iris looked a little startled. Her words had been spoken aloud but without the intention of conversation. "Thank you. What are you good at?"

Tommy did not have to think: he was missing his book that day, having been occupied on other things. "I'm good at reading. And writing. And delivering letters – that's what I've been doing this afternoon."

"Very good. You are a boy to be trusted. Tell me, have you delivered any letters for Teddy?"

"Just one."

"Was it for that girl? The one in the village pub?" Seeing Tommy nod, she continued. "Do they talk together? Do they meet?"

Tommy shrugged.

"Did you see them? What were they doing?"

"Oh just talkin', I spect."

He felt the need to change this subject, it made him embarrassed though he did not know why? Was he revealing secrets? *A secret's only a secret when you know it's one.*

"Will you write in my book?" He drew the green book out of his knapsack and held it towards her.

"Another day. I might not say the right thing now."

Iris got up and left the room. He could hear her walk quickly up the stairs. Now that he was alone, he opened the letter again, hoping that this time he could savour his mother's closeness through the words on the paper. But he could not hear her voice in these distant words, no matter how many times he read the few sentences on the page. He sat there feeling sorry for himself, holding the letter in one hand, the green notebook in the other.

"Hello, Tommy." Teddy stood above him, looking down at the disconsolate figure slumped into green velvet. "You look a bit glum."

Teddy sat down. "Can I see?" He took the letter from Tommy's loose grip. "That's a nice letter," he said after reading it quickly. "Your mother must be missing you. And you must be missing your mother. What's that?"

"It's the book I showed you, the one your father gave me to get people writin' in."

"Let me see that too. Perhaps I'll write in it now."

The written word had never come easily to Teddy. He had always dreaded compositions at the school he had been sent to, but he had been schooled there to overcome dreads. Now he sat on the sofa, pencil in hand, thinking hard. Then he wrote:

Do what will earn you trust.
Speak only when you must.
Strive always to be just.

He read it through to himself, shook his head and wrote some more in a less mannered style of handwriting. He was neither a writer nor a calligrapher, so the following words would be hard for Tommy to decipher. Teddy read them aloud when he saw Tommy struggling to read.

Sorry, Tommy. I'm no poet. Better to be a good friend. Nellie says Sorry for being a bad girl.

"Nellie wasn't bad. I just wasn't very good at lookin' after her."

"You did fine. Nellie loves you too."

Later, upstairs in his room, he read his mother's words for a third time, this time a little more able to imagine her saying them.

Mr Hardinge tells me you have been a good boy. He says any parent would be proud of you. He says you try hard. That is all a mother can ask.

7

FRIDAY

Sunlight was sliding like a butter knife through the curtains, and Winnie brought in a jug of hot water for Tommy's washing basin. She chatted to him about getting up.

"It's a lovely day," she said, "an' it looks as if the itchiness has gone. D'yer want any calamine put on?"

He shook his head: the stings and bites of other days had faded with a good sleep. "But you could write in my book." He kept the green book next to the bed and now he held it up towards her. "Me?" she asked and he explained what the notebook was for. Winnie found a space at the back of the book and after a visible effort she wrote:

"Remember every thing you can."

He thanked her though he thought it was a tough suggestion to make. He suspected there were things he might not want to remember, including parts of this week. Today he wanted to make sure that he had more time in his own company and less time with the adults.

"What's your plans for today, Tommy?" asked Rodgers over the now everyday sausage.

"Just wanna go t' the woods."

"Well, sneak out before they nab you for somethin' else."

So he did, though he passed Iris on the stairs. They looked at each other kindly without exchanging a word, so Tommy achieved his objective of making his escape out of the house without having to talk to Mrs Hardinge. He made straight for the woods, walking past the cottage, grateful not to have the responsibility of dogs or errands or expectations. After a short walk he came to the tree that he liked to climb, where he could sit and read out of sight. Soon he was back in the world of water rats and moles, badgers and toads, in the adventures of imagination that seemed preferable to those of reality, disturbed only by the occasional buzzing of a fly.

Getting to the end of a chapter, finding himself less entranced by the tales of a wayfaring rat, he paused to look around. The scene was enjoyable from this height and through dense leaves that made a canopy around him. This world was distant from that of the adults outside the woods, and he was pleased to think of this as his territory, but he began thinking about Rosie and Iris. Tommy liked Rosie but he did not think she was nearly as pretty as Iris. Rosie was ordinary, like a girl from his own street at home, but Iris with her pure white dresses seemed to him more like a fairytale princess. He liked to hold her eyes with his, almost like a game of dare, though she was generally quick to move her eyes away. He noticed how this always happened when she was talking to the adults, so it became more of a challenge for him to hold her gaze. He recalled her eyes, a deep brown like the bark of a tree in the shadiest part of the woods, summoned them into his mind as if they were the centre of a dream he wanted to revive. His memory shifted to her mouth, remembering her speaking kind words to him.

He blushed at the thought; he had never had such a thought before, never had a reason for his cheeks to redden like this, to his own surprise. He knew mysterious things happened between men and women, he knew it must involve kissing, but he could not really begin to understand it. It had never been a subject to ask his mother, and now it was already late to raise in the playground for fear of being laughed at for his innocence.

Another hour passed with a background of insects buzzing and birds chirping. Despite his long sleep the previous night, he began to feel a little drowsy as the midday sun warmed the air in the enveloping shade. He came awake to watch a rabbit on the ground below, moving in small hops from plant to plant, its twitching whiskers not detecting the observer above. Then he heard the sound of voices getting closer. Pushing aside the overhanging leaves he recognised the figures that went with the voices. He wondered what Teddy and Rosie were doing there, seemingly so friendly, right underneath his tree.

"All this is yours, then?" she said.

"What? This? Oh, the woods. Yes, I suppose so."

"Got so much you don't even know what you've got. You should care more."

"Really? The woods are fine but they're just woods."

"There's other things."

Rosie reached her hands to the back of her head and released a long cascade of golden hair that fell to her waist. It covered half her face. Teddy pushed it aside, like curtains, and kissed her mouth. Tommy was puzzled by the mystery of this. *Why do it?* Yet it seemed to have a tenderness if you put aside the unsavoury coming together of mouths. Rosie had dropped to the ground the blanket that he recognised from days earlier.

"Your hair is beautiful."

"And me?"

"You?"

"Am I beautiful?"

"You are very pretty."

"That'll have to do then."

"Very pretty – and game?"

She nodded a smile. "As long as you come out in time."

Rosie lay down on the blanket that she spread out across the ground of dead leaves. She lifted the skirts of her dress, exposing the petticoat beneath, with its lace fringe. Lowering himself, Teddy raised the petticoat to see the silk knickers that he shifted down below Rosie's knees and slid past her feet. While he did this Rosie was unbuttoning his trousers, reaching inside, pulling him down closer. Soon they were joined together, like one animal, with four legs and two voices bubbling with laughter. Tommy watched, fascinated and puzzled. For a short time they simply bounced, it seemed, Teddy on top of Rosie, the white skin of her legs wrapped around his dark-brown trousers. Then he pulled away and collapsed onto his back alongside her. Holding her hand, he raised it to his lips and kissed her sticky fingers.

They lay there for some minutes, simply breathing, faces turned towards each other. Then Rosie asked: "How do you feel? Was it good?"

"Ecstatic," said Teddy. "That was good."

"Oh no, it wasn't," Rosie replied with a pout. Teddy gave a start, disappointment clouded his face. "It was very bad. We'll just have to confess our sins on Sunday."

They both laughed as if they had heard the world's funniest joke, and they rolled towards each other to kiss again, closing their eyes as if to remember better.

Up in the tree Tommy was absorbed in the scene below but now he felt a sharp nip on a finger. He became aware that there was a whole army of ants marching down the branch where he was sitting, and he shifted his position, standing up on the branch to avoid the ants.

Rosie's eyes opened, staring upward – into Tommy's gaze. She shrieked.

"Pervert," she called out, "What yer doing? Should be ashamed of yerself."

"Who is it?" Teddy shouted. "Come down whoever you are."

Tommy clambered down the tree trunk. Recognising him, Teddy's embarrassment was no match for Rosie's giggles.

"Yer little bugger," she mouthed, still with a bubble in her throat.

"How could you, Tommy? That's spying and we don't like spies."

"I weren't spyin'. Honest. I was just up the tree readin' then you came along." He held out the book, as if to introduce his own evidence. Teddy read the title on the spine.

"So, you like this? Is it good?"

A literary discussion seemed unlikely, given Teddy's efforts to button his flies, Rosie's attempts to straighten her dress.

"I bet you can keep secrets," said Teddy to the boy. "Can you?"

"Course I can."

"Then this, whatever you saw here, that's our secret and you must never say a word to anyone. Do you swear?"

Tommy nodded. "Cross your heart and hope to die." As Tommy waved his arms across his chest, Teddy continued: "You must never tell my mother. And not a word to Iris."

Tommy knew it would be easy to say nothing to Mrs Hardinge. It was one of his aims in life. He hoped Iris would not ask him anything because he knew it would be harder to lie to her.

Teddy bent down and picked up the blanket from the ground, shaking it to loosen leaves and twigs that had become attached. Rosie watched on, then bent over from the waist so that her hair hung down. Now she could gather her hair, straighten up and press her tresses into a bunch on top of her head. Dishevelled clothing rearranged to order, Teddy handed the blanket to Rosie and blew a kiss towards her.

"We'd better be off," he said.

•

Back at Hall, Tommy and Teddy went to their separate rooms. It seemed better to avoid any invitation to questioning. Later in the afternoon, Tommy decided to go downstairs as the house seemed quiet. He wandered into the small drawing room, expecting emptiness but finding Muriel.

"Oh, it's you," she said. "What do you want?"

"I was just going to read."

"What? What are you reading?" Muriel took the book and opened it at his bookmark, then started reading aloud: *"Sitting up, he rubbed his eyes first and his complaining toes next, wondered for a moment where he was, looking round for familiar stone wall and little barred window; then with a leap of the heart, remembered everything."* Muriel stifled a yawn. "You like this? What a strange little boy."

"It's a good story," Tommy insisted.

"I wouldn't know. I don't really like stories. Though Father read this to me when I was smaller. The parts with Toad were best."

Tommy was not sure about that. He preferred it when Mole and Rat were the centres of the story. Muriel, perhaps out of boredom, seemed prepared to accept Tommy's company, and now she offered to share the cherries she had on a plate. Spitting out the last cherry, Muriel spoke the rhyme: "Tinker, tailor, soldier, sailor. That's you. Rich man, poor man, beggar man, thief. Boo-hoo, poor me. They'll put me in jail for thieving. Like Toad."

"Only if you steal something."

"Perhaps I will. Anyway, that's when I grow up. I think you're going to be a sailor like the Seafaring Rat."

"Will you write in my book then?" he asked. It seemed the right moment. Muriel had never seemed this sympathetic before.

"Oh, your silly book. Let me see." She looked through it, reading all the words written so far, then drew out the pencil. She wrote: *"They say the sun never sets on our empire. You must explore it by sailing the seven seas. When you return you might be better company."*

It seemed he had exhausted Muriel's kindness, so he moved away, grasping the green notebook to his chest. Muriel went up the stairs to her room, perhaps in search of other forms of boredom to pass the time.

Tommy wandered the house. It was always quiet in the afternoons as people retired to their own rooms for a nap, and he felt that the woods were forbidden territory after the morning's happenings. He went from room to room, as long as they were not occupied, and he knew it would be the upstairs rooms where people were locked away to their own preoccupations if not to deep sleep. Downstairs were large rooms with smaller rooms leading from them: a library with a next-door study, a grand dining room with a simpler version attached; a drawing room that also had a door to the study.

Tommy was curious about the different decorations of the rooms. He would have asked questions but he could not decide who would be best to ask. He might have asked Iris but thought she might not know either. He would avoid Teddy for a while and Mrs Hardinge for as long as possible. He had used up his time with Muriel, at least for today. So he explored the rooms like a museum visitor, not even knowing what a museum is, questions stored in his memory but then, when he remembered, into the black notebook where he wrote in pencil. *What is a landscape? Where does a bird of paradise live? Where is paradise if the bird lives there?*

The dining room was characterised by a glittering chandelier and paintings of countryside scenes on the walls; the drawing room had green walls and oriental prints; the study had watercolours of birds from different parts of the world; the hallway was gloomed over by large portraits of unsmiling people from another century. If he had imagined these as family heirlooms, collected by the Hardinges over generations, he would have been mistaken. When they bought Hardinge Hall – by auction in a distress sale – they had acquired all the previous owner's domestic belongings. The house had come ready equipped for occupancy by a country gentleman. So the Hardinges became the incurious collectors of another family's cultural heritage. The truth was they knew hardly anything of what now belonged to them – nor even its value – but they acquired an inherited patrician provenance rooted in the English rural tradition.

Tommy went up to his room and started writing in his black notebook. He did not really know what he was writing but the words started to flow. Words about the house, the week, the woods, arranging themselves into clusters on the pages. *Is this a poem?* It took him by surprise later that he had become so absorbed in his writing, deaf to the world. Like Rat, alternately scribbling and sucking the top of his pencil.

There was a bit of a commotion downstairs. George Hardinge had made a noisy return home for the weekend and he wanted to know how plans were progressing for the next day's high tea.

"Where is everyone? Why is the damned house so quiet? Are they all up to silent mischief? Not you, Tommy, not you, thank you for coming to say Hello. You have the makings of manners."

"I was in my room," said Tommy, heading off any accusations.

"Well, I'll show you what I've got you. I went to Jermyn Street to make sure you had the right things to wear tomorrow. You heard about our gathering? I want you to look smart. Look at these, I asked your mother about sizes," unwrapping clothes from a paper parcel, "so they should fit you perfectly well."

The long trousers were held up for him to see, then the white shirt. Tommy had never had long trousers to wear before, he had not expected to wear them till he was more grown-up. *Perhaps I am now?* The new clothes made him uneasily aware that he might now be deficient in other aspects of his wardrobe. His eyes followed Mr Hardinge's gaze down to his socks and shoes.

"You'll do. You can try these on in your room, make sure they fit. But they seem right," holding them next to Tommy. "Off you go."

In his room Tommy puzzled that his mother had helped by supplying clothes sizes. His mouth puckered with a touch of sour jealousy that he could not explain. It seemed close to a betrayal but he could not even contemplate such a charge. The clothes fitted but they felt uncomfortably alien. But he knew there would be no escaping the wearing of them next day. For now there was another family dinner to endure because Mr Hardinge insisted that he should be reinstated at the dinner table after his banishment to the kitchen in recent days.

"Sit here, Tommy," said Iris. "Next to me," she whispered, "we can be interlopers together."

Tommy wished he understood the meaning of that word.

But there were so many words, like the cawing of rooks in the treetops, conveying no specific meaning but expressing a threat. What could a boy do except read and read and read to improve himself? He looked at Mr Hardinge at the head of the table, listened to the distant conversation about arrangements for tomorrow's tea, and realised what he could not yet pin down as a fact known by the adults at this dinner table. *Mr Hardinge doesn't fit in, no more than I do.* There was an uneasiness there, the head of the house no more certain of his place than Tommy was. This became clearer with each passing course, leaping from salmon to chicken to trifle, with words criss-crossing the table and the supposed patriarch bemused in a white-linen no-man's-land.

It was true, though admitted to himself only in moments of painful self-knowledge. George Hardinge was never sure how he fitted in, whether he was really accepted. It was the main reason why he smoked cigars – it was what other people did in the circle where he wanted to belong. But he had never become that comfortable with the practice even though it was now close to becoming a habit. He waved the smoke away from his face, disliking the stinging it brought to his eyes, but this had become his custom at the end of meals.

Tommy, if he had been allowed such an opinion, might have declared it bad manners to smoke cigars and fill the air with such a pungent smell. If the thought flitted to the point of his lips, it was soon suppressed by Mrs Hardinge declaring "Cigar smoke – it's a masculine perfume."

She allowed herself a single cigarette, fitted into a black cigarette holder, when satisfaction with her world allowed. As it did tonight.

8

SATURDAY

Tommy woke to sounds of bustle in the house. Almost as soon as he opened his eyes, Winnie opened the door, bringing hot water for his wash basin.

"Come on, sleepy head. It's a big day. Mr & Mrs H are up and about, and in a right flap over the party."

When he was washed and dressed he went downstairs, heading for the kitchen, but was intercepted by Mr Hardinge.

"Not the kitchen today, Tommy. Or any day when I'm home. You must learn better. You will not learn the manners needed for company by consorting with the kitchen staff."

It seemed that Mr Hardinge had adopted the character of his wife. Tommy saw there was no escape; he saw Mrs Hardinge looking vindicated behind the disguised weapon of a raised tea cup.

"Perhaps manners cannot be taught," she remarked, apparently to no one in particular, not deigning to look at Tommy. "Perhaps one is born with them – or not."

"He is a good boy, Catherine. He will do us proud when the guests arrive."

Mrs Hardinge looked him up and down with distaste on her face. "He is a ragamuffin."

"Ah, there you are wrong. This afternoon you will see, he will be transformed."

They continued talking about him as if he were not there. Tommy was content to give his attention to the food on his plate if it excused an absence from the conversation. So they discussed the arrangements for the afternoon, who would be there and why they were invited. There was a reason for the high tea that Tommy could not quite understand but he realised that he was a large part of the reason. Words like charity, philanthropy, contribution were spoken and stored away by Tommy for later investigation.

Words could be investigated in a dictionary. But a person's background and motivations need deeper digging. For now there was the feeling of something being locked out of sight; only maturity might reveal the real reasons for snobbery.

"George, you are generous to a fault," his wife was saying in a particularly intense way. "You do good works. Here is another one, this ragamuffin you raise like yourself to heights of personal discomfort. You give money, you buy, or you hope to buy — what? I am not sure. Privilege. Influence. Standing. A knighthood, you hope, eventually. But you are an ordinary man that some would call a good man, but say so without respect. You work hard — for some, that counts against you. These people you invite today do not share your industriousness. Yours comes from something deeper. Like coal burning beneath the surface, it fuels your will to do good."

"That much is true, Catherine. I have that will. It burns inside like guilt."

"You have no need for guilt. Your money is earned."

"Nothing is possible without money. But money creates a sense of guilt in me. It breaks out like a rash on a hot day."

"Pah, you are getting sentimental. Look at the boy. You have raised him a little but he knows nothing better than the sausage on his plate. To him that is luxury — he needs no more. And he will return to his mother in a week's time hardly aware of the experience that was gifted to him."

"He needs – or at least he will get – this occasion. It is something he would not know otherwise."

They became aware that Tommy had stopped eating to listen to them talking. He knew that their subject was himself, and it made him flush.

"Finish your breakfast, Thomas. We have much to do." She drained her tea like an item on her list of things to do, leaving the dregs to be cleared by others who had that duty.

"Come here," she said to him. She put her hands on his cheeks and squeezed them. His mouth opened at her bidding. "Do you brush your teeth?"

"Yes. Every day."

"Good. But your teeth could be better. Do they teach you about teeth at school?"

"I'm in the Toothbrush Club."

"Winnie," she turned to the maid, "provide him with a new toothbrush and some chalk powder. Then," turning back, "go and brush your teeth properly. You don't want to lose them. After all, you enjoy eating. Or so I observe."

•

The afternoon party was under way. *How do you do? how do you do?* it seemed there was nothing more that needed saying in the guidance given to him by Mrs Hardinge. Tommy, embarrassed by the attention forced upon him, edged away from the small group that had assembled around Mr Hardinge. The conversation revolved around crops and gardens. As a landowner, Mr Hardinge felt it was his duty to take an interest in such matters, though his lack of knowledge was obvious even to Tommy. The planning for a village fete allowed a more convincing display of managerial expertise through the deployment of numbers and the discussion of money raised for local good causes.

Tommy backed into the garden terrace unnoticed by those inside or outside. Here, near the French windows, were two men in conversation.

"The man has money, you can see that," said the red-faced man with the waxed moustache who, two days earlier, had almost chased Tommy from his grounds. "But money is not breeding, as we know, General. He's non-commissioned class."

The other man was in Army uniform with several medals attached in a row across his breast. He had the air of someone on the brink of issuing the order to attack. "Chorley, he is a rising man. What becomes of our country when he is the new order? Where money means more than history."

"Oh, he has history, I'm told. His father owned a coal mine, though he began as a labourer in the mine. Hardinge's bank is built on coal. At least he does not try to conceal that. The Newcastle & Durham Bank at least allows you to guess at origins."

"It explains a coarseness I could never quite put my finger on. And perhaps an accent disguised. Growing up in the northern coalfields."

"But it shows something. A kind of gumption. That could be useful. To us, to the country."

Inside the house a bell was rung, summoning them to its location in the dining room.

"We are called to serve," laughed the General. "Perhaps for enlightenment or entertainment? Who knows? We do our duty. For a show or simply showing off. Are you there, boy? Seen but not heard, as it should be."

"It has that air of the *Titanic*. Summoned to the lifeboats." Far from panicked, they shared a comfortable chuckle.

Tommy observed their mutual satisfaction with their places in the world, their willingness to laugh at others. If the ship was sinking, they saw no need to go down with it; self-preservation was their natural right. They brushed past Tommy and went through the doors inside.

George Hardinge was already standing on a dais in front of the large painted landscape of a lake fringed by heather-covered hills.

"Come closer my friends. Take your places at the table. I have no wish to shout…"

As he looked around the room, George Hardinge had more than a moment of self-importance. He saw the dignitaries of the local establishment, brought here at his bidding. Leaders of church and industry, the state and the aristocracy, with hands on the levers of power, at least at this parochial level. It must, he thought, add to his earnt ledger in the departments of Government. These leaders must lead to something, some of the things that he desired. He contemplated that prospect even as he stole a glance in the mirror to check that he was well enough presented. He straightened his tie, touched his hair, while thinking that an honour would improve his bearing.

"The world has known great heroes," Mr Hardinge began, looking up from his notes. "The history books tell us. Nelson. Wellington. Clive. We teach their deeds in school, and our children learn by their examples. Children like young Tommy here.

"I invite you to consider his situation. His mother is a good woman, a cleaning woman. She does her job, as we expect people all across our nation to do their jobs. We ask little more of them than that – except we do…they raise children who grow up to serve their country.

"They might not become the clever men at Oxford but we still need them. They might not become the generals whom the Army all salutes – but still we need them. If we go to war, we need them to fight for King and country. If we remain at peace we need them to plough the fields and scatter the good seed on the land – as Reverend jones will tell us in church on a Sunday.

"Our society needs the likes of Tommy. There is an order to it that we all rely on. That is why I have Tommy under our watch, why he is with us for two weeks. He will see that there is a wider world with wider opportunities, if he works hard. It is a sign of our respect and gratitude, and I am proud to welcome Tommy alongside all of you this afternoon.

"Tommy comes from an impoverished part of London. His mother lives in Covent Garden. I do not recommend it as a place for the ladies here to visit but it is clear to me that our Empire is great because of the people who live in such places.

"But we need to give them more than silent gratitude. I will do my best for Tommy but he is just one example among many. So today I announce here, among you all, my friends, that I am establishing a charitable fund to give a helping hand to the Tommys of our world. I establish it with a personal contribution but I hope, dear friends, that you will wish to contribute to such a good cause.

"For now – forgive me if it is early in the day for this – your glasses have been charged. I invite you to raise your glasses to the future of this philanthropic enterprise. I give you a toast – to the Tommys!"

Tommy wished he could become invisible. He wondered about sliding from his chair and hiding beneath the table but he was transfixed by the gaze of his benefactor who lifted a glass of white wine in his direction. There was a smattering of applause then General Carstairs rose to his feet.

"Words liberally spoken, Hardinge," he said. "Now I give you this toast – the King!"

Food, and the eating of food, is often the saviour of

awkward situations. There was a clattering of cutlery and crockery as the guests began to be served. Later, in his room, Tommy would struggle to remember what he had eaten. Once he had finished he remembered Teddy taking him outside to walk in the garden.

"Sorry about that, Tommy. I'm sure he meant well but it must have been difficult for you."

They were walking at the edge of the woods, which reminded Tommy of the last time he had seen Teddy in that place. On top of any social embarrassment, there was a blushing memory, and the physical discomfort of sweating in his unaccustomed clothes. He was not used to long flannel trousers and the stiffness of a white cotton shirt.

"Teddy, I want you to tell me. I really want to know. What were you and Rosie doin' the other day?"

"Which day? Oh, that," as if it was almost forgotten. If Teddy had forgotten, Tommy found it hard to keep the image from his mind. He had written the words in his black notebook: *Like a spider on its back. Legs waving.*

"What was it?"

"It's what grown-ups do to say they like each other. But it's always a secret. So we never talk about that. It's part of being grown-up, so you must be too."

That closed the subject as definitely as turning back towards the house. Iris was waiting for them on the terrace, perhaps taking refuge from the indoor conversations.

"Are you settled, Tommy? It was an unsettling speech as you were the centre of it."

They went inside with a nod or two. The guests were leaving, to the relief of everyone, it seemed to Tommy. Even he could tell that this had not been a good party. He stared at the

General with suspicion. *How can he be a soldier? I could fight him.*

"Where is your green book, Tommy?" asked Mr Hardinge. "We must ask General Carstairs to write in it. I'll explain while you go and fetch it."

So it was that Tommy acquired the latest written advice, perhaps from the most unwelcome quarter so far. *"Serve your King and Country. There is no higher calling."*

9

SUNDAY

"You are up at a good hour, Tommy," said Mr Hardinge. "Breakfast is not yet ready. Let us take a stroll."

Tommy had been sneaking down the stairs, heading for the kitchen. After the previous day's high tea, he had suffered an early night, boredom and a lack of food.

The dew was heavy on the grass, and droplets of water were scattered like seeds as they walked across the lawn. The sun was rising in the sky above the tops of the trees where birds were making the only noise apart from the squelching of Mr Hardinge's footsteps in the grass.

"There is so much to be thankful for. Don't you think, Tommy? Despite everything, despite disappointments."

Tommy did his best to reassure. He could sense an unease, perhaps even pain, in this man half a stride alongside him. The memory of yesterday's party was disturbing to both of them; Tommy felt that with certainty.

"They call this the Lord's Day. Thank the Lord. I tell you, Tommy, I would thank the Lord for a better sleep." He smiled a smile that aimed to create a bond between the two of them, and Tommy understood the need to return it. He even ventured a question: "Is it hard for you to sleep?"

They teetered on the edge of a conversation between equals. Tommy felt that he might understand, might sympathise. Seeing Mr Hardinge in this early morning light, with the professional assurance stripped away, seemed to bring them to a surprising closeness. Tommy looked at the older man and something, affection perhaps, gratitude, whatever they might call it, helped them understand each other better without words passing between them. Tommy understood that yesterday had been a disappointment. It had loomed with hope but had collapsed under the weight of expectations, and Tommy felt he might have to shoulder some of the blame, if that could help. He looked sideways at a troubled face.

As if reading his thoughts, the man said: "It is true, I expected a lot. I wanted them to understand. But people do not always choose to do so. It is not your fault. You behaved well. Now they leave me feeling as if I failed you, failed myself."

He rubbed his chest as if feeling for life there, as if doubting that he would ever find consolation in his own feelings. George Hardinge was acutely afflicted by mortality. He felt it more than most because he thought about it more than most, particularly on those nights, all nights now, when he slept alone, with his head on the pillow imagining indigestion as the onset of a heart attack, a headache as the symptom of a tumour in his brain. Yet there was part of him that welcomed the prospect of death, the opportunity to put nagging uncertainty behind him, the final end of insomnia. Particularly on mornings like this when he was still partly in recovery from the sadness of shallow dreams interrupted, in a half-waking state like the orange sun that was just beginning to remind him of greater responsibilities that come with wakefulness.

"We must go back, Tommy. It must be time for breakfast now. I am sorry to have burdened you with my troubles – and really they are nothing. Life is fulfilling, if only we allow it to be."

•

Tommy had never before felt this kind of sympathy with an adult, except his own mother at those times when she felt most alone, times when he knew he had the power to comfort her by cuddling close. But this was strange, because Mr Hardinge was a stranger, someone he hardly knew. Yesterday he might have looked forward eagerly to their farewell. Now he was less sure what he felt.

He went to his room after breakfast, his mind made up to write to his mother. So he sat at the table by the window, taking advantage of the light in this room of dark furniture. He had been furnished – in Mrs Hardinge's words – with letter-writing materials: ink, pen and headed paper stamped Hardinge Hall in gold, with an embossed envelope to seal his words inside. The words came no easier than his patron's sleep in the midnight darkness but he forced out some well-worn platitudes that he had imbibed from his surroundings. These were words drained of emotion, almost a disguise for his own feelings, but he still felt tears in his eyes as he wrote *"I trust you are well."*

The problem was that there was so much that he could not write about. The sights he had seen from the vantage point of the tree spread a sense of secrecy across all his thoughts. The memory of what he had witnessed was foremost in his mind but could not be written down for his mother. It was easier to retreat to food eaten and animals seen. He managed to fill a page with words of little meaning, then sealed the envelope with a lick of his tongue.

A bell rang to summon everyone. It was time for church. They set off, the whole household, as the previous week in a double file, but with even less animation than before. The whole family party seemed overcast by the greyness of their feelings as they walked down the road that wound between the trees towards the village church.

As they reached the village and marched past the pub, Tommy watched Iris's head turn to observe the briefest of glances between Teddy and the girl leaning on the gate. Then inside the church, sitting in the front pews, he looked back and found himself in the line between these two pairs of eyes. He shrank a little to avoid being caught in the cross-fire of sight.

When the service began there was a rousing singing of the hymn. As if released from bonds, Teddy's voice led the congregation:

> *"All good gifts around us*
> *Are sent from heaven above.*
> *Then thank the Lord, O thank the Lord*
> *For all His love."*

The service passed without Tommy listening to the words spoken by Reverend Jones. He was in a reverie, automatically following the ritual movements of those around him, to sit, to bring hands together, to stand, to kneel, to file out down the aisle.

Again Tommy was told to wait outside until Mr Hardinge was ready to walk back to the house with him. Hardinge had approached the vicar again, buttering him with the title Reverend. He had wondered, with disarming directness, where were the signs of God's love?

"They are all around if we choose to see," replied the vicar. "That's why we sang 'We plough the fields and scatter'. You mentioned it yesterday, for a reason, I felt, because you are ahead of the season. But God's love is not bound by the seasons. It is all around you, you must bring it inside you. He has a response to your questions, allowing you to see His goodness. The thankfulness we bring and sing at Harvest time are ours throughout the year. We thank God for his gifts. For all his gifts."

Hardinge scratched at his beard, as if shaking reluctant words from his mouth. "If you were looking for a sign, there seems to be a shortage of gifts. I reached out and received no response from those who were present but chose not to hear."

Reverend Jones looked serious behind his automatic response of a smile. "You must stop demanding them as your right. Think of blessings you can bring rather than being blessed by gifts that men might give you. Even disappointment may be a gift if it spurs us to try harder."

"I always try hard. I think you know, I do not look for gifts for myself, and not for now but for the future."

The Reverend ploughed on. "A wondrous time is coming – Autumn is the time when we feel God's bounty most. I always look forward to Harvest Festival. Do you? It makes clear the abundance of good things for which we are grateful. And we can all sing those words...all good gifts. Already we have planted seeds, already we are blessed with the fruit of those seeds. We need to remember that every day of the year."

Hardinge shot a look at Tommy, suddenly aware that the boy was waiting and listening. "Do you have a Bible, Tommy?" He shook his head. "I think you should. Reverend?"

"I hope your mother is bringing you up as a good Christian." Reverend Jones went back through the doors of the church; he returned with a Bible. "Read it regularly, young man. It will teach you to be good."

"There is advice, Tommy. It must be sound advice because Reverend Jones is sincere and not an empty vessel. Have you asked him to write in your notebook?"

Tommy slipped the Bible into his knapsack and took out the green notebook, which he handed to the vicar. Rev. Jones wrote: 'A good man out of the good treasure of his heart bringeth forth that which is good.' Luke 6:45

•

When they returned to the house, Teddy was in earnest conversation with his mother. She was reclining on the chaise longue in the drawing room, her pose drawing a posture of submission from her son sitting in the high-backed chair at her side. For Teddy it was not a comfortable conversation, so his father and Tommy held back from making their presence immediately obvious.

"Feckless is not a word I wish to use against my son. But it fits you rather too well."

"That is not fair."

"I saw you look at that girl. Her eyes had a knowing look."

"It would be rude to avoid her. She is one of the village, and she performs a role valued by many of our tenants."

"Does she perform such a role for you? Her eyes say she does."

"Mother, this is impossible!"

"George, come in, do not loiter in the shadows. This is your son, he needs paternal counsel. He is in dereliction of his duty, his duty to you, to me, to his intended. He has eyes only for the village slut. Explain to me, George, why men are like this. Does it come with the wearing of trousers?"

"Catherine, please. The boy…"

"You care more for this boy than for your own son. Your son is errant in his behaviour, he needs to be corrected. He cannot chase after village girls. It brings shame on us."

Sex had never been a subject for conversation in the family; relationships between the sexes were considered only in terms of partnerships formed by marriage, a business deal. Anything more physical could not be referred to, but here it was dangerously close to the surface. Congress, as his wife termed it, however irregular, was the duty George Hardinge had performed to ensure the continuation of his name and legacy. Teddy and Muriel were the result, Adelaide the unspoken one, a baby who had never properly opened her lungs to life. Sex was the constant temptation that he succumbed to in London, never in Kent. He might have been shocked at the thought of its existence away from the tightly packed streets of a metropolis. It was a transaction that normally involved the payment of money, an assertion of a power he wielded outside his house that he could not enjoy inside it.

The bell rang for Sunday dinner and it was hard to say which of those present felt the greater relief.

•

That afternoon was languorous, only the flies were active as they flitted from drowsy face to face. Members of the family were slouched in different parts of the house or on the terrace, avoiding the perils of words and honesty and activity. Eventually Teddy roused himself to play croquet with Iris and Muriel, while Tommy watched them from the window of his room until, bored, not understanding the rules of the game, he curled up in an armchair to read his book. Perhaps the only exuberance of his day was the return of the friends to Toad Hall, but this came tinged with the sadness of 'The End'. *What will I do now?* He wondered and no doubt the Mole did too.

He stayed in that world for a time, closing his eyes as he lay on the bed. When he woke he went downstairs, finding Iris sitting alone in the drawing room.

"Have you finished the game?" he asked.

"Silly game," she said. "But it amused Teddy for a while. I see you have your notebook. I am ready to write in it now."

She opened the green book that he handed to her, reading through the messages from start to finish. Then she wrote carefully in pencil, spelling out the words so that he would be able to read her handwriting: *'Always – show kindness and helpfulness and truthfulness for they are qualities which will make you a good man in time.'*

Tommy read and nodded to show that he had understood.

"Will you do me a kindness?" asked Iris. "I will write a message for you to deliver to that girl tomorrow. Will you do that? That will be helpful to me but it will be best if you tell no one else."

Iris smiled at him. It was a smile that he would remember and always strive to win again.

10

MONDAY

John Everett Millais. Tommy read the painter's name on the frame's brass plate. *Mill-ace?* The painting itself was a highland scene with purple heather and brown sedge. To Tommy's eyes this was as unfamiliar as the jungle with brightly coloured parrots on display in the small dining room.

"You could do drawings in your notebook too, Tommy," said Iris who had entered the room quietly.

"I can't really draw."

"Of course you can. You just need to look at things – look really hard. Then draw exactly what you see, especially the shadows."

"I've only got a pencil."

"That will do. The best artists start with just a pencil sketch. But wait here, I'll get something for you."

Tommy wanted to please Iris so he was willing to consider the idea. *But what to draw?* Iris returned with a tin box containing twelve coloured pencils.

"Try these," said Iris, "they're Derwent, good pencils."

Tommy opened the tin, noting that the picture on the box was like a much brighter version of the painting on the wall. The range of colours made him want to try them.

"What shall I draw?" he asked. "A rainbow?"

"If I were you, I'd go out to the woods. There are lots of things to draw there. What about a leaf?"

He nodded and Iris smiled. He would do his best with these pencils, sketching a leaf, a rainbow smile, gratitude.

"And one more thing. That message I mentioned to you. I have it here. Please deliver it to that girl. I forget her name."

"Rosie," said Tommy, just to be clear.

"That's it. Put this in your knapsack, out of sight. The pencils too."

Tommy went upstairs to get ready. When his bag was packed, he collected a cheese and pickle sandwich from Mrs Rodgers in the kitchen. As he came back through the hall, on his way to the front door, he overheard the voices of Mrs Hardinge and Teddy in the dining room on the left.

"So your father has taken the early train to his work. As usual. He is a stickler for his duties. While you remain here, with no visible occupation. As usual."

"I have things to do. It is very quiet in father's offices at this time of year."

"So are you not having a day in London this week? Not at all? A day at work?"

"How can I, ma? I am here, attending to Iris according to your wishes."

"Despite ignoring her for the most part of your time."

"I try, I do my best to live up to your wishes."

"Your attitude leaves a lot to be desired. To work and to life."

"I try my best."

"It matters not a jot that you try, Edward. I expect more than effort. Particularly when the effort is fruitless."

"Fruitless? My efforts do bear fruit. Iris sees that."

"Feckless is the word I am obliged to use again. Again against my wishes. Again it is not a word I would wish to use to describe my son. You must stop your behaviour matching its meaning."

The conversation was winding down and Teddy had no

wish to prolong it. Tommy slipped out of the house before either of the Hardinges could see him.

The woods looked dense that day. He chose to walk through them rather than along the lane that skirted them. The light was flickering through the trees like a guttering candle, as grey clouds scudded across the sun, as sunbeams sometimes filtered through the leaves. He wondered about stopping to draw, but to draw what? The envelope in his knapsack was too much on his mind so he decided he must discharge his duty first by delivering the message.

As he drew nearer the pub, he became anxious that Rosie might not be there – or that she might need to be summoned from inside. Tommy wanted to avoid that situation because it would lead to questioning. *I just wanted to say thank you, she was very kind.*

He need not have worried as she was mopping down the table outside. She looked up with curiosity, putting down the cloth and wiping her hands dry on her pinafore.

"Hello," she said. "What brings you here?"

"This." He passed the envelope to her, which she opened eagerly.

"Oh, not what I was expectin'," she told him after she had read it. "Does she trust you then? Must do. So you tell 'er we can meet at the shed in the west woods. Tomorrow. 3 o'clock. OK?"

"You mean the hide."

"I mean what I mean. You know it. If she don't know it, you bring her there."

As Tommy walked away, Rosie called after him. "And not a word to anyone else. Specially not Teddy."

He felt unsettled by this conversation with Rosie. He felt that he was being drawn deeper and deeper into a place where he would be uncomfortable, perhaps made to do wrong. Yet he wanted to please Iris; he felt an attachment there that he did not want to jeopardise. After all he was simply doing what adults asked him to do, and no blame should be laid upon him for being obliging. He told himself as much as he walked away from the pub into the centre of the village.

Still he worried that what he was doing might not be counted as good. Otherwise why would he avoid questions? He always wanted to do good, to be good; he was not one of those boys in his class at school who took pride in misbehaving. His mother expected this much of him: *be good* was her constant reminder. Conflicted by the demands of others – Teddy and Iris, Rosie, Mr Hardinge – he was unable to see a way through, like being lost in the darkness of the wood at night. But who could help him? *None of them want me to say anything to any of the others.*

With a sense of desperation, and driven by a sudden shower of rain, he sought shelter in the porch of the church. He stood within the grey stone columns, the heavy dark door at his back, watching the rain spattering onto the gravel path that led from the lych-gate.

"You can come inside," said the voice behind him. Reverend Jones was standing in the doorway. "The rain will not last long but it is dry inside."

The vicar's voice sounded different. He was not delivering a sermon; he sounded gentler, kinder. He was not wearing the surplice that he wore to conduct a service, so Tommy followed him inside the church. They sat in a side pew but the altar with its golden cross was just a few steps away.

"You seem a little nervous, Tommy. No need, you are in the house of God, He is here to guard you and to guide you. Tell me, do you pray? Shall we pray?"

Reverend Jones brought Tommy's hands together in prayer, then formed his own hands into the same shape.

"We are all troubled. Even a boy as young as you are. But God can comfort you. You must trust me as the true messenger of God."

They bowed their heads in silence and closed their eyes. When Tommy opened his, he found the vicar's eyes fixed intently on him as he knelt before him, his face close before his own.

"I will instruct you a little because I see you do not know many of the teachings of the church. Our Sunday services are the only ones your guardian attends but there are others, services that bring us closer to the Lord Jesus. Closer to the sacrifices he made for us, his body and his blood. Here we worship the body of Christ. It brings us comfort because we are human, because Christ understands our humanity, because he died for us all. I will offer you this wafer as a symbol of Jesus' body, the body that you see taut and muscled on the cruel cross. Do you see? Here, Tommy, take this."

He held the communion wafer out to Tommy in his hand. He brushed it against his lips but Tommy did not open his mouth; he stared, even more confused, at the man kneeling in front of him. What was he being offered? A biscuit, it seemed. This is my body. *I don't want it. I don't want it.* The wafer was still pressed insistently in the vicar's hand, held between his fingers towards him. The man's larger hands closed over his small hands, there was a squeeze, of reassurance or comfort or something more that words could not express. *Is this what they mean by the mystery?* As never before it made his mind confused. The hands clasped around his, lowering his fingers firmly while he felt the piercing pressure of the clergyman's eyes upon him, willing him towards a submission that he knew, instinctively and instantly was not what he wanted.

"No!" he shouted, surprising himself by the sound of the echo he created. He wrestled his hand out of the man's grip and ran out of the church, down the tiled aisle, through the wooden doors that he had to pull open, out into the daylight whose very brightness, with its suddenly restored sunburst, seemed like a Biblical revelation. Relieved as he was by the light, he carried on running, across the road and into the woods.

Although the woods were dark he found they offered security. He seemed to understand these trees better than he could understand the humans who were on the other side of them. He ran and ran, his knapsack bouncing on his back, his boots sliding a little on the newly-muddied surface. It was glorious to run, to run fast, faster and faster, the tree trunks passed second by second, flashing by, eventually to stop in the clearing where he had been with Teddy a few days earlier. He listened. What could he hear? Only the winds in the leaves, punctuated by the croaks and calls of the crows.

He wondered what had made him panic. Why had he run so fast? It all now seemed like a dream but dreams can have a frightening reality. He looked around, as if he really were waking from a nightmare. The woods had a familiarity he had not felt a week ago; now they seemed his friends. He had very few others in this place.

Sitting on a tree trunk, he shrugged off his knapsack. Its fabric was wet on the outside where he had brushed against bushes, but he reached inside to find that everything was dry. He took out the black notebook, turning the pages past the words he had written in tiny handwriting, as if they were secrets shared with himself. He stopped at a blank spread of pages, flattening the book open to make the area as large as possible, then he lifted a green pencil from the Derwent tin. He started to move the pencil tip across the paper but the sharpness of the pencil was scratching the white surface. He turned the point of the pencil sideways and slid the pencil horizontally across the paper, enjoying the sensation, observing the softer effect of the pencil lead when he held it more loosely between his fingers. Up and down, from side to side; he had begun by attempting to draw a leaf but now he was content simply to create a pattern.

He looked at what he had drawn. It was meaningless, just a scribble, and suddenly he was aware of his own dissatisfaction. *Enough. Put them away. You can't draw.* "It's as much as I can do to draw my breath," he remembered his mother saying, as if discouraging artistic aspirations.

The pause for drawing at least had allowed space for calmer thoughts to reassert themselves. He found the cheese and pickle sandwich – pickle was a recent discovery for him. If allowed he would eat only pickle not the cheese.

Later, returning to his room, sneaking in because he had no wish to encounter anyone, he told himself with some relief that soon he would be home again, reunited with his mother whom he was missing more and more each day. His mother brought a certainty that was missing here, the certainty of knowing what it was right for him to do. For now he could only grit his teeth and bear whatever was put in front of him, delivering messages to others if they found him useful in that role. Certainly Iris seemed pleased when he reported to her the arrangements that Rosie had suggested.

"Where is that? I don't know the hide."

"It's OK, I'll show you to it."

"Tomorrow?"

"3 o'clock," he repeated the message he had been given,

the message that had not been written down, that he had remembered.

"Good boy," said Iris. Her smile warmed him and made him feel better. "You are the best."

11

TUESDAY

It seemed unfair to Tommy that he could not sleep. He lay wrapped in the itchy coverlet of darkness, turning this way and that, thinking of all the people he had delivered messages for. It was hard. He could not be easy when the consequences of those messages were uncertain. He could not sleep for thinking that life was unfair. But eventually he did.

As did Iris. As did Rosie. As did Teddy. Consciences can be put to sleep. Just as they can be wakened as one day slips between the sheets of another.

When he woke in the morning he was worried about the clandestine task he had to perform, to take Iris to the place where she was due to meet Rosie. His worry was increased by the need to wait until the afternoon, which seemed a long time away. But he was realising that life was a matter of waiting. His two weeks in Kent had become waiting time but he was not sure what he was waiting for, except the time to return home, reunited with his mother. Now that he had finished *The Wind in the Willows,* he had only the Bible and *The History of the World for Children* to read, and these books seemed only to make time pass even more slowly.

That morning the house was made up entirely of women, a situation he was used to at home but puzzled by here. "Where is Teddy? And Mr Rodgers?" he asked. Mrs Rodgers told him that her husband had been told to drive Teddy to London to the bank. "They think he should do some work," she explained, laying before him the family's belief that work is a masculine duty close to punishment. Along the corridor in the dining room Mrs Hardinge, Iris and Muriel sipped tea in silence under the attentive gaze of Winnie.

"This is what it's like, my dear," Mrs Hardinge started saying. "The men go off to work and leave us to our own amusements. If we can find any. I expect we can, with this and that."

It was quite easy for Iris to catch Tommy alone to confirm the afternoon's arrangements: which made it all the more necessary for him to avoid any conversations questioning his own plans for the day. He needed to be in places where Mrs Hardinge would not find him.

Knowing that he would be in the west woods later, Tommy made for the east woods. He liked them better anyway; they were not so wild, not so dark. But the crows were all around, black and ominous, with a harsh threat in their throats.

Caw. Caw. Crow. Crow. Rook. Croak. Caw. Croak. Caw. Tommy tried talking to the crows. It felt like being brave, like going up to the bad boys in the school playground. As they strutted, he slid, shoe leather slipping on the muddiness underfoot. But still they ignored him. Only the waving of arms brought a weary flapping of wings, a contemptuous air, as they flew into the trees and cawed to each other, not to him.

Soon he was at the climbing tree, so he scuttled up to sit in the cleft between the lowest branches. He scrabbled around in his knapsack, bringing out the black notebook and its pencil. As he no longer had a book to read, he would write something instead; after all there had been poems in *The Wind in the Willows*. Opening the notebook, pressing flat the pages. *I can write one like that.*

He concentrated hard and wrote the words down slowly, pausing at the end of each line to think about the coming rhyme. He felt poetry had to rhyme, and he discovered that he enjoyed the search for the right chiming word. After half an hour he had finished.

> *"Tommy's best at climbing trees*
> *Cos he never hurts his knees.*
> *He shins up and down*
> *So he can see for miles around*
> *And look at what he's found*
> *He brings it down to ground."*

Tommy knew there must be much wrong with it, for reasons he could not understand, but he was still proud of his poem. It bothered him a little that he could not see very far in the tree, that he had found nothing, and brought nothing down to ground – but he put this down to poetry not being real.

There was a penknife in his pocket – not something he had found up the tree. Teddy had given it to him yesterday and now he carved his initials TGS on the bark of the tree. Walking on, as an afterthought, he carved IF into the bark of another tree. This brought him back to his afternoon task, feeling a shadow pass across his eyes. He returned to the house to be ready to take Iris to the hide, but headed to the kitchen for something to eat.

At half past two, the hall grandfather clock struck once and Iris came down the stairs. "It's OK," she whispered to him, "she's having a nap in her room."

Tommy felt a surge of pride that almost overcame his discomfort. Iris was at her most elegant, her long white dress rustling at her booted ankles. He felt a little shame-faced that he was dressed in this ill-matched mix of old and new clothes, the jacket and boots his own, but showing signs of wear, the shirt one of Teddy's boyhood cast-offs that hung loose on him so that he had to turn up the cuffs, the trousers those that had recently been bought for him. He had decided to wear the long trousers to give him a sense of adulthood, that might *who knows?* be needed.

It was not far to the hide, perhaps only a quarter mile, but it was not easy walking. The nettles and brambles scratched at his trousers and Iris's skirt, so they had to make frequent detours to avoid snagging.

"I had not realised it would be quite so hard, Tommy."

"It's OK. You get used to it. Except at night."

They glimpsed the wooden walls of the hide ahead, in the tiniest of clearings between the trees.

"Is this it?" asked Iris. The hide was empty; Rosie had not yet arrived. They went inside, Iris's curiosity easy to be seen. She stood at the open wall, like a window with no glass, pretending to be looking for wild life. "There's a pretty bird," she observed. "Do you know what that is?" Tommy shrugged, his bird knowledge restricted to sparrows, pigeons and crows. He could sense Iris's nervousness, her eyes flickering from side to side, eager to spy the woman she would meet, anxious at what she might say, even though she had practised the words.

Rosie took them by surprise, approaching from the woods behind them. She smiled at her advantage.

"You found it then. Or he found it for yer. Now you can scarper, young man."

Tommy went out through the door but felt no inclination to go far; he would have to escort Iris back afterwards so there was no point in retreating any distance. He sat down under the opening, out of sight but not out of hearing. He tried his hardest to be silent, even as he crouched and leant back against the outside wall.

"You asked to see me. So here I am. But why here?"

"I wanted to see you – and this place. Is this where you meet?

"Not yet. Though you're puttin' ideas in me now."

"Leave him alone," Iris said, with a firmness that surprised her.

"Why should I? He's a grown man, can make up his own mind."

"A grown man? Only in one way. In other ways Tommy is more grown-up, perhaps more than he'll ever be."

"So why do you want 'im? Seems to me you can do without. He's only a silly man but you, you're like those votes for women."

"They are brave women, worth more than many men. Yes, I do admire them."

"So do you go around London smashing shop windows like they do?"

"Of course not. I am here. My family needs me to be here."

"But why? Do you love him?"

"Let's just say, he is spoken for. He is said to be mine by those who can say. And I shall make him mine."

There was a pause. Tommy wondered what they might be doing in this silence. Were they just looking at each other? Were they circling each other like prize fighters?

"You don't love 'im, do yer?" Rosie broke the silence.

"No, you're right. I don't. But that does not bother him nor me."

"I'll tell. He oughta know."

"You dare not. He will hate you if you do."

Rosie considered and another silence agreed more clearly than any words.

"Why do you do it?" asked Iris at last. "You know he will never marry you, you know that is impossible."

"Perhaps not. But it pleasures us both. We like it. I don't suppose you've ever done it, have you?"

"I will wait until we are married. And that will happen. It will happen more easily if you stop tempting him."

"Tempting? Huh, that's a good 'un. He needs little temptin'. And he's good-lookin' anyway, more so than any of the others round here."

"But why do you need that? Is it a need?" A long pause. "What is it like?"

"Like nothin' you've ever known. As you've just admitted. If you had, you'd know it's not somethin' you just decide to stop. It takes hold of yer. Here. Here."

There was the sound of rustling fabric. Tommy wondered if they really were fighting.

"If you like that," said Iris, "there must be other men who will do. If it's just carnal."

"Oh my," Rosie laughed, as if Iris had made a good joke. "Oh my. Whatever next?"

"Next, you must leave him alone. I insist. Find a local man, someone of your own station."

"There's no young men worth the lookin' at, not round here. Just raggedy lads. Not even got a change of clothes. They're only good for diggin' spuds or marchin' up'n down if they take the uniform. Not enough work to keep 'em here, least not to earn a proper wage. Barely enough to keep 'em in beer, but that's what they care about more'n anythin'."

"Do you think Teddy is that different? He just has better clothes."

"And sometimes he has none. And that's when I like him best. That's why we do what we do. You'll find I've taught him well."

"But only the one thing."

"I don't want the things you want. You can keep those things for yourself – the money, the house, the motorcar. I'll take what's left when you take those things away. It's just him an' he is worth somethin', he's worth more than all the others."

There was no more to be said, or at least there was no more said. Tommy could hear a sound that was like tears suppressed. He could not tell which of them it was, or whether it came from both of them. After a few minutes Rosie hurried out of the door on the other side, and Tommy, peeking around the corner, saw her brushing through the undergrowth towards the village. He walked away in the same direction, stopping when he was at a distance that seemed to imply discretion.

Iris stepped outside, gathering herself to a greater height, or so it seemed to Tommy. A sun shaft pierced the foliage above, lighting her face, showing a pink puffiness on her cheeks, around her eyes.

"Not a word of this to anyone at the Hall. They might not like me meeting people from the village. You wouldn't want me to be locked up, would you? If they said I'd done something wrong. I would hate confinement."

Tommy shook his head but thought he would find a way to rescue her if she were put in prison – Toad had shown him the possibilities. They walked side by side through the trees, lifting their feet over any thorny plants, suddenly conscious of the need to maintain appearances, even if they both felt that something had been taken from their world, that something as intangible as innocence had been lost.

Later that day, alone in his room and looking out of the window with the evening shadows thickening and colours darkening, the clear purple sky promised an exuberance of stars. But first the car purred down the drive and came to a sputtering halt at the entrance stairs. Teddy skipped out onto the gravel; looking up at the window, he gave a cheery wave. Tommy liked Teddy, he decided at that moment. He felt this bond suddenly reinforced. He liked his cheeriness, yes, but more than that, he liked the feeling of being united in an undercover resistance to the rules of the house.

12

WEDNESDAY

Next day Tommy woke to bright sunshine, but by the time he had finished breakfast in the kitchen heavy grey clouds had rolled in. He was wondering what he should do that day, when Teddy beckoned him into the small drawing room. Without saying anything, with a single finger raised to his lips, Teddy handed over a sealed envelope on which he had written 'Rosie'. Tommy simply nodded.

"Good man," said Teddy quietly. "Soon as you can."

There was nothing to delay him. The sooner he left the house the safer he would be from other errands. He set off through the woods, his preferred way to the village when engaged on a secret mission – at least that was the extra *frisson* of adventure that he gave to these excursions. As he ran through the woods, hiding behind trees every so often to avoid detection by imaginary enemies, his subterfuge was aided by the relative murkiness in the woods that day. The grey clouds were turning black in the sky above the trees.

The Badger's Inn was quiet, its doors closed to the world until opening time a couple of hours later. Tommy hesitated to knock on the door, as it might not be Rosie who answered. Keeping close to the walls, he edged his way around the building, maintaining his game of being on a spying mission. So it was that he came unobserved to the pub's back yard where, behind wire mesh, Rosie was feeding the chickens.

"You made me jump," said Rosie when she saw him, his nose pressed against the wire. "What brings you here?"

Tommy held up the envelope. "Push it through," she said, pointing to the gap between door and frame. She ripped open the envelope and read the letter inside.

"Just tell him Yes."

"Is that all?"

"Yes. Off you go."

Tommy expected little from these errands, certainly not a tip. But he thought politeness might be shown, particularly as he was constantly being schooled in politeness by the Hardinge family. Iris would say Thank-you. He found more and more comparisons that put Iris in a better light than Rosie.

Still, he had a job to do, so he returned to the woods just as lightning flashed over the village rooftops. Rain poured down suddenly as if from a tap. Inside the woods he was sheltered a little at first by the dense covering of leaves that slowed the fall of rain. But soon the rain was streaming down in cascades rather than droplets, forcing him to quicken his pace until he reached the edge of the lawn. Standing under the trees that formed a border, he stared at the house a hundred yards ahead, tantalisingly close but almost hidden by the curtain of rainfall. The sky was black, with no promise of the storm ending soon. Daunted by the sudden illumination of lightning, he still decided to run as fast as he could to the house, arriving in a deep roar of thunder.

Although it had not been far, it was far enough to get drenched. Staggering up the entrance stairs and through the front door, he was relieved to arrive but aware that he was not in a state to be welcomed. His heart sank when he saw Mrs Hardinge standing in the hallway.

"Stop there!" she shouted. "Stand in the porch."

She ushered him backwards into the porch with his feet

squelching inside his boots, his shirt plastered to his skin, and the wool of his jacket hanging heavy from his shoulders.

"You look like a drowned rat," she said. "Whatever possessed you to go out in such weather?"

"It was dry when I left."

"Winnie, get a towel, take off his wet clothes here and give the boy a bath. You hardly deserve such kindness."

So Tommy was stripped to underpants and wrapped in a rough white towel. His clothes were whisked away in a galvanised iron basin, to be washed or dried. Feeling humiliated, Tommy padded up the stairs to the bathroom. His only consolation was that Winnie left him alone to bathe himself. After five minutes she brought him one of Teddy's old dressing gowns, retrieved from his childhood wardrobe.

He had no choice but to sit in his room, wrapped in the dressing gown. He had no clothes left that were not being washed but he enjoyed the soft, velvety touch of the dressing gown's fabric on his skin.

"You look the part," said Teddy, entering his room without knocking. "Quite the young man."

"I like it." Tommy made no effort to suppress a smile.

"Good. Did you get an answer?"

"Yes."

"So what was it?"

"That was it. She just said Yes."

"Oh. Good. The right answer."

Teddy walked to the window to look at the weather. The rain had eased off and there were patches of blue between the clouds in the sky. "Very good," he said, to himself, to the window and the world outside. Then he turned back to Tommy.

"So, young man, what shall we do? I have time to spare until this afternoon. What are your plans?"

Tommy explained that he had to wait for his clothes to be brought. So he would just sit there to wait. Perhaps he would read.

Teddy said he had an idea and would come back soon. Five minutes later he returned carrying a large wooden box.

"Take a look at these, Tommy. These are good."

He slid the lid of the box open, revealing the toy soldiers inside.

"These are the best things that came with the house. Unfortunately just a bit late for me. I would have loved them at your age."

They sat on the floor, taking out the lead cast soldiers one by one. Some were in red uniforms, others in blue. British and French. "You can be British," said Teddy with an affectation of indifference that might have been generosity.

What do you do with them? Just imagine. You are the British Army. It's Waterloo. What will you do to win the battle? My men are here. Up on a hill. Yours are there. Charge. You don't have a chance. Boom!

Tommy could not help but feel this was a contrived game. Teddy was bound to win because he had the advantage of knowing what to do and there seemed to be no rules beyond those you stated as your own. "Sorry, Tommy, I just shot him so you can't use him any more." Even so he enjoyed holding each soldier in his hand, running his finger over the undulations that made arms and legs, the colours that made uniforms, touching the sharp tip of the musket.

"I'd best be off," said Teddy. "But you can keep these here to play with."

Now that he was free to make his own rules, Tommy warmed more to the game. Picking up one of the red-coated soldiers with puffed-out cheeks, he had the idea to base his game on *The Wind in the Willows*. He thought of the battle to recapture Toad Hall in the book. *You can be Toad.* Other figures suggested different characteristics. *Ratty. Badger. Mole.* Badger fell naturally into the General's role but Tommy regretted that Mole had to be an ordinary infantryman. On the other side, the men in blue were weasels, stoats, ferrets, but as he played, the thought crossed Tommy's mind that he might just make them the winners. *As long as they're good to Mole.* Perhaps Toad might fall bravely in battle.

So the game proceeded. It involved no great movements of soldiers. Tommy simply picked up a soldier from each side, one in each hand, bringing them into a conflict that he acted out through dialogue. In this way Toad was soon agreeing to share Toad Hall with the weasels. This appealed to Tommy's sense of humour for a while but then he was distracted again by the sound of rumbling thunder outside the window.

The thunder crashed more violently than any guns that Tommy could yet imagine. Lightning zigzagged across the sky, bringing sudden illumination to the scene of rain pouring down. In the white flickering of the lightning flash, he saw a figure running across the lawn and he soon realised that it was Teddy, dressed in a green oilskin cape against the pounding rain, sliding down the grassy bank into the trench that separated lawn from wood, then charging in his leather boots off into the blackness ahead.

Behind him the door opened and he turned to see who it was.

"I came to see if you are coping," said Mrs Hardinge. "A thunder storm can be frightening even when you are sheltered in a house."

Tommy was surprised. He had not expected kindness from this quarter.

"Thank you, m'am. I don't like it but – it is interesting."

"That is an interesting way to describe it. Certainly it is better to be watching from safety than to be outside in the thick of it. You have to respect storms and never venture out in one."

Despite her softer tone, Tommy was not tempted to betray Teddy by saying he had seen him out in the storm, though he had a shadow of fear for this woman's son. She would have to make her own discoveries, and she seemed intent now on doing that. She pointed at the toy soldiers.

"What are you doing with these?"

"Playing. Teddy let me."

"Well, he was wrong. Put them away carefully in their box, they are not for playing with, they are much too valuable for that. These are heirlooms. One day they will belong to my grandson."

"I didn't know you had one."

She looked sharply at him. *Was he being cheeky?* She gave him the benefit of the doubt while standing and insisting that he tidy away the soldiers.

"Are you going to be all day in that dressing gown? Where are your clothes?"

After all the explanations were done, she accepted that he would remain in his room for the rest of the day to read.

"What are you reading?"

He showed her *The History of the World for Children*. He thought it would be the most acceptable answer he could give, even though he found it a boring book. He decided he would begin reading *The Wind in the Willows* again later.

"I hope you will learn from it. It will teach you about the Empire, and that is something you need to know."

As he replaced the book on the chest of drawers, he saw the

green notebook. He could avoid it no longer; he was running out of people to ask.

"Will you write in my book, please?"

"Oh, that silly book. Show me." She took it and flicked through it, frowning at one or two of the entries. "I suppose I must."

She had left the room saying that he would be served food in his room for the rest of the day. She seemed to have exhausted her unexpected wells of kindness. Yet Tommy was a little relieved that he would not have to talk to her again that day. He opened the notebook to read what she had written. *Boys should be seen and not heard. This advice does not change as you grow older. Follow it and you will live a useful life. Mrs Catherine Hardinge*

He sat in his room. He listened to the train chuffing in the distance on the other side of the wood. He ate the food they brought. He read. He was happy enough. He even wrote a story about a mole who travelled on a train to find the home he had left. He began to write not knowing where his words were heading, simply enjoying his thoughts being carried along on the words he put down in the pages of his black notebook.

13

THURSDAY

Tommy was feeling cooped up, like a chicken behind wire mesh. Had Rosie brought this on him, had they discovered his secret mission? He knew that was just his game not reality. But it was now nearly 24 hours that he had been deprived of clothes to dress in.

"Where's me clothes, Winnie? " he asked.

"'Sbeen too wet to get 'em dry," she replied. "I'll ask again."

So Tommy sat in the crimson dressing gown all morning. He had nothing to do but read and he had nothing to read but *The Wind in the Willows*. He enjoyed the story all over again, even though he knew it well. When Teddy popped in briefly he simply asked "Are you still reading that?" There was too much to explain and Tommy did not want to venture too far into a conversation that might lead to oilskins, Rosie and the hide in the woods. So he said nothing about the book beyond a nod.

At least Teddy went away promising to do something about his clothes. And within ten minutes Winnie appeared, carrying them before her like a tea tray.

"They's a bit stiff," she said. "Overdid the starch. But at least they's clothes."

He went down the stairs quietly, trying not to be spotted in his starch-stiff white shirt. He wanted to go outside but first he needed to see Mr and Mrs Rodgers, because he was very hungry. Over bread and sausages, he talked to Rodgers.

"We should get out a bit, you and me," said Rodgers. "Let's

go for a spin in the car. Just down to the village so as we don't use too much petrol."

Tommy always enjoyed the sense of importance conferred by riding in the car. He liked to observe the heads turning at the sound of the approaching car, and sometimes to wave at people if they waved first at him.

"Just like the king," scoffed Rodgers. "Don't get carried away with yourself. Or you might just get carried away anyways."

"Where to?" Tommy had to shout above the puttering of the engine.

"Oh, far away. The white slave trade, I 'spect. Or pressed ganged into the army."

Rodgers stopped the car outside the pub. It gave a cough, as if to show it had done some exercise, shuddered and fell quiet. Rodgers stepped down and Tommy followed after. "Here we go. Told you 'bout the press gang." Rodgers nodded towards the man in uniform marching towards them with a polished stick under his arm. "The recruitin' sergeant, dead on cue. Told yer. Mornin', sergeant, what brings you this way? Goin' to sign up the lad?"

"Your time will come, lad, don't you worry. You'll get your chance to serve King and Country." He spoke certain words with the pomposity of capitals. Then he saluted and strode past into the pub. Rodgers watched him enter before saying "I fancy a pint. Lemonade for you?" Rodgers got Tommy to sit on the bench outside the pub while he went inside for the drinks. But before he went inside he tossed Tommy a cloth pouch — "Here you are. Ever played Jacks? Try these."

Tommy took the spiky metal pieces out of the pouch, along with the rubber ball. He had watched the game being played but had never played himself. Now he had the jacks and soon he was absorbed into the game, bouncing the ball then scooping up jacks before the ball bounced again. The game captured Tommy's concentration so he did not notice that Rodgers had failed to reappear with his lemonade. Eventually he came out, glass in hand.

"There you go. How yer getting' on? Got the hang of it? Just need to practise."

He knelt down and showed Tommy how it should be done. "Thirsty work. Think I'll get another pint."

When he returned later, he brought out a little gang of his mates, each with a glass of beer in hand. In their midst was the sergeant, the only one who now seemed sober, the only one not carried away by beer and the heady prospects of glory. The sergeant was talking in a tone that commanded attention.

"Join the Territorial Force and you get the respect of everyone. All the girls like a soldier. Course, there's no war either, so you won't be sent away. Just keep the jobs you're doing and train to be more of a man."

For a reason Tommy could not understand the six civilians, all young men from the village, kept bursting into laughter. As if someone was telling them a joke, but a joke that Tommy could not understand, could not even hear.

"Come on, lads," the sergeant said, pulling out some forms from inside his tunic. "You can soon be enjoying yourselves, mates together and meeting new mates."

The half dozen men looked at each and carried on giggling or trying to suppress their laughter. By now they had fresh beer in their glasses.

"You gonna be first, old chap?" the sergeant asked Rodgers. "You look like a responsible sort. Someone who loves his country."

"Me? Why me? Bit long in the tooth for this sort of game."

His mates laughed and swigged more beer. One of them called out "Sign up the old 'un first" and then started a chant, just for a laugh, so the others joined in: "Sign 'im up. Sign 'im up."

"How old are you?" asked the sergeant.

"Not thirty-five yet," said Rodgers, not wanting to be thought old.

"Sign 'im up!"

It became irresistible. Before long the sergeant gathered in the signature 'J. Rodgers'. Once he had signed, the others followed after.

"Well done, lads. You can be proud of yourselves."

Tommy had suspended his game of Jacks, caught up in the scene acted out before him. *Is this real? Or are they pretending?* A familiar voice cut in, making Tommy look up.

"What's all this about then?" asked Teddy.

"Sir!" the sergeant saluted. "People of the village doing their patriotic duty."

"Quite right." He looked around the group, his eyes acknowledging Rodgers; then, sideways, seeing Tommy with a surprised air. The group started to disperse, the atmosphere changed by Teddy's arrival. "Funnily enough, I've been thinking about this myself. Always best to be prepared. Who knows when our country might need us."

Rodgers, sobering rapidly, put on his cap. "Best be off, sir," he said. "Tommy, pick up the jacks."

Hearing a different voice, Rosie had come out into the garden, shooting a quick smile at Teddy. They went through into the pub, and the recruiting sergeant followed them, intent perhaps on the capture of one more pledge of loyalty or the reward of a final drink.

When they were both sitting in the car, Rodgers turned

round and addressed the boy. "It's all right, Tommy, it's just a way of giving something to our country. It won't come to war, that's not gunna happen."

"So, are you in the army now?"

"No, course not. Just the Territorials. Just grown men playin' games. No harm in it."

"Will you get a gun?"

Rodgers was thinking. Second thoughts are always uncomfortable. Perhaps there might be a way back?

"Mind you," he said, "I'll have to get permission. But Mr H will be all for it."

"Mrs won't be."

"No? Why's that?"

"She says you get killed in the army."

"Not if you're in a good army. The British army."

"She don't want Teddy to join. She said so."

"Expect her scruples apply just to her own."

Scruples? What are they? I'd like to see them. Is that how you tell good from bad? Tommy was confused, not knowing whether to be pleased or not. The boy in him looked up to a soldier, but he worried that it would take Rodgers away and into danger. As if reading his mind, Rodgers said "It'll never happen."

When they got back to the house, Tommy saw Iris as soon as he came through the porch into the hall. She insisted that he join her for lunch as there was no one else around. They helped themselves to bread and cold meat with pickles.

"I wonder where Teddy is," Iris wondered.

"He's joined the army," offered Tommy, enjoying that he had some real gossip to give.

"What? He can't have."

"Ask him. Tell him he can't."

"I can't. I don't have that power. No woman has the power to tell a man what to do. He'll do what he does regardless."

"You could try."

Iris looked doubtful. Perhaps it struck her as absurd that she was listening to the advice of a nine-year-old.

"There is a power that comes to your sex at birth. There's no changing it. The vote won't, whatever they say."

Tommy did not know what to say so he concentrated on the ham sandwich he had made. The pickled onion made him wince, though Iris might have misread the cause. She questioned him about 'the army' and found the mention of 'Territorials' reassuring. She smoothed away the thought of battle and vinegar, so that Tommy was able to go outside without a feeling of betrayal.

There had been a brief shower during lunch but now the sun was bright again. Tommy had no firm intentions except to disappear from sight within the woods. He was used to being solitary and these two weeks had reinforced that tendency. At the edge of the woods there was a dead tree, gleaming in the sunshine like a sculpture wet with rain. It was just a few days since Tommy had passed by here with Teddy but those days already seemed like weeks. He felt that something had changed inside him, and probably there was no going back to those original feelings when he had wandered in the woods. He now knew they held much more than he could speak of. But it was not that Tommy now knew more; he knew from experience that there was more to understand than he had first imagined.

He spent a pleasant hour by the bank of the river, that he now recognised as just a stream. Reading his book again on the river bank brought him closer to his favourite characters in the story. *Perhaps they'll say Hello*. Reality and imagination merged together as the sun parted the leaves to sparkle on the water surface.

He did not want to return to the house yet so he decided to cross into the west woods where the tangle of the undergrowth caught at his woollen socks. It became a game to take higher steps to avoid the entanglement of nature's thorns. Soon he found himself at the hide, where there was less need to step high but a greater need to tread quietly. He listened at the door and heard nothing, then stepped slyly inside, sniffing the air and recognising the lingering scent that was Rosie's. Once a place of refuge, now it seemed a place of secrets. Fearful of discovery, he stepped outside and headed back to the house.

There were secrets everywhere. Without meaning to be he found himself a spy, listening from the hallway to Teddy in conversation with his mother.

"I went into the village," he was saying. "I might be joining the Territorial Force."

"Such stupidity," Mrs Hardinge said. "Anyway I am not sure I believe you. Unless your recruiting sergeant is a Nancy boy." She puckered her nose in distaste. "There's no hiding the smell of cheap scent. No resisting it either, it seems."

"It's not cheap. I know that for a fact."

"It is cheap. I am not talking about money."

Tommy edged backwards. He did not want to hear any more, so he made his way downstairs to the sanctuary of the kitchen.

"He's not here," said Mrs Rodgers. "Sleeping off his foolishness." As Tommy hung around she asked "Want a bit of cake?" So he sat down at the scrubbed wooden table.

"Not long now, eh?" she said. "Soon see your mum again. Guess you'll be pleased to go."

Tommy smiled and remembered something. He reached into his knapsack and took out the green notebook.

"Please, will you write in it?"

She wiped her hands on a tea towel, as if to say 'don't expect much'. Mrs Rodgers did what all the others had done – she read through the messages, then she wrote her own. Her handwriting was painstaking but clearly legible.

"Never go soldiering. No good ever came of war. Mrs M. Rodgers"

14

FRIDAY

Heading down to breakfast in the kitchen, Tommy was greeted by Mr Hardinge at the bottom of the stairs.

"Surprised to see me, eh? I came home late last night. My work this week is done and I wanted to spend some time with you."

"Really?" Tommy asked.

"Really. It is your last day after all. Tomorrow you will go home to your mother. Are you looking forward to that, my boy?"

Tommy's surprise, and a sudden welling of relief, made it hard for him to say a word.

"Good. So, come in. We shall breakfast together."

Mrs Hardinge was already seated at the table, a cup of tea in front of her.

"Being nice to the boy is all very well," she said to her husband, "but do not forget your duties to this family."

"Catherine, how could I? Not with you to remind me. I am determined, we are determined. It shall be settled today."

"Good. First you might have to capture your son. Lock him up if need be for his own good."

"I doubt it will come to that."

Tommy had to ask. "Has he done something bad? To lock him up?"

"No, no, it's nothing. He is young, as you are young. He does not always understand obligations."

Tommy did not either. He wondered if 'Obligations' was a subject he would be taught at school.

"I will spend some time with Thomas," Mr Hardinge was saying. "As we discussed. Then Edward. Then Iris. Then both together. There is no cause for agitation."

At Mr Hardinge's silent motioning, Tommy had another sausage and a second slice of bacon. It was easier to convey kindness through extra helpings of food, particularly when words were in short supply. As Tommy studied the sausage on the gleaming prong of the fork, he wondered again who this man was, this provider of good breakfasts.

"I don't suppose you will eat like this at home. Make the most of it while you can."

"But do not over-indulge," cut in Mrs Hardinge. "You will make yourself sick."

Benefactor. Is that the word? It was a word newly learned, one of many gifts still to be fully unwrapped. It did not yet slip past his tongue as easily as the sweet tea he now sipped. More time and vocabulary would quench that thirst.

"Have you finished? Let us go to the library."

Tommy understood the need for obedience. It would ease the journey through this last day. In the library it was impossible not to feel the weight of words, the instructions bound inside books. Yet he had found something lighter there too, the release of imagination. The older man and the young boy shared the thought without words.

"Did you enjoy the books you borrowed?" the benefactor asked, as if he might recall the debt if given the wrong answer.

"I liked *The Wind in the Willows*."

"Did you read it all? Did you finish it to the end?"

"I read it twice."

"Twice? You liked it that much?"

"It was good."

"How did it make you feel?"

Tommy paused to think. He wanted to choose the exact word. "Ecstatic," he pronounced.

"Ecstatic? That is a good word. One from the book I imagine."

"I looked it up in the dictionary. Like you showed me."

"I am pleased to hear that. Will you read me the ending?"

Tommy had to go upstairs to fetch the book from his bedroom. With the book's spine nestling in his hand he had a sudden concern that open-air reading had caused some ageing to the book's cloth binding.

"It has been well-used, I see. But well-looked-after. Read to me. Not the ending – read your favourite passage."

Tommy opened the book at random, wanting to avoid the agony of selection. He began reading about the Rat looking for the Mole lost in the Wild Wood.

"He had patiently hunted through the wood for an hour or more, when at last to his joy he heard a little answering cry. Guiding himself by the sound, he made his way through the gathering darkness to the foot of an old beech tree, with a hole in it, and from out of the hole came a feeble voice, saying, 'Ratty! Is that really you?'"

"And it was," Mr Hardinge almost shouted. "Indeed it was. A charming story, and very well read. I can tell you are a clever boy. Any parent would be proud of you."

The man gave a deep sigh. "I would like to see you grown beyond a boy, Tommy. Though I'm not sure I will. Death is apt to intrude into life without warning. We can never expect life beyond its natural course. Sorry. Thinking out loud."

Tommy worried that this man might show his mortality by dropping dead before him. But a hand on his head, tousling his hair, supplied reassurance of a sort. *Why do people die? It doesn't seem fair.*

"Let me see your notebook, Tommy. The green one. I would like to see how many people have written messages for you."

Mr Hardinge read through the messages, sometimes nodding approval, sometimes frowning.

"What have you learned Tommy?"

"I tried to be good. I did my best."

"Is that good enough?" Mr Hardinge said these words almost with a smile. "Tell your mother you have been good. You are a good boy and I…" Tommy imagined he saw a tear glistening in the man's eye. He watched him turn to the next blank page and write. *"The boy does his mother credit. GH."*

Tommy was released, taking the books back to his room. Looking out of his window there was a grey sky and an empty lawn, but he sensed that there was activity in the house, perhaps more than usual. Curiosity got the better of him so he sneaked out of the room and sat at the top of the stairs. From here he could see the hallway and whoever might be visiting any of the rooms on the ground floor. If nothing else he felt that these two weeks had trained him to be a spy.

He saw Teddy cross the hallway, from the drawing room to the library. He closed the door behind him so Tommy could hear nothing; the servants crossed into the other rooms on their tidying duties; a bell rang and Winnie went into the library. She came out soon after and Tommy scurried into his own room before she could see him. He listened at his own shut door, heard Winnie knock on the door of Iris's room, heard them both go down the stairs. He resumed his place on the staircase's top step, just as the door of the drawing room closed behind Iris. Tommy wondered who might be in there with her. *Mrs Hardinge?*

The house became very quiet. It had an air of feeling the tension – creaking in the floorboards, rattling in the doorframes – while it waited for the next movement to happen. The ticking of the grandfather clock in the hallway seemed to grow louder, then it chimed the hour. One, two, three. Tommy counted up to eleven. He rose from the step to peer down into the hallway, around the corner. Unusually all the doors of the rooms were shut. He could just make out the murmur of voices but no words. Then, as if at a signal, the dining room door was opened by Winnie. Soon after the drawing room opened and Mr Hardinge came out with Iris, moving through into the dining room. Then Mrs Hardinge emerged from the library with Teddy and entered the dining room. Rodgers carried a bucket filled with ice packed around a bottle. There was the sound of laughter, a little embarrassed at its own jollity, and Mr Hardinge's voice louder than usual.

Whatever was going on, Tommy was not part of it. He went back to his room, waiting until it was lunchtime. Fifteen minutes later, keen not to be seen, not to be drawn into the dining room, he glided down the stairs and continued into the kitchen.

"Is it lunch?" he asked Mrs Rodgers.

"Yes, but you won't get much today as somethin's happened. Looks like they've done the deal, there's a wedding agreed."

"Really?"

"Mister Edward and that poor girl Iris. Not sure either of them wants it. But Mr & Mrs is pleased. Champagne, would you believe?"

All Tommy wanted was sausages, but it looked as if he would be unlucky. Mrs Rodgers cut a rough slice of bread for him, and put it on a plate with cheese. "That'll have to do today."

He was desperate to get out, and he was not going to be detained by the lure of hot food this lunchtime. He tore at the bread and gnawed at the cheese, feeling sorry for himself. It was almost a relief when Teddy found him and beckoned him away into the garden. Teddy had a way of making Tommy feel grown up just by talking to him as he paced up and down.

"One last message, Tommy. If you would. Take this to Rosie. It's all up with me. My life's signed away."

He slipped the letter to Tommy, pushing it inside his jacket. "Secret, as usual. You know the drill. But I will have one last moment."

Tommy did not know what to say so he said nothing, just nodded to show he understood. Then he hurried off before any other duties were put upon him. The walk from the house to the pub seemed shorter with every day that passed, with every message that he delivered. Tommy found Rosie wiping the wooden tables outside, the few lunchtime drinkers sent on their way by the closing time bell and the call of their work.

"What's'at?" she looked up from the damp cloth that Tommy felt now defined her. She slipped the letter suspiciously into the pocket of her pinafore.

"He wants an answer," said Tommy, though this had not been Teddy's request.

Rosie went around the side of the pub to the chicken cage at the rear. It seemed a pointless deception: Tommy could see her and so too could anyone passing by. *If that's the way she wants it*. He sighed to himself, tiring of these adult ways that seemed so childish to him. When Rosie returned a few minutes later, she simply said: "Tell him I know it."

With his time at Hardinge Hall nearly expired, Tommy felt he should show his independence. At this time tomorrow he hoped he would be home with his mother. The thought made him tearful so he decided to seek a familiar, quiet place in the wood, on the bank of the stream where he had spent time reading and imagining that he saw characters from his book. He wished he had the book with him, but he had left it in his bedroom, determined not to surrender it unless he was forced to. But he knew it so well that he could summon up any of the stories while watching the dragonflies hovering and darting above the water. Much as he longed now to go home, he also thought he might miss this place in a future time.

Eventually he made his way back to the house, aware that Teddy would be anxious for his return. He had no real wish to make an enemy of this young man who seemed at times like an elder brother. He was waiting, as Tommy knew he would, sitting at the white iron table on the terrace, awkwardly with Iris and Mrs Hardinge taking tea.

"Show me your book, Tommy," he said. "The one that people wrote in. I want to see if anyone's left."

"It's in my room," Tommy replied.

"Well, let's go and take a look. Excuse me for five minutes," he called over his shoulder, leading the way upstairs. Teddy opened the door to the room and quickly shut it behind them.

"Well? Did you give it to her?"

"Of course."

"How did she seem?"

"She said – 'I know it'."

Teddy wanted to ask more but could not without revealing more than he wished. He simply muttered "Good" and told Tommy he had done well.

The rest of the afternoon passed slowly. Champagne brought a state of torpor to those who had drunk greedily, allowing the alcohol to relax anxieties. Only Teddy still moved with a nervous energy while the women, even Muriel, dozed under parasols.

Later they sat down at the dinner table, with Mr Hardinge making a great show that "this is Tommy's last supper with us". He laughed as if he had made a joke but no one else seemed to see the funny side. Over the brown Windsor soup, he suggested: "We must make arrangements to visit your parents, Iris."

Before Iris, in mid-sip, could smile agreement, Mrs Hardinge cut in: "Edward first."

"Of course. But we shall not be far behind. Oh no, there will be no lagging. We must press on now. I look forward to discussing matters with your father, Iris."

She smiled a smile as dim as a guttering candle. It struggled to keep any light beneath the cold breath of her future mother-in-law. The clearing of the soup bowls rescued her from any further communication, then the serving of the main course.

"Roast chicken, Tommy. One of your favourites, I believe."

"It is the potatoes he likes," observed Mrs Hardinge. "Is his mother Irish, George?"

"Irish? No. What a strange thing to ask. Why did you think so?"

"Potatoes."

There was no more to say, so they concentrated on eating. Everyone was surprised when Tommy asked a question, because no one had told him and he wanted to know the answer for sure. "Is Teddy going to marry Iris?"

They all looked a little embarrassed. Perhaps something had been forgotten? Or someone. It fell to Mr Hardinge to reply.

"Indeed. It is remiss of us not to have told you. We had assumed. Wrongly. Edward is engaged to marry Iris. Marriage is a very good thing. And we are all very satisfied. So now we raise our glasses again to wish them happiness."

"Wealth and happiness," Mrs Hardinge embellished the toast. They raised glasses, the crystal glinting in the candles that now lit the table top. Tommy brought to his lips the glass of lemonade he had been supplied with instead of water for this special occasion. Iris looked embarrassed, Teddy hid his awkwardness in the rim of the wine glass with its deep-red wine. There was not much appetite for dinner that evening, though Mr Hardinge tucked in, as did Tommy. The others picked half-heartedly at the food on their plates, their appetites still satisfied by the large lunch and the size of its news.

As the plates were being cleared, Mr Hardinge felt the need for sentimentality. "When some years have passed, the gap between you, between your ages I mean, will seem to close and you will be young people together. We have that hope, I might say belief. And friends we will all be."

"Nonsense," muttered Mrs Hardinge.

Teddy looked anxious as the apple pie was brought in.

"Is there anything wrong, Edward? No appetite or too much?" asked his mother.

He hesitated, not wishing to speak, forcing a "Well?" from deep inside. Teddy could not escape, because he longed to escape. "I'm afraid I have to go. I'd arranged, long time ago, a card game, with some of the chaps."

"Life's a gamble still, Edward. For you at least. That has to change soon."

"But not now, ma."

"A card school. I didn't know you liked that kind of game."

"I said I would meet James and Reggie to celebrate."

"Are there three-handed card games? I did not know. Perhaps you plan to play it with a dummy?"

His mother's sarcasm was not able to trump his desire to go. "Forgive me, Iris. I must go. It is getting dark and I will walk."

Watching Teddy rush through the dining room doorway and up the stairs, Mrs Hardinge said: "Perhaps we should follow his example? Iris, do you play Rummy? Muriel does. With myself and George we can play our own games while Teddy plays his. It will bring us to a better understanding perhaps."

"Perhaps."

Tommy was dismissed to his room and bed on the grounds that he had a big day tomorrow. He would be driven to the station by Rodgers after breakfast.

Up in his room, the curtains were not yet drawn, his night light was glowing on his bedside table. The red sun was nearly out of sight behind the trees and the spaces between the trees were thickening with darkness. Minute by minute the sky's colours were changing until deep blue became black and stars appeared like faraway matches struck by invisible hands. Tommy knew he was inventing but he had discovered that there was pleasure in the making of similes, a joy in the solitary exercise of imagination. He stood at the window, staring, his eyes seeing less and less in the blackness outside, a blind moth beating its wings against the pane, eager to come inside and shelter even at the risk of being consumed by fire.

A shadow crossed the lawn, though. He saw that, a shadow in the shape of a giant, growing bigger then smaller as it carried a lantern into the depths of the woods, then became a receding point of light until, as if blown out by a whispering breath, it disappeared altogether.

15

SATURDAY

"Where is he?" asked Mr Hardinge.

"Playing games? Riding his luck? I've no idea but why should I? I'm only his mother."

Tommy could say nothing. He knew nothing, or at least that would be his protestation if it came to it.

"Do you know, Thomas?" she asked and Tommy shrank a little inside.

"." There were no words, just a reluctant shrug. *Am I my brother's keeper?* He remembered the words from his recent reading of the Bible. They seemed to fit the situation but he would not say them in case they invited explanation.

Iris came in to breakfast and started helping herself from the buffet on the sideboard. She sat at the table with toast and scrambled eggs, and received a cup of tea.

"Is Teddy coming?" she asked in all innocence but, for the first time, with a hint of ownership.

"Who knows?" replied Mrs Hardinge.

Muriel came in, and brought a boiled egg to the table.

"Where is he?" she asked.

"It's too much, George. Where is he? He should be here."

"I agree. It's Tommy's last breakfast. And soon he will be leaving."

They ate in silence. *Let me go.* Tommy hated every silent, hard-to-swallow minute.

"Tommy, you will be off soon," said Mr Hardinge. "Before you go, you should return the books you borrowed."

Tommy pretended not to hear, concentrated on cutting the bacon on his plate, slicing himself from the company around, choosing to focus on food; bacon first before moving on to the saved, savoured delights of the sausage. "The book, Tommy," insisted Mr Hardinge. "You have to return what is not yours. As soon as you finish."

In a few minutes Tommy pushed back his chair and hurried from the room with a display of sulkiness. It was the natural state that morning. Returning more slowly, he placed the History, Bible and *The Wind in the Willows* on the place mat in front of his 'benefactor'.

"Good. But the Bible is yours to keep. No need to return it."

"What if I don't want it?"

"You must," a steely look. "Take it, keep it, learn from it."

"I'd learn more from this," said Tommy, holding up *The Wind in the Willows*.

"Indeed? Show me."

Tommy handed over the book, and Mr Hardinge flipped through its pages. He smiled as he did so, at a returning memory. He took out a pen from his jacket pocket. He wrote on the title page 'To Tommy nine years old' with a wavy line underneath for a signature that no one would be able to read.

"Now it is yours." He looked at the boy with an expression that said 'nothing more to say'. But he looked at the watch in his waistcoat pocket, sharing an exasperated moment with his wife. "We have an hour."

Tommy knew he had to be quick. He was sure he knew where Teddy was so he went out the front door and ran across the lawn into the west woods. Twigs snapped under his boots as he ran and he brushed past dry shrubs that left seeds and petals on his woolly clothes. He was dressed for home, in the clothes he had arrived in two weeks ago; sweating, he was conscious of being overdressed in his long socks and grey flannel shorts, topped by his worsted Norfolk jacket and a baggy cap on his head.

He stopped when he saw the hide ahead of him, standing under the trees panting and wiping his face with his handkerchief, taking off the cap and holding it in his hand. The door of the hide was shut and there was no sign that anyone was there. Perhaps he was wrong? He stepped forward, doing his best to be quiet, and pushed the door open.

There was a shock in nakedness that took Tommy's breath away. Teddy had leapt from the mattress on the floor ready to fight off intruders and he stood there, muscles flexed and in boxing pose, with sweat glistening on his pale skin. Behind him Rosie sat up on the mattress, her breasts pointing at Tommy as if in accusation.

"What are you doing here?" Teddy demanded.

"I" *thinking* "I just" *staring* "I just came to say Goodbye."

Rosie giggled as she wrapped herself in the sheet. It did not strike Tommy as such a laughing matter but she could not stop. Eventually she asked Teddy for a cigarette. This made him conscious of his own nakedness and he picked up a discarded blanket and knotted it around his waist. He tossed Rosie the cigarette packet and a box of matches, and watched her light up.

"Keep them," he said but Rosie's expression was irritable. She did not seem to regard the gift as a reason for gratitude. She threw the cigarettes and matches down next to the oil lantern by the wall. The still air was filled with the smell of burning tobacco and phosphorus, mixing with Rosie's scent.

"Step aside a mo, Tommy, just need to get dressed. Will be right out and we'll go back together."

Tommy was pleased to escape. He found the unexpected nudity embarrassing; it was not something he was used to. *Why do they do this?* He could not explain but felt, at least, there would be no pressure on him to explain. Silence, as so often in this place, would be acceptable. He sensed the redness in his face and thought the heat might explain that to anyone who might wonder.

Where is he? Tommy wondered, fidgeting as he waited in the trees, his boots kicking at dry leaves on the ground. Minutes passed and he was getting anxious about the time. He wanted to catch the train and could not bear the thought of spending even more time with these people. He longed to see his mother again.

Teddy emerged alone, pulling on his suit jacket, banging the wooden door behind him. "Come on then," he said. "You must have a train to catch." They walked quickly through the woods, not speaking. There was nothing to say.

Mr Hardinge was in the hall as they entered. "Bad behaviour, Edward," was his greeting.

"Couldn't help it, pa. Unavoidably detained. You know what it's like."

"I am not sure I do. And I am not sure your mother will understand, let alone Iris. Tommy, go and get your suitcase, you will have to leave soon."

In his bedroom Tommy crammed the extra books and clothes he had acquired into his battered suitcase. He took a last look around the room, even feeling a touch of affection for it. He would not return home to anything quite as comfortable but there is always at least a small sadness in leaving. He looked out of the window, knew that he would miss that: the woods to either side, the village in the distance, the green lawn in the foreground. The white-walled cottage at the fringe of the woods where Mr and Mrs Rodgers lived. There would be memories.

When he opened his bedroom door, he found Rodgers in his grey uniform and peaked cap waiting for him.

"Here, let me take that, lad. It must be heavy." So he took the suitcase that Tommy had struggled to manoeuvre out of the room, and he carried it down the stairs to the empty hallway.

"Where is everyone?" asked Tommy.

Rodgers nodded towards the door. "Come on, we've got to go."

Outside they were all lined up to say goodbye, like a cricket team being presented before a match. He shook hands with Mrs Rodgers and Winnie, and they both curtseyed to him. Muriel mumbled something that hovered between indifference and politeness, putting the pleasure of meeting him behind her. Iris wished him well; but he wished she had wished him more, hoping they had established something closer to friendship. Teddy stepped forward into that space, shaking Tommy's hand as if he were an adult. "You've been a pal. Like my own little brother."

"I hope, in times to come, you will appreciate the benefits you have been given," said Mrs Hardinge, not quite able to smile. Which made Tommy smile for reasons he did not understand. Then he came last in the line to Mr Hardinge who bent down towards him, a hand on each of Tommy's shoulders. "Well done, my boy," he said. "Well done." Then he walked Tommy down the stone steps onto the gravel drive where the car stood with Rodgers holding the door open for him.

He could not trust himself to speak. Finally his emotions had swelled beyond his ability to contain them. He quickly stepped into the back of the car and Rodgers walked around to the driver's side. Mr Hardinge was at the window, saying some last words that Tommy found impossible to take in, swept away by the pounding inside his head. All he could do was wave at the window as the party on the terrace receded behind the car.

"You'll be pleased to get home," shouted Rodgers from the front.

It was true but first he had to catch the train and Rodgers had stopped the car in the village by the green, pulling to the side of the road on the grass verge. Tommy wondered why but then he heard the clanging bell and saw the fire pump being drawn by a galloping horse. It was one more excitement to add to the others of that morning, and Tommy loved the white horse straining to pull the fire engine as fast as it could.

"Will have to see what that's all about when I get back," said Rodgers. "But better not miss your train."

When they got out of the car, the train was visible down the track. It came clanging into the station with whistles and steam blowing from the engine. There was no time for an elaborate farewell but Tommy thought that just as well. He did not want to shed tears at saying goodbye to his friend – for he had come to regard Rodgers as a friend and now he suddenly realised that he might not see him again.

"Don't worry, Tommy," said Rodgers. "You'll be back. We might all be different and older but…anyways, you'll see. On you get and settle down."

The whistle shrilled, doors banged shut, the train shunted forward. Tommy stood up at the window and waved at his friend in grey, now at last with a tear rolling down his cheek. The couple in the carriage smiled at him and offered him a boiled sweet, for which he was able to say 'Thank You'. He leaned back into the upholstery of the train's wide seat.

Looking out of the window as they skirted the now-familiar

woods, he saw puffs of black smoke drifting above the treeline. His knowledge of the area identified that the smoke was rising from the west woods, where he had been only that morning. He worried a little that the woods had caught fire, and hoped that the animals would be safe, but as the train chugged forward the smoke now faded into the distance behind him as everything else would. The house, his room, the bed, the woods, the people. He rattled away inside the carriage, with relief and regret, leaving much behind that might, as memories do, return one day, wanted or unwanted. And the train chuffed to him in a voice that might have been his mother calling *goodgoodgoodgoodgoodgood*

PART TWO

1918

Extract from
THE END OF WAR
A novel by Iris Fakenham, 1923

11.11.18

So Vanessa Bowen told herself, it could *not* be missed. Over the last year most conversations had been inside her head. This time, unusually, what she told herself silently she also spoke in so many words to her mother. *It could not be missed.* Her mother looked surprised, doubtful then pleased; looking at her mother's expression Vanessa thought, with a shiver of recollection, back to an earlier, warmer season, with the sun playing in and out of clouds on a breezy day; so different from this damp November.

The previous day had brought news, though news was often rumour in these wartime years. There was a rumour of peace that found its way even into the censored newspapers, and they allowed the dream to linger this time, plumping the cushions on the sofa as if expecting company; would company at last be allowed again to this reluctant widow? Yet she felt she could almost touch the change, with her fingers on the patterned velveteen, that this was approaching a moment of resolution, decision even, and that moment needed to be called out in public, marked in a notebook and observed in person.

"I will go," she said.

"You haven't finished breakfast."

So Vanessa thought, no need for breakfast, buttoning up the tweed overcoat that had lasted the war and outlived a husband, pulling on the black veiled hat she had worn for the last twelvemonth and would wear one last time on this anniversary. Did she need more? She stood at her bedroom window and urged bravery – or was it just boldness? – upon herself in case the doubts mounted. It was still dark outside, the November day was reluctant to show itself through the mist that hung over Kent, but she determined to take the first train possible. What an adventure! What a change one happy day might make after hundreds of days that were impossible to distinguish one from another, except by degrees of darkness, by relative levels of dread.

She escaped before her mother might decide uncharacteristically to accompany her. It was a short walk to the station where the clattering board announced the London train to an almost empty platform. If there were excitement in the air, it had not yet penetrated the drizzle; but inside herself she felt an unaccustomed flutter of anticipation. For once there was no ominous arrival of the postman to await; she would be gone before his suspenseful delivery. Just London – the vast untrusted, unfamiliar city – lay before her, at the far end of this railway track. For now it was time to forget, and in the forgetting there would be enough remembering to salve a conscience and require the service of a handkerchief; she checked inside her bag; finding the handkerchief she raised it reassuringly to her nose.

So Vanessa thought, dozing at the urging of the rhythmic chugging of the train, *I want to find another man*; there, she startled herself awake, the thought like a carriage uncoupled from its buffer and now it was out, released at least into the world inside her head, running away down the incline. She looked beneath her eyelids at her fellow passengers, wondering if they had sensed or even heard her thoughts. She closed her eyes, as if to stop anything worse escaping, while smiling to herself, recognising her innate innocence and wondering whether she might stretch it that day like elastic to new possibilities, perhaps beyond previous borders, to places outside her experience.

Stepping from the train at Charing Cross daylight gleamed dimly through the smoke-grimed glass above. She turned right, down the hill towards the embankment, wanting to see the river, like an old friend she looked to rediscover after a long time away. She gazed up and down the river, with St Paul's on the near-horizon to her left; and Chelsea with its chimneyed power stations visible only as fog around the curve of the river on her right; and across the water, in between bridges, the sooty warehouses, breweries and wharves that seemed to her like another country, a country not to be visited. A sickly yellow light pushed at the grey clouds that filled the sky; the sky is sombre, she thought, but it will brighten if we give it enough reason.

In Embankment Gardens leaves stripped from trees by the wind soared then drifted then plummeted straight to the earth like birds shot out of the sky. As the wind gusted, leaves and seeds came spiralling to the muddy ground, the liturgy of life; death and renewal, despair and hope. *Amen*, her mother might say; but not her, she had renounced such established comforts, discarded with the memories of a forsaken childhood. People were gathering, walking down the path through the fallow flowerbeds, and she followed in the same direction. *Perhaps they know something I do not?* From nearby churches in the Strand – how she remembered St Mary's and St Clement's with unexpected fondness at that moment – bells tolled by the handful and added a flourish as if to say 'because we can'.

Savoy Hill seemed steeper than she recalled but she was now in a group, as if marching with a purpose, and they burst into the Strand with cries that also rose as if to say 'because we can'. Noise and movement all around yet the Strand displayed no exaggerated signs of excitement; it was determined to be phlegmatic and British for as long as peace remained unconfirmed as a prospect still in the future not a reality in the present. The current reality was the smell of vegetables, rotten vegetables, wafting into the Strand from Covent Garden where the market did its best to pretend life might soon be back to normal, all passion spent, all strewn with cabbage leaves forming a carpet where revellers, given the time and the news, might later dance a knees-up. *Will it come to that? And what will I do?* The outfitters' shops along the Strand, the restaurants and theatres, the Savoy Hotel; she had always longed to have lunch at the Savoy, perhaps this might be that day. She trotted again in her criss-crossing of the road, passing behind a horse cart, to stand outside the Savoy under the metal awning, feeling like a schoolgirl at the windows of a sweetshop.

In the Strand a lorry trundled by, making a great noise as if its load were too heavy; that load was an anti-aircraft gun; the sudden sound of its firing should have been a shock – was there an air raid? – but no one seemed perturbed at the booms; exhilarated rather. So Vanessa thought, this is queer, why are people not running for shelter? Then the dawning realisation, the cry caught up, 'Peace! Victory!' And immediately, as if the whistle had blown to send the troops over the top, the crowd swelled and broke into a run down the roadway in between and around the omnibuses, taxicabs and motorcars. The vehicles, forced to be stationary by the press of the crowds around them, now found themselves clambered over as people sought a vantage point on top, to shout, to sing, to wave a flag.

What shall I do? So thought Vanessa Bowen, not even aware that her cheeks were wet with tears. *And so, at last, it is here, it is peace. For myself, I am glad to be here, glad to have survived when so many did not.* There was nothing for it but to walk, carried along by the impulse of the crowd down the Strand, past Charing Cross station, into the wide space ahead. In Trafalgar Square there were still workmen erecting barricades and platforms. Around the base of Nelson's Column a four-sided sign had been erected and on it were the words 'Victory Bonds'.

The crowd swirled around the square as if on a mass pilgrimage, as if the crowd had a single brain that was directing them until they were stopped in their tracks by a surge of people from the opposite direction, a tide of khaki soldiers linking arms with munitions girls in their uniforms, and all singing:

> *"I live in Trafalgar Square*
> *four lions to guard me,*
> *the fountains and statues all over the place*
> *the Metropole staring me right in the face,*
> *I own it's a trifle drafty*
> *But I look at it this way, you see*
> *If it's good enough for Nelson,*
> *then it's quite good enough for me."*

They got to the end of the chorus and lifted their arms to the sky, turning to point at the Metropole on the corner of Northumberland Avenue. So Vanessa thought to herself, every emotion opposed by a contradiction, now it's been requisitioned, now it's a government annexe kitted out like a stone soldier for the war effort. But the crowd cheered; and she cheered too; it would be a day for cheering without questioning, without too much questioning.

But she could not quite let go; she wanted to abandon

herself to the moment, knowing she might never feel this again; but there was a voice inside that urged caution, that said *still I must question.* Otherwise the war has won; otherwise we cannot win peace. While another voice countered *forget forget forget make new memories to drive out the old.*

So Vanessa Bowen thought these were weedy men with the stunted stature of boys, yet not natural, shrunken by short rations and deprived even of the glory of warfare by callowness or disability or cowardice; so might the women with white feathers have said in those cruel days before reality allowed kindness to slip through the cracks. Yet we are, we are a pitiable crew, so she really thought though she might not speak the thought aloud, we survivors of this war that deserves no label of greatness. The hollow-eyed boys, caps pressing down on foreheads, leer and prowl like alley cats, sniffing the air for beer and sex and at the very least the chance to laugh and not be questioned for their sanity; because they have earned at least that right, learned at least that lesson, by the very act of survival.

Joshua Joshua sweeter than lemon squash you are how they sang those munitions girls in their dungarees, linking arms and dancing in a line down the street, swerving into Trafalgar Square each with a soldier interlinked. The khaki uniforms bestowed a hero status higher than the left-behind boys would ever now attain, and the gazes that met them mingled respect and envy and came out as a kind of staring lunacy. Except the one, standing at the fringe with a woman clutching tight to his arm, his stare fixed on the far distance, still watching the scattering of mud and whizzing of shells all around in his head. So the realisation sank into Vanessa, *we have to pity the shell-shocked above all today.*

Without waving a baton, without even lifting a hand,

simply standing there with hands on hips, there was one soldier who seemed to conduct the singing and the dancing. Men go bald in different ways, so Vanessa thought, but none so bald as the three-striped sergeant who shaves his head, who inflicts baldness on himself as a deliberate and defiant act. It was his signal of not caring what others thought; the way he raised his peaked cap to take the cheers of the crowd around him, rubbing his gleaming bare head as if for luck, knowing by experience that he would need no luck and not be crossed, whatever he said or did, there would be no argument to brook today; knowing, they all knew, that he had won the war by his own bravery.

The clanging bell of an ambulance forged a path through the crowds. How awful to fall ill at such a moment, how dreadful to die so publicly amid such jollity. The bell sounded continuously, the ambulance inched forward. Vanessa knew she wanted to move from here; she was not ready to be an observer to unwelcome tragedy in this place. She took advantage of the vacuum behind the van to push back into the Strand and walk against the flow towards the Savoy. *If not today, when?* Trudging along the pavement, she thought of Edwin, feeling guilty that she felt such little sense of loss for they had never been a true couple, would never have been, even if battles and bullets had not come between.

Though there had been nothing in it, after Edwin had gone, she thought of Gerald, missing in action in those last hot days of summer. How typical of Gerald that he could not even be certain of his own death. Gerald who might have stepped into the breech of her emotions, might have smoothed the crack and made it close again, given the time and the opportunity. *But no, it was hopeless. In truth, he was hopeless.*

Inside the Savoy, under the chandelier, she did her best to

appear at ease. She entered the door of the grill restaurant, where the *maître d'* summoned an indeterminate smile of warning or welcome, waiting to hear her accent. His raised eyebrows greeted her request for a table for lunch.

"Have you reserved, madam? We are quite full." Though she had a pleasant voice, she was well-to-do, he thought, prepared to make an effort in the circumstances, noticing her widow's hat. "Perhaps I might ask. One minute."

Approaching a table, he spoke to three young officers in uniform. One of them got to his feet and bowed his head in her direction; she allowed herself to be shown to the table's empty seat by the *maître d'*s beam of satisfaction and padding footsteps. The officer on his feet, soon joined almost at attention by the other two, said that she would be very welcome to join them. Their identical hair partings glistened under the lights.

"We have not ordered yet – not the food in any case. But we have a bottle of pre-war Claret on its way."

They introduced themselves as George, Roger and George, all officers who had somehow, miraculously, certainly not by any degree of expertise but simply by luck, so they confessed, scrambled out of the trenches ten days ago. Congratulations, she murmured, directing her smile particularly at Roger who seemed to take the lead in everything; who was, to her eyes, the most handsome. They toasted the future in Claret, soon establishing that there was another bottle in the cellars that could be released from its dusty seclusion. She found herself imagining the cellars below the Strand, brushing aside cobwebs, and speaking the thought to Roger. *Bizarre*, did they both think? She determined to be open to the bizarre, and *why not?*

The meal progressed pleasantly enough, the men on their best behaviour, their eyes sunken not gleaming, a yearning there, suppressed and longing to break free, nervous in female company. Moustaches, as well as memories of recent hardship, lent a mournful look to their faces, as if they knew more than they might ever express in this changed world. Inevitably they asked about her situation, broaching the uneasy question of her solitude, soon explained by the loss of her husband in Flanders a year ago. They sympathised, nicely enough, using the tropes of their upbringing, stiff upper lips modelled in the forge of battle and public school. Bad luck, hard lines. So Vanessa thought, *it is as if I have lost a hand at Rummy*.

"I hope I have not spoiled your lunch plans? Or indeed your mood?" Vanessa felt the need to venture towards apology.

"Not at all. It is charming to meet you and to have more civilised company than we have become used to. We should apologise for our roughness; we are out of certain habits."

"I imagine so. You have been deprived of all comforts."

Indeed, indeed, they agreed. There was comfort in a baked apple after the supreme de volaille. *Such food, how did they make it, how did they get it?* She thought of the rations she had saved in recent weeks, the shortage of foods that seemed here in abundance. The sharp thought of payment made her suddenly uneasy; seeking her purse, where had she put it in this bag of many compartments?

"You must allow me," said Roger, as if reading her mind. "The pleasure has been ours."

Gratitude should have softened her; custom should have moved her towards politeness; but such feelings had become rusted by disuse. *Polite society, they will call this*. But there was mischief in her today, perhaps emboldened even as her cheeks were reddened by two glasses of Claret.

"Now what are your plans? What will you do this afternoon? You must have thought?"

"Oh, yes," Roger sounded wistful but his eyes were evasive. "As you say, we have missed comforts."

"More drinking? Tobacco?"

"Perhaps. There is the club. And the crowds outside, a chance to mingle. We have not seen friendly faces for a long time."

There was more, she knew; she could see it in the shifty glances of the two Georges, there was the prospect of mingling in their eyes. Raising the last of the red wine to her lips she looked at them through the distorting glass of cut crystal that seemed to her to reveal a certain truth. *I must call it out.* She knew she was doing wrong, a crime against politeness, but could not stop herself; the Savoy lights pointed the way.

"So I expect you are all off to seek some kind of carnal comfort?"

The question stunned them to silence, unable even to look each other in the eye; certainly not to look at Vanessa. They looked down at their napkins below which she sensed a shrinking; but they would rise again, from this table to go their separate ways. *Or perhaps?* She observed their flushes. *A hit, a palpable hit.* If only Ophelia had been there to see how this might be done. Roger fingered the bill and fumbled in the breast pocket of his jacket.

"So will you pay or seek it for nothing?" she asked. There was a hesitation in her, staring at Roger's face for a response. She wondered how she had dared so much; but these were extraordinary times. *There is nothing there but embarrassment.* The three men prepared to rise from the table, a chill over the occasion that none of them had foreseen just minutes earlier. She wished them well and thanked them – how could she do otherwise? – and made her way out into the Strand, casting glances behind her, just in case one of them followed, as if rising to the challenge, and if so what would she do, what should she say if words were needed?

She was well-fed but dissatisfied, unable to understand her own feelings. *What came over me? Am I that desperate?* Yet part of her was defiant, thinking that this now needed to be a new world; what had previously passed muster would no longer do. *Is it down to me that our men do not come up to the scratch?* she mused. *Have I set a bar too high?* She told herself, as if ticking herself off, that she sought only the hale and hearty – though heartiness was not really an absolute requirement, indeed it might easily be foregone. Four years of war and isolation had set her against heartiness; she could be satisfied with much less.

The streets were still heaving with people, with no intent but the pursuit of long-denied pleasure, all the more desperate for the long period of denial. The throng was too great for her; she felt herself becoming flustered by the noise and the numbers. Approaching the square again, with Nelson high on his column, she knew she must make a detour.

At the top of Villiers Street, at the side of the station, stood a one-legged accordion player, his wheezings about Italy nudging her with dimly remembered words from another age. He played as lustily as infirmity would allow, reminding her from a time before current history blew up in their faces; she sensed an echo that filled a space that was now missing, like the emptiness in the accordionist's trouser leg, its grey flannel pinned up where a thigh might once have bulged. She escaped down the hill again to Embankment Gardens, seeking a place to sit by herself.

Here she sat in solitude on a bench as darkness covered her; she hoped the natural dark blanket made her invisible; people did not disturb her, wrapt in their own encounters, more alone among crowds than is ever possible in isolation. She watched the plump pigeons waddling along, oblivious to all events except the furtive stalking of a mangy cat; a cat that pounced too early and scattered the scavenging birds, then licked its fur with a nonchalant air as if to assure anyone that it could do without food, this kind of food, something better would surely turn up while he waited. *Even the cats have been on short rations.* The drizzle became too much to bear; her coat was becoming heavy with rain, she had to move on, to find somewhere dry; to become one with the crowd again.

In the unlit alleys off the main streets, brick rubble, wet gutters, the detritus of a city only just managing to keep itself in order after the keepers of order had been diverted to trenches overseas. Here in these alleys men in silhouette groped fingers inside girls' dresses while ten yards further on, back to the illuminations of the main street, omnibuses crawled in dense traffic packed to the open roofs with people standing and shouting and waving their flags as if there might be no tomorrow; which was the way of the war; but Vanessa thought, that way has reached its end, we can think differently now, this is a new present, the past is behind us, there will be a tomorrow. So she wonders why, if that past was characterised by madness, why does she now feel herself in this present teetering so close to the brink of a broken sanity?

So Vanessa Bowen thinks, forcing herself into the present, as she steps over the kerb and strolls along the Whitehall roadway where the flags flutter on buildings and look smugly down on the manic waving of smaller flags below. She turns into Downing Street, thinking she will see Mr Lloyd George, but not knowing what she might say, particularly as she is swallowed into this swaying crowd of American soldiers, loudly proclaiming their yankiness and not caring what the prime minister might think though ready to give him a cheer. On the railings there is a silent proclamation that she stops to read, an official claim of victory and a licence to celebration, under the imprint of Government.

There will be tomorrow; as long as I can always slip away from today. So Vanessa will think later, on another day when her thoughts can turn more comfortably to the past and the future, as she might turn on a tap, as soothing as soaking in her hot bath.

There was a beeriness in the air, even walking down Whitehall; a street that you might think sober in all but the most exceptional times; these were exceptional times, or at least an exceptional day, she thought, congratulating herself on the bravery of being there, this small personal victory, stepping over puddles of spilt beer that were signs of happiness but also inevitably of bitterness. Because the war had left a bad taste in the mouth and no amount of kissing with strangers would take the taste away.

"Come on, love, join in, let your hair down."

Oh, I'm tempted, she thought, her finger instinctively touching the bun at the back of her head.

The warm lights of the pub, almost in the shadow of the War Office, looked inviting at that moment to Vanessa; she knew she must go inside, if only to seek the dry and the warm if not the more dangerous comfort of humanity. *Had we met before?* was the question that sprang to Vanessa's lips, wishing to swallow it even as it rose in her throat, a question that came so vacuously into the light of the pub. On such an unusual occasion it seemed impossible to find the right words for conversation, for wars do not end every day; everyone smiled desperately, cheerfulness bursting out and served with the sausage rolls struck that day off the rationing because no one would tell or dare tell; a meagre spread put on with such a desperate spirit of defiance that could not be, yet, an utter celebration of the end of war. Yet a party, a party of strangers made friends, a party that became a single body that smiled *it's nearly all over*.

Had we met before? The object of the question had been a young man with a golden moustache on a handsome face that at first managed to hide its scar in the low light; and a missing arm, his officer uniform with its badge of rank as vacuous as her question. But no, she could not stomach this conversation at this time on the anniversary of her own husband's death in action.

Had we met before, had we met earlier, had we met before stupidity plunged the world into this pointless conflict, before acts of mutilation were randomly inflicted, we might have meant so much more to each other. We might have embarked on an affair, I might have kissed the still unblemished skin of your cheek and touched it tenderly with my fingers, you might have folded two arms around me; I might have taken you in, a mad consuming affair that could have taken us to secret assignations and beds in hotel rooms but never to marriage because this kind of love would go up in flames at the very thought, would be puffed instantly out of existence.

I would never dare, so thought Vanessa at a sudden moment of clarity, to embark on such an affair; not even to contemplate its reality, so locked inside the fragile shell of her own timidity. Reggie had told her – you're a good egg. I know, she thought, I might crack.

She pushed past the officer, unwilling to venture into the scars of his story; pushed through the chattering, babbling crowds of voices talking above one another; the faces creased in laughter, red cheeks flushed by alcohol. At the bar, for the first time she ordered a drink, *a beer*, so she thought; beer as these people drink, with a flat head no froth because, to be honest, it was past its best, but also to be honest, no one was really caring. Sipping it, grimacing, she had not acquired the vinegary taste for want of trying, in her twenty-one years of existence sheltered by the war, sheltered from the war, the war that still had sealed her off from what might pass as a normal life.

She looked at the faces, wanting to like them, the shining eyes of people drunk on ale and liberation; liberation from the daily fear of death intruding in a telegram from the front line of a battle elsewhere, floated through the channel of a desk in the War Office, a life and a death beyond her experience and imagining but not beyond her conscience.

A loud cackle made her turn, a whoop almost of madness dragged out into the open by excitement. She looked at the face and it seemed she saw a skull, the white bone and hollow black eyes, while the face continued to laugh, the sound rang in her ears; the sound rang all around her, like a tuneless carillon of bells in this confined room, too close to be borne. *This might be hell*. This place that on this November day many saw as paradise; that next day they would through the blackness of a hangover claim to remember forever for its happiness; yet it could not yet persuade her to that. More beer might do it but she found herself gagging at the thought and the liquid already swilling inside her, putting down the glass, pushing again through the packed bodies, parting the seas between them with her hands outstretched before her in panic, placing her faith in the redemption of moonlight and fresh air or even the dampness of the drizzle that was still falling. Fresh air, cold rain, she gulped them down, like a newborn greedy for the stuff of life.

"Hold up! Hold up, my dear." The man in cap and muffler held her by the elbows, suspecting she might faint for joy of life on a day like this.

"It's nothing, thank you," whispered Vanessa with a voice as pale as her skin. It was all too much emotion for a girl's body starved of feeling to contain.

So Vanessa felt gratitude flow through her in a pink flush returning colour to white cheeks, like an application of rouge; and this emerged in no time at all as a smile that spread across her features and lit up her eyes as if from deep inside. And she turned her smile to the man who had helped her, this smile as a gift of gratitude, holding his eyes in her gaze then realising that she was staring into the milkiness of a glass eye, unseeing in his eye socket, so she had to suppress a scream into a shudder that might still pass for faintness; but emerged in an instant as an expression of tender kindness towards this man who had stepped forward to help.

"Thank you," she managed, and it was enough, to allow her to move on.

The rain had ceased, and there was a feeling that the party in the streets was ceasing. The inflammation of high emotions and unaccustomed alcohol was dying down as Vanessa observed from the top deck of the omnibus that she had jumped onto simply because it had been there, and *there* was a place she wished to escape. Her thoughts turned to home, though she was unsure how she might ever return, least of all tonight.

Down on Regent Street, for that was the route of the omnibus, a shindy of brawling boys, worse the wear for drink, sprang her to judgement. *Is fighting never finished?* But there was excuse enough today, today of all days, she could see the wildness of justification in their eyes, so she herself set aside judgement, at least in that moment looking down from above.

Two seats in front of her on the open deck of the omnibus, now starting to make faster progress, a man struck a lucifer to light a cigarette and passed it on to the woman's lips before lighting his own. They sucked in and blew out with a shared satisfaction. Careful, she wanted to say, those are dangerous, they start fires, you never know where they might lead.

She rose to her feet, went down the narrow stairs, and dinged the bell so she could step back into the street.

PART THREE

1927

1

MESSENGER

I tried not to think about it. But the memory always bubbled up inside like indigestion.

It was getting on the train, though the train was different. It was standing in this station with the clouds of steam. It was heading south to Kent, though to a different part of the county, on different tracks. The memory of that time, half my life earlier, and the memory of that place. The woods mainly, I always remembered the woods more than the house; more than the people, funnily enough. The house, the people, they were an impression, an impression of a house much grander than anything I'd seen before or since, but an impression fading like one of those early photographs in sepia, the detail at the edges washed away like sandcastles before the advancing tide. But the woods were real; I felt I could touch them still.

It had only been for two weeks. Two weeks out of 24 years. I always felt like screaming *Leave me alone, bloody leave me alone*. You owe them nothing, I told myself. You owe them everything, I argued back.

Bloody don't.

Do.

Of course it was complicated. Life is. It's complicated more than anything by memory. By the tricks of memory. What was I really remembering? Was it a memory or a re-imagining? Was this from the mind of a 9-year-old boy or a 24-year-old man?

The train juddered to a clanking stop. The announcer called

out 'Tunbridge Wells', whistles blew, carriage doors slammed shut, and my reverie puffed away out of the station.

I came here regularly. This was where the *Messenger* had its offices and I worked more for them than any other paper; after all it was where I'd started as a trainee reporter nearly ten years ago. It was a local newspaper where stories often found their way into the nationals – and that was now my real interest. I wanted to see my by-line 'T.G. Shepherd' in the Fleet Street papers not here among the parish notices. They'd offered me staff jobs but I'd turned them down. I was after bigger and better, stories that had meaning beyond the borders of Kent.

It made for a more precarious living but that suited me. A regular salary might be useful – more so for mum than me – but I was young and rising and there were no ties to hold me down: no wife, no girl friend at the moment, just me. My needs were few, and they could be satisfied by the occasional bonanza of a story I could sell on to other papers.

Bert Sermon was the *Messenger* editor. He'd not object to being called a seasoned hack, he might even revel in the title; it might suit his cynicism. He'd got so used to the job that no news was new to him any more. He'd seen it all before. He wasn't bored by that; it was just the job, that was what he did. Not subject to wide-eyed wonder nor disbelieving horror, he steered a straight course between extremes, never too distracted by a rigid adherence to the truth. The truth, his truth, was whatever sold more papers.

I walked in to his office, rapping gently on the glass in the door frame; as I opened the door some of the tobacco fug escaped over my shoulder. The 'I' of EDITOR was peeling off the windowpane. Bert saw no reason to replace it; he would rather the paper's money was spent on essentials not fripperies:

stories not housekeeping. Suited me if it meant more money for stories.

What sold papers was important because it also kept him in cigarettes. Bert smoked instinctively, incessantly, lighting a new one without thinking, almost as soon as he stubbed out the old one. But here was the thing, the way he smoked them, no one else smoked like Bert. He held the cigarette in his cupped right hand, with the lighted tip of the cigarette pointing inwards. If I'd been more of a smoker myself I might have admired his dexterity. But I smoked because everybody smoked and I didn't want to stand out too much. So I only ever smoked with other people; left to myself, I never bothered.

Now it meant I could offer Bert a cigarette and that was worth doing. A gentle reminder as we puffed away that *now you owe me something*.

"What you got for me, Bert?" I asked.

He shuffled some sheets of foolscap on his desk. "Something here," he said. "Could be interesting. But not worth us tying one of our boys down on what might be a goose chase." He looked at his scribbled notes on the lined paper.

"It's like this," he said. "They found some baby's bones in the wood. Who? How'd they get there? Is there something suspicious? Police not forthcoming. Got their *Don't ask me* faces on. *Don't ask* – so no one does."

"And?"

"Go and ask. That's what you do. What happened? What are they covering? Doesn't smell right. Find out, it's a story, I think it's got legs."

"Where is this?"

"Place called Luckhurst. Little village down the road."

"I know it." I paused, looking down at the sheet of paper he'd given me, brushing away grey tobacco ash. "Good." Such a useful word; it could cover my feelings so easily, inhaling the word with the smoke. "Good."

"It's near a place where there's a military hospital." He cradled the cigarette even more outrageously into his palm as if it held all his secrets. I bet Bert had a few, but never mind. Don't bite the hand that feeds you.

"Old soldiers? All these years after the war?"

"Nutcases," Bert said as if that was it, said it all.

"Shell shock?"

"Nutcases. Doesn't need a name to make excuses for them. Perhaps one of 'em kills babies but the doctors don't like to let on."

I wrote down all the details in my notebook, copying from Bert's bit of foolscap. There were names. Police officers. Coroner's office. Addresses. A cottage near the scene. The doctor in charge of the hospital. Not much but I liked it that way. More of a puzzle.

"You sure about this, Bert? Doesn't seem much there. And lots of effort to end up with nothing much."

He looked at me over the rim of his glasses. "Believe you me, there's something. I just asked one or two questions and they backed away like there was a bad smell."

"So it won't be easy. And it'll take time."

"You're a crafty bugger. But I can't do more than exes."

"I'll need a car. And I'll have to work it between other jobs."

"I'll ring Bentley's – make sure you get the rate. One of their jalopies, up to five days' use. By then, you'll know if the story's gonna fly."

"Could be five days wasted."

"That ain't gonna be my fault. You'll work out an angle. Take it or leave it."

I left him phoning the garage. Truth is, I fancied a job

with a car and there was a curiosity inside me about the place. Luckhurst. I remembered it but the memories were not pin-sharp. I was curious to see what it was like, to see what memories might be stirred.

Police station first, just a stroll away. Thought I might as well make it official. But Bert was right: they were hiding something. These were people who'd trusted me with tip-offs many times and I'd made it worth their while, always a good name check in the story – if that's what they were after. But here it was *mum's the word*.

"George," I pleaded. "How am I gonna earn a living? Give us a break."

"Nothing in it, Tom. We're not investigating."

"Why not?"

"Cos there's nothing in it."

"So there were bones, a baby's bones, you admit that."

"If there was, it's innocent. Nothing to uncover."

"That's what I heard. The bones were uncovered."

"If so, it was all natural."

"As in, a baby went out for a walk, dropped dead, buried itself."

"If you say so. But I never did."

They were giving little away but I could tell there was something. George's words to send me on my way were: "We have no reason to suspect a crime."

Next stop the coroner's court. The coroner was no more forthcoming except he let something slip: "I can't go back into historic cases to satisfy curiosity."

"Historic?" I asked. "When does history start?"

"Yesterday, you might say."

"So it's recent?"

"Not what I said. No, no, no. Not at all what I said."

"But it's a case you've looked at?"

"Not what I said. Afraid there's nothing to be said. You can consult the records if you're looking for something specific. But you'll need details – name, place."

"Luckhurst," I said. "Bones found in Luckhurst."

"Not my patch."

The morning was nearly gone and I'd found out nothing. But felt there was something to find. The only thing to do was to go down there and have a nosy around so I walked to Bentley's, just off the high street, to pick up the car.

"Best you can do?" It was a little black Austin 7.

"It comes at Bert's rate. That or nothin'."

"Won't be breaking the speed limit in that."

"You're not Gordon England. On your way before Bert says No."

It was a good enough little car, good enough to get the few miles down the road to Luckhurst and back again. I was happy enough; this was independence; and I was curious.

It was funny pulling into the village. I had this memory of being here before, which wasn't that surprising; after all, I had been before. But I hadn't expected to remember being driven down this street by Rodgers all those years back when. Rodgers. I hadn't given him a thought since those days. Now I wondered what happened to him.

I knew where to start. Always start at the pub; you can have a drink and find out what you need to know at the same time. I parked the car outside. But before going in, I had to walk around the pub. It looked run down, and from the lack of lights and noise, I wasn't even sure it was open. There was a bit of a garden out the back, a yard really, some hollyhocks growing and stirring like memories in the breeze.

I tried the wooden door of the pub and it opened inwards.

The gas lamps inside were turned down low, but there was enough light to see that there was no one there. I went up to the bar and called out 'Hello'. Eventually an older man appeared, wearing a jacket and a muffler, looking at me in a way that did not say 'welcome'.

"We're shut," he said.

"But it's opening time. And I could do with a drink."

"That might be so but we're shut. The pub don't pay. And I'm movin' away."

"Really? Why's that?"

I didn't really want the full story but I had to listen to get close to what I needed. It seemed the village had been in steady decline since the war and now there were not enough people in the village to keep the pub going. Now he was just going through the motions until the brewery took things over – as soon as that happened, he would be off.

"Where will you go?"

"East coast. Daughter's got a place; she don't want me but she's gettin' me."

"That's a shame. What'll you do?"

He shrugged and I looked around the room. It was hard but I had a vague recollection of the place. In those times it would have been full of people and warm light and warmer beer.

"Rosie."

The landlord looked up. "What about her?"

"Is that your daughter? It was Rosie, wasn't it?"

"What if it was?"

"Let me have a pint. And one for yourself."

So I got my drink after all, not the best of beers, but good enough to loosen his tongue a bit. I slipped him a shilling for the beer and the chat. It seemed that Rosie had moved away before the war – 'she had to go,' was the way he put it.

"Why's that?"

"Trouble. She was trouble, always was. But trouble with the gentry. They never took to her, not that they had to, they stayed away from here. Things happened, she moved away. Got married, had babies."

"Is she all right? I knew her, you see."

So I had to tell my story: about staying at Hardinge Hall for two weeks one summer, about the night I'd got lost in the woods and Rosie had helped me. But his face remained blank, remembering nothing.

"Tell me, I heard that a body was found near here. A baby's body – well, bones really. Did you hear anything of that?"

"I did," he said quickly. "I found it. My dog found it, started barkin' and brought me to it. Over there in the woods. Only a couple of weeks ago."

"So, what happened? Seems a strange thing."

"I told the police, the village bobby. Useless. Just blustered and said it were animal bones. It never were. But not my business. I reported it and that's that."

"So the police didn't follow up?"

He shook his head. I asked if he would take me to the spot. It was only a five-minute walk from there. I was surprised how sparse the trees were. In my mind this had been a dense wood, with tall trees, but now the branches overhead offered little shelter from the sun that was high in the early summer sky. The spot we reached was one of the denser areas of the woodland, under trees that formed a triangle of earthy space.

"It was just there," he pointed. "You can see the earth's darker, been turned over. The police did come back, just to take a look. Perhaps to tidy up, take away the bones, cover over the traces."

"Why'd they do that?"

"Your guess. Anyways that's all I can say. Don't know any more."

He left me there. I'm no detective but I knelt down to rub at the earth with my hand. There was no point in doing more, not even any point in doing that. All I could do was walk around and while I walked my memory was stroked to life by the surroundings. There was an eerie familiarity about it all, these woods, the birds in the trees, the carving on the bark. It seemed that lovers in previous times had been here to record their affections; however fleeting they might have been, these letters remained on the tree. IF said one; if only, I thought.

I sat down on a tree stump to gather my thoughts. It seemed to me that Rosie might be the key to unlock this. My suspicions, on very little evidence, were that Rosie had had a baby, and that she had disposed of the baby. I could imagine reasons for that. My most vivid memories of that time were looking down on Teddy and Rosie from my perch in the trees, watching them while they did everything that could lead to a baby further down the line. Perhaps that was why Rosie had had to get away; perhaps she had been driven away by the scandalised Hardinges.

I needed to find out more. I reminded myself I was a reporter not a writer of melodramas. *Keep digging.*

Through the trees ahead of me I could see two buildings: the bigger one was Hardinge Hall, and then there was a white-painted cottage, another image that seemed to come out of a dream. I walked to the edge of the woods where a wire fence, with stakes every five yards, made a half-hearted attempt at security. There was a gate onto the lawn, with a sign announcing King George V Military Hospital. I gazed at the building, feeling something like nostalgia washing through me. My eyes scanned along the windows on the first floor, half-expecting to see a familiar face staring out, my self looking at myself.

But to my left was the cottage, and I decided to head there first.

2

SEEDS

A stout woman opened the door. Her face was open and rounded in all its features, her hair grey and pinned back in a bun, ready for service, like the pinafore she wore. I thought to myself that she must be prematurely grey because she had a face that was not yet ready for old age. A familiar face. Although she was changed I recognised Mrs Rodgers from my memory of long ago. But I decided to say nothing yet, certain that she wouldn't recognise me. I explained I was a reporter and had some questions to ask.

"What is it?" came a voice from within.

"It's a young man asking questions."

"Ask him one then. Who is he?"

I adopted my foot in the door technique, just in case. The voice was one that carried from a room inside but also across the tracks of time. It sounded no more welcoming to me than it had ever been, which made me all the more determined to persist.

"Here you are, Mrs Rodgers. Can you give Mrs Hardinge my card?" The face in the doorway switched from polite to puzzled. Then excited as she raised her hand to her mouth in surprise.

"My dear Tommy," she said as she put her arms around me. "It's been such a long time."

"Who is it? I demand to know." That voice again, like a knife grinding on my memory.

Mrs Rodgers beckoned him inside into the low-ceilinged

hallway, then through the door on the right into the sitting room. There Mrs Hardinge was enthroned on a green floral armchair. She wore a shawl and a pair of fluffy slippers that seemed incongruous when compared to my memories of her. She cut a reduced figure from the formidable matriarch I remembered. Or perhaps it was simply that I had grown and she had shrunk a little. But her tone when she spoke reminded me of who she had been, someone who was still used to getting her own way without argument. Mrs Rodgers showed her the card and bent down to whisper.

"It is you, I see it now." She stared at me like royalty inspecting the troops, even from her armchair. "You've grown up to be presentable. For which we should be grateful if somewhat surprised."

"Happy to pass muster."

"You carry yourself well. And you know how to wear a tie."

"Shall I get Tommy some tea, Ma'am?" asked Mrs Rodgers.

"Tell Iris too. But don't say why."

"Nowadays I generally answer to Tom not Tommy. Only Thomas on official forms. My reporter's byline is TG Shepherd."

"I will call you Mr Shepherd. We adopt familiarity too easily through names. This did not use to happen. The war has changed much, seldom for the better."

We were alone and I knew I should say why I was there. But she made me a boy again, even if I wanted to be as defiant a boy as I hoped I had once been. The fact was these days I needed to show defiance less often; I was out of the habit and reporters needed a wider range of deceptions.

"You might as well sit down at the table. If you are staying for tea."

The table was well-scrubbed wood, rustic in style. It took

up rather too much space in the room; there was a feeling of too much furniture fitting into too small a space, and none of it really fitting, all clashing styles. I was becoming aware that circumstances had changed a great deal from the days when I had stayed in Hardinge Hall like the orphan child. Everything there and then had seemed so grand. The furniture then had been polished but now was scrubbed; the ceilings had been higher than anyone could ever reach without ladders whereas here I was tempted to touch the white plaster above with my fingers.

"We have suffered," Mrs Hardinge said, reading my thoughts. "George was to blame. I hope you have not come to ask about that. There is no money left, you know."

I sat down and got out a notebook, as a signal to myself more than to her that I was here to do my job. On the table was a vase filled with flowers from the garden. To make sure there was no mistaking its role in life, the vase was also decorated with flowers painted on its surface boldly yet crudely, as if the artist had had no patience with an unwanted task. The bright natural colours of the real flowers overshadowed the fading painted ones, but any sadness in that was not immediately evident. Mrs Rodgers brought in the tea things on a tray and set it down on the table.

"These are lovely," I said. "I remember them like this in the garden."

"Dahlias, zinneas, marigolds, hollyhocks," Mrs Hardinge recited.

"The country garden flowers of memory. My memory."

"You do well to remember. Mildred will be pleased."

"Mildred?"

"Mrs Rodgers, as you knew her."

"Milly," said Iris, coming in. "I call her Milly. She prefers that." Iris sat down opposite and looked at him intently. "Why do I know you? Do you loiter in the woods? I see you have muddy shoes."

Despite my own wishes, I was excited to see Iris again. She had changed least of all of us, seeming to age hardly at all. But of course she was still young, perhaps only just thirty, and still as beautiful as my memory told me she had been. She picked up my card, read the name and stared at me, hunching inside the long blue cardigan she wore despite the season: the stone walls made this a cool house in summertime.

"Tommy? The little boy?" Mrs Rodgers had willed her towards this recognition; perhaps she had said something upstairs. "Now grown up. And handsome."

"Mr Shepherd is now from the gutter press. Is that an improvement on the gutter where we found you before?" Mrs Hardinge's mood seemed to have been soured further by Iris's presence. She would strive to be unpleasant. And she pulled it off easily enough.

"I never knew," said Iris, " – perhaps I did but forgot – that your name is Shepherd. Perhaps we are your lost sheep."

"You are the black sheep," put in Mrs Hardinge, ushering Iris into the pen.

"The whole flock might be black sheep. In which case the good white sheep will stand out – whoever that might be. Millie perhaps."

"Mildred has enough to occupy her already. She should concentrate on looking after us. Particularly those of us in advancing years."

A sense, not really an odour, of dusty lavender seeds emanated from the older woman, as though she might pass her time out of sight in a dresser drawer. I wished she would, but I needed to ask my questions first.

It struck me more and more with every sip of tea across the Spartan table: this was a house of few comforts, and the residents gave little comfort to each other. So they all took seeds of pleasure from the flowers – Mrs Hardinge even reached out to touch the petals and squeeze them into shape.

"It was a bad war. Dreadful things happened and we have not recovered. We try to forget. But you, of course, were too young. You were spared but not poor Edward."

"I was sorry about Teddy," I said. "He was always good to me. If the war had gone on another year or two, I expect I'd have been drawn in too. But I was never a tommy, only in name."

It always bothered me. I had escaped the need to fight. That turned into a source of guilt rather than regret. And guilt distorted things, like the bowl of the silver spoon in my saucer. I looked at Mrs Rodgers, waiting at the back of the room, and I knew her news from the war at that moment. She stood like a widow at the cenotaph, her face as white as its Portland stone.

"What about Muriel?" I asked, aiming to spare Mrs Rodgers' pain, directing my question between Iris and Mrs Hardinge.

"Muriel? She got married and moved away."

"To a husband who expected nothing from us."

"There was nothing to expect."

"She moved away."

"Married a man called Reggie."

"We don't miss her."

"She had already moved away."

"There was a difference."

"A difference of opinion."

"We are used to it now."

Iris's sentences seemed let out on a tight leash, like the dog

I remembered, as if fearful the words might run away from her. Mrs Hardinge's words came yapping along in irritated pursuit. Perhaps they had both got out of the habit of free-flowing conversation in this house of competing suppressions. I decided I had to try: for curiosity, for professional reasons, for the hint of a deeper connection than a cup of weak tea with two lumps of strained conversation.

"Something happened nearby," I said. "It sounds a bit gruesome. Apparently the bones of a baby were discovered in the woods."

"Apparently? No such appearance was ever made. I am sure we would have known about it otherwise."

Mrs Hardinge did not seem to me an objective witness. My job had trained me to sniff out trouble and she gave me the impression of wanting to keep a secret buried.

"Nothing you heard either, Iris?"

She shook her head. Nothing to say. Lips sealed. *Anything you say may be…*

"Do you ever see Rosie?" I asked. "The girl from the pub. I don't suppose she hung around."

"Certainly not," spat out Mrs Hardinge. "We wanted nothing to do with her. And we had nothing to do with her."

"Whose baby might it have been, do you think? Someone said it could have been Rosie's."

"There was no baby. You have been misled."

"I suppose that's possible. Though the police seemed sure enough. That there was something."

"There was nothing."

I could see Hardinge Hall through the window that was framed on the outside in trailing flowers. I was curious to see more of the house, perhaps all the more so now that I had revived the memory of that time. On the lawn I could see soldier-patients, some walking, one on crutches, one pushed in a wheelchair. I saw this place and became Tommy again, a boy eager to do well, to be seen to be useful.

In the hallway, a clock struck with a familiar chime. I knew instantly it was the grandfather clock that had once stood in the much larger space of the big house.

"Some things were moved, then? The old clock."

"Never seek to ask," said Iris. "It tolls for thee." These words – from a face like Louise Brooks, framed by dark bobbed hair – were portentous as title cards in an epic film. And you had to take them with an ironic smirk in just the same way.

"Indeed," said Mrs Hardinge. "We must release you, Mr Shepherd. I'm sure your bloodhound tendencies need to be exercised elsewhere. Though I do hope you will not sniff around the woods too long. These poor men deserve a little respect in their sanctuary."

"I'm sure. But I will ask my questions carefully. And perhaps, if I may, return another day to ask one or two more?"

"I cannot see the point. What's done is done. Sleeping dogs must lie."

There was something then. I had not been sure until those last words of Mrs Hardinge. She had just let her guard down, relieved at my departure. Yes, I told myself, I will return. And, yes, I knew, looking at Iris, I wanted to return. I would try to unseal her lips.

3

CHARITY

So I went back just a couple of days later. I already had the feeling that this story was not going to add up to much apart from frustration. I'd stumble around, like I had all those years ago, lost in the woods. If I found anything – well, I doubted I would use it.

But what drove me back, like a moth, was the bright light in Iris's eyes. Seeing her again had revived a feeling in me. It was a long time since I'd been this drawn to someone. Iris was so different from anyone else I'd known.

Mrs Rodgers showed me in, a bit more cagily than before. Mrs Hardinge had no doubt put her on her guard. But it was Iris who greeted me in the sitting room.

"You're back? What brings you? Nostalgia?" asked Iris.

"I hope you don't mind."

"Yes, I do," a voice waylaid me from behind. Mrs Hardinge shuffled into the room.

"Just a few questions. My editor insists I follow up."

"Does he never get out? He should, rather than just sending you to do his dirty work. Reality is a good antidote to fantasy."

"I don't think a dead baby is fantasy."

"Where is the baby then? Or the body? This is madness. You should leave us in peace."

"It's true, Tom," said Iris. "There is nothing to find."

"You're right, no doubt. But I have to satisfy my editor. And myself too."

Iris smiled a smile that might have offered friendship or withheld it for good behaviour. She could play me, and already I knew she would win.

"Some tea, then, I think. Millie – would you be so good?"

Mrs Hardinge was in her armchair, scratching the brown liver spots on the back of her hands, perhaps showing signs of eczema and not just the wrinkles and wattles of age. Might I have to feel sorry for her, to give her the respect demanded by her accumulation of years and entitlement?

"She's not really old," said Iris, reading me, speaking as if there were no one else in the room. "She just likes to act it – she feels abandoned – to the clutches of the living – by the thoughtlessness of the dead."

"Iris, you can be cruel. You see, Mr Shepherd, how she has no feelings for me? It is a sad state of affairs."

"Yet we manage. Strangely we manage to rub along together – bobbing along – jolly on the surface like two corks in the same bathtub. Don't we, Ma'am? Don't we have fun? Don't we, Catherine?"

The Christian name came as a shock. She might never be anything but Mrs Hardinge to me. Memory and history would restrain me. And the tightening of my skin sent a shiver through me as I looked at the coarse grey hair that clung tight to her head like a metal helmet. She would never encourage softer thoughts.

"Names are so tricky, aren't they?" said Iris. "I can never really be so familiar – hard to 'Catherine' her. But I could never bring myself to 'mother' either. Mother is such a word – so fraught with meaning. And motherhood was never easy – not in this house."

"Iris. This is cruelty. Mr Shepherd has not even asked."

"Not asked because really – well, because he is too nice.

He has a kind face. I could never see you as mother – but mother-in-law does not slip comfortably between the sheets of conversation."

Iris spoke quickly, squeezing her words out as if she could not bear to own them.

"In time," she mused, aloud but as if to herself, "'Ma'am' seemed most natural. Close enough to Ma to indicate a relationship – a maternal one. But showing a deference that might be deemed acceptable. Is that not so? It seemed her due – as the family queen."

It allowed Iris the dry pleasure of irony, like a morning Martini, but it seemed too close to goading for my comfort. I felt uncomfortable as a bystander, even more so when I realised Mrs Hardinge had slumped into silence, her gaze looking through the window at the world beyond. Outside the cottage the woods offered sanctuary of a kind, as they had all those years ago.

"Thank you, Millie – we shall pour." As polite a dismissal as Iris might manage. She swirled the teapot. "As you hear, I call her Millie. Every time Ma'am calls her Mildred it seems like a reprimand. To me – and – I'm sure – to Millie. What do you think?"

So she forced me to take sides, and I was not quick or clever enough to avoid it.

"I like Millie," I said.

"We all like Millie. She is a good woman. But we cannot make her say which she prefers. Apparently Jack – Mr Rodgers, you'll remember – used to use both."

"Mildred," Mrs Hardinge put in, "is a mark of respect. A quality rare in the world."

"That" said Iris "depends on whose mouth it comes from."

"People are given names for a reason. I do not see why you

should change the name by shortening it, by changing it to sound more childish. There are adult names for adult people, and children should be encouraged to be adult as soon as possible." Mrs Hardinge looked at me, a challenge in her eyes. "Do you not agree, Mr Thomas Shepherd?"

"I prefer Tom," I stated. "But will answer to any name if it takes me to the truth."

"Now there's a grand ambition. We might fall short if that's the hurdle we have to jump."

"Tell me, what is the truth about this baby?"

"There was no baby," insisted Mrs Hardinge, wincing that the tea had become stewed.

I pressed on with questions but it was like pushing at a locked door. Nothing would emerge today; tea and conversation were drained. I got to my feet and pinched the tip of my hat to take my leave.

"Already?" asked Iris. "Let me show you out." She led me to the door and through it, closing it behind her. "Let's take a walk."

We walked down to the fence, and then along it until we reached the gate on the roadway. Iris had slipped her arm through mine, which sent a shiver of pleasure through me. To be honest, I felt proud walking along arm in arm with this beautiful woman; but it did complicate my job and I told myself that I still needed to dig out a story.

The gateway had a temporary look about it, made of wood and wire rather than stone. Staring down the drive that led up to the house stirred a memory of sitting in a car driven by Jack Rodgers.

"It has a military air," I observed.

"Not really what we like to see in a hospital. But they do good work."

"Tell me, did Mr Rodgers – Jack – I suppose it was the war?"

"Passchendaele."

Her eyes glistened even more brightly with the moistening of tears. "But come, no more of the past."

"I'm only here because of the past. I wonder when that baby died."

"Oh Tom, don't be Tiresome Tom. We are here now – and perhaps as well as the present – perhaps there is a future."

She squeezed my arm and I felt any professional commitment draining out of me.

"Let's head into the woods. A walk in the woods is good for me. I remember it was what you did – all the time."

"You remember? I'm not sure I can."

We headed into the woods on what seemed to be a path made by the footsteps of people. The trees were denser on this side, and there was a feeling of being enclosed with the wood's natural inhabitants. We had stopped talking, and it was surprisingly comfortable to be with Iris in silence. With no words between us, only a glancing smile, we listened to the sounds of the forest. "Birds," I said, foolishly, every inch the city boy. Some were trills, some shrill single notes; some deep-throated pigeons, some croak-mouthed crows; most unidentifiable; from the low branches and from high up in the treetops.

"Do you remember?" she asked. "These woods were your playground. I always wondered – what you did all day here."

"I read a lot. That's the main thing I remember. I read *The Wind in the Willows*. Then I read it again."

We reached a glade and the sun slanted down into it. The sunlight illuminated a dead tree. Its chopped down branches formed a shape that was almost like the figure of a dancer.

"I love this tree," said Iris. "It's like sculpture."

"But it's real, a real tree."

"Like a sculpture by Picasso."

"Do you like that stuff?"

"Enough. Enough to know I like it. Because it moves me."

I looked at her with sunlight on her face, and I could see a tear on her cheek like a raindrop on a window. "Hey," I said, "no need for tears."

"How do you know?" There was a sharpness in her voice. I didn't know what to say; it seemed that any words might upset her.

"People call me highly strung. Whatever that means. To be honest I don't know. Sometimes I change, I say the wrong things. I can't help it. Anyway I get by."

I felt I had to say something. "I can see you do. But it can't be easy with Mrs Hardinge in the same house all the time."

"Not all the time. She gets out a surprising amount. Charity work." I was simply nodding to keep the conversation going. "She runs the hospital board. They have meetings. And there are others."

"She didn't strike me like that."

"She's difficult but so am I. We know each other – and I'm not good with people I don't know. We've been through things together."

We sat on a bench that was positioned at the edge of the glade. Side by side, able to face each other, I watched her in the shade. She half-turned away, lifted her chin as if to pose 'this is my best side'. I was happy simply watching her, all thoughts of investigation blown away by her presence.

"We had to sell the woods," she went on, talking to the trees rather than me. "It was no wrench. They're public now – not that we ever kept people out. But the sale was forced by our circumstances."

"Really? It was that bad?"

"Oh, it was bad. Nearly everything went. The fortunes of two wealthy families. And death – to make it worse. Or perhaps better. Who knows? I could get bitter, and sometimes I am. But there's no point. I need to live again – I have not lived enough. Frozen in time for ten years."

"And now? You're ready for change?"

"Yes. Yes, I am," she looked deep into my eyes, as if daring me to hold her gaze. "It's time to move on."

I thought she was talking about her life. But it seemed she was calling our afternoon encounter to a close. "I must get back," she said. "Ma'am will become suspicious. I need to maintain her trust – enough to break it when she doesn't realise."

She walked on with more purpose towards the cottage, then stopped when its white walls came into sight through the trees.

"There," she said. "I must go back in. That is your direction," she pointed with her finger towards the station.

"I will go. But I want to come back. We never touched on half the things I wanted to."

"Must you be so full of questions? Could we not just forget about them?"

"I can't. I have a job to do."

We were standing just inside the woods. I had no wish to ask her questions about the corpse of a baby but I did want to enter her life, and this excuse of a job served my purpose. I needed to see her again.

"Mrs Hardinge – Ma'am herself – though that's not easy – well, she will be out. Tomorrow. She has one of her charity duties all afternoon. Would you, I hope – if possible. It would be good, I think, to talk – without –" she nodded; I understood how one person's absence might loosen things. "And Millie too

– Millie is visiting her mother for a few days. Come tomorrow and we will have time. Time to ourselves."

"Of course. Though I will be working. Might I find out more?"

"You might find out more than you bargain for." She smiled, like a lantern in darkness. "Tomorrow."

She kissed me on the cheek, a simple gesture that would puzzle me until the next time we were to meet. But I was pleased that I would need to wait only 24 hours, and pleased – smiling inwardly at the irony – that I was now receiving secret messages myself rather than delivering them.

4

ROSES

I still lived with my mum in the buildings in Covent Garden. It embarrassed me at times but on the whole she didn't intrude. If I was away she accepted it was part of my job. If I was around she'd cook me something to eat. Though she had her work too. The only constant refrain was "When you gonna get married?" She meant well.

That morning our neighbour was sitting at the table with a cup of tea. Edna had a face that reminded me of the dough for a currant bun but I liked her and she was a good friend to my mum. She had been out to the market to get her flowers but was in no rush to get off to the work of selling. She sold flowers on the streets where she could: the Opera House in the evening was a good spot. Nellie and Edna were in and out of each other's flats all day, so they didn't mind me and I didn't mind them. I just poured myself a cup of tea and with a slice of toast that was breakfast. Mornings were a quiet time for mum these days as she'd given up the cleaning job that used to get her up early. Now arthritis had set in to her knees and she had a job that involved less kneeling: she sold evening papers in Kingsway, and she had a little stool to sit on.

The advantage was neither of them took any notice of me. That suited me as I didn't want to talk; I didn't want to explain that I would be back down to Kent 'on the story'. Seeing Edna and her flowers had given me an idea, but I didn't want to buy flowers from Edna as it would involve some questions; and I had no wish to give answers. I felt flustered, not really wanting to be there, thinking of where I was heading, who I would be seeing. So I got ready and set off, buying a small bouquet of roses outside the station. It's only polite, I told myself.

You've still got work to do, I kept telling myself too as I sat in the train carriage puffing past the backs of houses in south London. I was looking through my notebook, wondering how I could uncover any new information. Even as I thought to myself that Iris might be the answer to the mystery – if indeed it was a mystery.

When I got off the train at Luckhurst, I walked into the village. Opposite the pub was the church. I avoided churches; I simply didn't like them. They were alien places and they made me nervous. I had managed to go to a church school without religion making any impression on me, or at least that was the story I told myself. But this church was a magnet, pulling me towards it.

I walked through the church's lych-gate. Somehow I had dredged that word up from my memory, and now as I approached the church doors a shadow seemed to pass over me. Seeking an explanation, I looked up at the scudding clouds that had just obscured the sun. Another shiver passed through me.

"You are welcome. Feel free to enter."

I was surprised to see the priest there. My intention had been to slip inside the church, to be by myself, perhaps to see if anything seemed relevant to my quest. There would be tombstones, inscriptions marking the deaths of local people, record books even. The church might be the haystack and it might show me the needle.

Going through the doors, then seeing the pews and the aisle leading up to the cloth-covered altar, stirred a memory. It was not a pleasant one. I would not be tempted to drop to my knees in prayer.

"You seem troubled," said the priest. "Can I help by listening?"

"Not really. Perhaps you can help by talking?"

Of course, he said nothing to that. His face was blank, not even registering curiosity. I could see from his grey hair and the wrinkles around his eyes that he must be sixty at least. But that did not seem the right age: I studied his face trying to find features to recognise.

"Are you local?" he asked eventually. "Are you new to this village? I cannot remember seeing you here before."

"Oh," I replied. "I have been here before. But it seems a world away." I looked even harder at him but there was no familiarity in his face. "You are not the same vicar, you must be new."

"Hardly new. I have been here for twelve years. In the general reckoning that's a reasonable stint." He pointed to the flowers in my hand. "For a loved one? Is someone buried here, someone that you knew?"

"Perhaps. It wouldn't surprise me. What was the vicar's name before the war? I know the church from then."

"Ah. That would be Reverend Jones."

"That would be him. What happened? Did he find another parish?"

"In a sense. He became an army chaplain. He joined the war effort in 1915. A little impulsive, he left rather quickly. I came for a short while, just to cover, but it became permanent."

"Tell me then, where is Reverend Jones now?"

"With his maker. The war did not spare God's ministers any more than His soldiers. A grim harvest that autumn. I'm afraid the Somme saw to him, as it did to so many. God rest their souls."

I wasn't sure I completely shared those feelings. Reverend

Jones had not left a favourable impression on me but I had no wish to rake the ember of this particular memory.

"We remember him every year. His memorial is in the churchyard, and we lay a wreath on it in September, when he died. A sniper's bullet as he held the cross before his eyes."

"I wouldn't have wished that on him."

"No one would. He was much loved, a good man. Are those to lay on his tomb? I can show you to it."

"No. Not at all. Something else altogether."

I started backing away, then decided to give it a shot. "Are there any other graves? Outside the church – or the churchyard. Does that ever happen?"

"There's a strange question. Not that I know of. No one would want that – certainly not the family. You are thinking of local people? We all wish for a Christian burial."

"But what if you're not yet a Christian?"

"Not everyone is. But we are all God's children and recipients of His love."

"What about children? What if a child was not baptised? Too young, say?"

"It sounds as if you have an example in mind."

"Perhaps."

"There are procedures. God does not abandon children, and we find ways to meet His wishes."

"Really? Have you ever wandered the streets of London by night?"

He became silent. The conversation had not led to a conclusion other than prayer. He closed his eyes and knelt before the altar. It was clear that our audience was ended. As I walked away, back through the wooden gate, the bells struck twelve times. Iris had been precise. Not before 12.

Even so, I was fearful of arriving too early. I had no wish

to encounter Mrs Hardinge leaving the house. I was here to see Iris and no one else. So I wandered into the woods, to kill time, and to approach the cottage from the rear. That way, even if someone was inside the cottage, I could see and not be seen.

The previous night I'd taken *The Wind in the Willows* off the shelf next to my bed. Now the woods were all around me, as they had been again in my reading. I don't have many books – the public library serves my needs. I was surprised at how remote that book's language was from my own: full of long words that needed a dictionary, some complex sentences, references to mythology I didn't know, Latin phrases. Had I really read it and understood it enough to love it so much? Perhaps I had. I seem to live in a time of Perhaps. But I had started reading again last night and been captured again by its magic; and that memory added to my emotions as I walked through these woods.

I glimpsed the cottage through the trees. It seemed to be quiet. I judged that I had delayed enough past the earliest appointed hour. I longed for and dreaded this last part of my journey, pushing open the squeaky gate, treading on the stone path, knocking on the door, wishing each sound quieter; watching the door open inwards.

"So. You came. Come in."

It struck me: Iris spoke in short, sharp bursts, like a machine gun. I never thought of military things so *why now?* Perhaps in this place, with the hospital and its wounded soldiers, there was no escaping the war. Perhaps the church had summoned spirits. Perhaps Teddy was unspeaking, unseen, unheard in this place, ducked down below the parapet, tracer bullets passing overhead.

"You look glum," said Iris. "I didn't invite you for your

glumness. For a chat at least. A smile. For comfort. Who knows?"

"Of course. I'm sorry. Here, I brought you these."

The roses looked the worse for wear, or at least for being carried to too many places.

"How silly," said Iris. "I will have to hide them. What a sad little bouquet."

My face must have fallen. "You are a romantic after all. That's better."

She led me through into the sitting room, taking me by the hand. "See," she said. "No one else here. Not till much later."

"Good. So are you going to tell me the truth?"

She laughed, and there was something in the laugh that seemed cruel – to herself if not to me. There was a vulnerability that made me wary and anxious – and desperate to please her. Some men would run away from Iris but I was the opposite. The more she seemed broken the more I wanted to mend her. Not that she would have that.

"I asked you for a reason. And it's nothing to do with your questions."

I shrugged, trying to look disappointed. "What is it then?"

Her eyes were glimmering, as if she might burst into tears. I reached for her, instinctively, to comfort her; as she reached towards me. We embraced, holding each other tightly in our surprised, pre-determined arms. Then we kissed.

"I want life. I want a life."

I felt that I had allowed myself out too far, and was already out of my depth. I had no idea how to return to where I had been just a few minutes before. So we clung together even more tightly, desperately.

She laughed but her laughter was close to sobbing, her stare was intense enough to break down any remaining reluctant barriers. She took me by the hand again, and led me up the stairs, like a blind man.

"Iris, are you sure?"

She nodded, still on the brink of tears but not sadness, yet smiling as she took me into her bedroom. The whiteness of the sheets. The tears glistening on her cheeks. We kissed again, then stared at each other as if seeing our faces in a new light. Then, in a sudden racing against time, she pulled away and took off her clothes; her blouse, her skirt; stockings, underwear. She stood naked, trembling slightly; I stood there watching, engrossed, a spectator to a scene of some mystery, wondering at the sight before me, unexpected yet yearned for. She slid into the bed.

"Come under. It's chilly – even in summertime. This house is cold. No wonder no one's ever had a baby here. Poor Millie, she really wanted one. But not to be."

"Don't worry, I'll make sure there's no baby."

I lifted the sheet and slipped underneath its whiteness – Iris's skin looked surprisingly dark against the cotton. I almost gasped at the situation. I wanted to tell her she was beautiful – she was – but nerves got the better of me. The bed was narrow so there seemed no option but to go straight to it, laying my bare skin on top of hers. Her legs were spread open, waiting, the black triangle of hair, the slit warm and wet inside, I slid in with no effort at all just as an irresistible surge of feeling rushed through me, shuddering out of me in spasms; it was over hardly before begun.

"Is that it?" It was less a question than a sigh of disappointment from her lips. "After so long – so long. Now so short. It might be funny. If not so – so hungered for."

She was babbling and I wondered if it was to cover her embarrassment just as the sheet covered her nakedness. But I wanted to see her, to touch her. And I did. She was glorious. I had never seen anyone quite so beautiful but I was aware that I had seen few naked women. I was innocent in these matters. Would she notice? Of course she already had; she had been married so sex was no mystery to her.

"I have wanted to do that. I have wanted to do that – for so long." She saw me looking surprised. "Not with you, silly. I've hardly thought about you since you were nine. And then I hardly thought of you at all. And never like this. Never like this. Though you did not reach great heights as a lover."

She ran her hands over me, as if in admiration, in compensation for any harshness, but she spoilt the moment by laughing.

"Just a boy. In many ways just a boy."

The sheet was over us. I was conscious of the sharp angles and crags of my body, and was happy to keep them hidden. Even though I longed for my eyes to linger on her body. Yet I could still feel, and there were hills and valleys, bushes and paths in which my fingers could saunter.

Stung by her comments, I moved my hands across her smooth skin, her breasts, kissing them, then lower, she was a mystery to my explorations, discovering the skin puckered around her belly – still taut but like a dress that was no longer pristine. The marks made her less perfect than I had first imagined, but there is always a beauty in imperfection.

I reached for the cigarette packet and passed it to her. She took one and bent her head towards the lighter in my hand. She coughed. "Are you not a smoker?" I asked.

"No. I never thought I would. Though doctors suggested it to me. When I saw them about my nerves. Highly strung – they said. Have a cigarette in highly strung moments. Is this a highly strung moment?"

"I hope it's not – not for you, anyway."

"Quite the opposite," she said. "Perhaps I'll put this out. Anyway we don't want Millie – or Ma'am – smelling our smoke. They might think we'd been up to mischief."

With that she snatched the cigarette out of my hand, opened the window and threw both cigarettes out. "That's better. Now we can breathe."

She clambered back over me into bed, allowing me the chance to feel the shapeliness of her body. I was lost in wonder, no longer caring that she might think me callow, luxuriating in my closeness to her. I kissed her and she returned the pressure.

"You will learn," she said. "In the right hands."

I forced a smile. "I'm not used to it. Need to practice."

"Sex," she said. "Is that what we call it? In the modern age."

"Love," I said, protesting instinctively.

She smiled. "Really? I don't think so. I don't think you think so."

"It's making love. In my book anyway."

"In your book? That's what you say – or what you read? And perhaps it can be the result of doing this. But I prefer to call it sex. Perhaps Mr Lawrence does too." She lay back, arms behind her head, dark hair like curtains at the side of her face. She seemed to take pleasure in sly words that disconcerted. "It's like a sense. It's like seeing or tasting or hearing. If I didn't have one of those senses – it would make my life impossible. Perhaps not worth living. If I could not see, for example – if I were blind, would I want to live?"

I wasn't really used to talking in this situation either. The wrong words seemed to come out. These were not words of love, as I had insisted; nor were they anything to do with sex. But I was responding to her words and I felt I owed her some seriousness.

"There were plenty of men blinded in the war. They survive, they live. One or two just over there in the Hall. You see them across the field there with their white sticks. You can't say their lives are not worth living."

She looked at me, listening hard; then leant over and touched my face. "Serious boy." She pulled a face. "That's them, Tom. I'm not like them. I need to feel with all my senses."

"And you do."

"But I haven't. For too long. It was as if I could not feel. Sex *is* a sense. It makes me feel whole. Not a fraction." My hands were stroking her, as if trying to heal an invisible wound. "I have lived for too long – without this. Whatever you choose to call it. It's just the joy – of being close to someone."

This was not a conversation I had ever come close to having before. Conversation of this kind embarrassed me, even as I lay naked next to Iris, even as her hand lay upon me. Embarrassed and aroused. She raised her face to mine, and brought her lips down on mine while her hand reached down below my stomach, feeling there until there was a swelling that filled her hand, then bending her mouth lower.

"Steady, Iris. Are you sure?"

Her eyes lifted to mine across the skin that lay between us. She looked quizzical, as if to ask 'Sure of what?'

"Are you sure you don't mind?"

She might have laughed but she could say nothing.

We made love again. I was sure of that term, there was no doubt in my mind at that moment of high emotion. Something had stirred inside, more than just the physical. But she scared me a little. I sensed she was on the edge of something but I didn't know what, fearing that it might bolt out of control. With a glancing thought I hoped it would not be a revelation about a dead baby. The sight of stretch marks on her beautiful body puzzled me.

Afterwards, lying there, looking at her feet peeking up out of the sheet, there were quiet companionable moments of reflection, the two of us relaxing into the strangeness of being in this embrace, confined by the limits of the bed frame. The two lines of her toes were like a family of different heights, walking in procession. It reminded me, a distant memory of processing from the Hall into the village, so many years, a distant childhood ago.

My stomach rumbled. I hadn't eaten, apart from a slice of toast for breakfast. Iris reached up into the glass bowl that held fruit.

"Here, take this apple. You must be hungry." I was. The apple was sour, too early in the year, but we took it in turns to take bites, until we met at the core with Iris's shriek of laughter. The grandfather clock, unforgiving as ever, chimed three times.

"Are we all right?" I asked.

She nodded. "But perhaps you had better go. In case I change my mind."

"About what?"

"You, of course."

I dressed quickly, under Iris's penetrating gaze. With my tie knotted, I sat on the edge of the bed. I smoothed her straight hair sideways, my finger curling it round her ears.

"I'd better go. In case. In case of Ma'am."

She nodded but lay unmoving. I bent to kiss her but now she did not respond. She turned her face towards the wall with its flowered wallpaper.

"Go," she said. "Skedaddle. Quick as you can."

I got up. "But Tom," she said, turning around towards me. "Come back."

"Another day?" I kissed her bare back, now hunched away from me; I had no wish to prolong what was now becoming agonising. "Today. No. Skedaddle," she half-shouted, half-chuckled. "You don't want to get caught." So I left, clattering down the wooden stairs and straight out of the door, pulling on my jacket and hat as I went.

Outside on the garden path I saw two half-smoked cigarettes: the ones Iris had thrown out of the window as incriminating evidence. Here the evidence was waiting for anyone to see. It made me smile. I heard the upstairs window creak open and a moment later the bunch of roses landed at my feet.

"Take them," Iris called down. "They'll only cause questions."

I picked up the half-smoked cigarettes and felt foolish holding the flowers that were more and more bedraggled with every exchange of that strange day. Flowers of romance, flowers of mourning, flowers of no certain purpose, flowers as refuse to be swept away by the brutal brushing of time. Then I knew where I might place them, at least to retrieve something for my own peace of mind.

The woods were re-establishing their familiarity in my mind. The recollection of a schoolboy wandering through this undergrowth, under the murmuring canopies of leaves, seemed sharper with every step. The birds called, seeming to guide me, but I knew the way. There, deep in the woods, underneath the dense foliage of a lime tree, was a darker area of earth and there I laid the flowers. I unwrapped the paper from them, crushing it into a ball that I put in my pocket, and I laid out the six red roses in a line, like sentry guards on the parade ground.

The sharp snap of a twig made me look round. I saw a young man with intense, staring eyes, dressed in the uniform of a hospital patient. He was studying what I was doing, his head shaking from side to side, rejecting my actions. Or so I thought at first. Then I realised his shaking movements were not intended, they were beyond his control.

"Hello," I said. "My name's Tom." I held out my hand to the poor soul whose body was trembling more and more uncontrollably. "Shall we take you back to the hospital?"

His wild eyes looked through me and past me, into a distance that was beyond any ordinary sight. Whatever he saw there was of no comfort. He screamed, a wail that sent a shiver of fear through me. "Billy!" he screamed. "Billy!"

Then he turned jerkily on his heel, set his face towards the Hall, and began to run, like a would-be, once-was athlete who was drawing on all his reserves of memory to rediscover this once-familiar activity of sprinting. A lost skill that was as remote for his body as serenity was for his mind. Billy Tree, once the fastest runner in school. He ran and ran, with high-stepping movements as he had not used to run, ungainly in style with elbows thrusting outwards, his booted feet clattering aside branches on the ground like skittles, until the birdsong that passed for silence closed around the trees again.

5

PATIENT

My encounter with Billy had made me curious to find out more about the hospital and the kind of patients they looked after. Next day I rang from Bert's office, to get the weight of *The Messenger* behind me, and I managed to get an appointment to interview the man in charge. Mentioning the word 'Press' can either open or close doors: in this case the door swung open for me, and Dr Vaughan was waiting for me in the hallway on Friday morning. He took me around the back to his office in the extension that had been built on. I was a little disappointed to find myself not in the building that was in my memory, so I asked him if it would be possible to look around the house after we had spoken.

"This is all irregular. What are you after, Mr Shepherd?"

"A better understanding."

"Of what?"

"The people here. Your patients. People who suffered in the war, and now they've been put out of sight. Treated well, I'm sure, but out of sight, and I want the public to feel a little more for them."

He was right to be suspicious. Newspapers were not inclined to tell stories from any point of view other than 'will this appeal to our readers?' I thought of my editor Bert, cradling a cigarette as if to disguise his intentions.

"If I write something – and I don't know if I will – I would put the hospital in a good light. No mention of patients' names. I wouldn't normally but I will check any quotation from yourself, just to make sure you're happy. It would be good for the hospital."

The doctor pondered, as if considering the symptoms, running through the possible treatment before speaking. "We are always short of funds," he said eventually. "I would not do this without Mrs Hardinge's say-so."

"This will help," I replied, myself puzzled by the reference. "Which Mrs Hardinge?"

"Which? Oh, the older one, of course. She's chairlady of the board. I'm only speaking because she said I should."

So we began the interview. He told me that the Hall had been requisitioned during the war with the co-operation of the Hardinge family: they had wanted to support the war effort. This small hospital was established away from the front line but close enough to the coast to make transportation easier. At that time, while the fighting was at its peak, the patients had the expected physical injuries: lost limbs, wounds that could be treated by surgery. But increasingly, towards the end of the war and afterwards, the hospital was treating damage to minds rather than bodies. They started specialising in psychological problems, a new area of medicine.

"Treating shell shock?" I asked.

"We avoid that term. But that is what the public calls it. And most of our patients have been damaged by the violence of war, the explosions of bombs and shells. A shock enough to anyone's equilibrium and certainly not – as some generals claimed – the condition of cowardice."

"Do they recover?"

"Some do. But most are permanently if invisibly scarred. They suffer a traumatic neurosis. The symptoms can become less severe over time but some suffer relapses, leading to breakdowns."

"Nervous breakdowns? Leading to behaviour that can be violent?"

"Rarely. I have no wish to generalise. We all suffer from stress. Life is stressful, it all depends on the degree of stress suffered and one's individual tolerance."

"Do your patients get out of control?"

"Of course not, they're not wild animals. These are men who have suffered. And not just the men, many of the women too – though we don't treat them here."

"Not many women served on the front line."

"Not what I mean. The front line for the women was at home, and the worry might even have been greater."

"Like the family there," I nodded in the direction of the cottage.

"Young Mrs Hardinge suffered certainly. I know you know her so I mention her. She was severely stressed, as we can all understand, by many things."

"What kind of things can bring on this kind of neurosis?"

"Marriage can, if it is not a happy situation. Unsympathetic families. The war, widowhood. Loss. Multiple losses. Husbands, fathers, brothers, babies. Then the financial situation, the loss of wealth – and property." Dr Vaughan held out his hands to point out the building. "But already I have strayed outside my bounds of confidentiality."

"You treat her then?"

"We referred her to a sanatorium. She is, I gather, much improved. But I am not referring to a specific case, just stating that patients can recover after treatment and sometimes the best treatment is simply to be seen as normal, to talk and to be listened to. To receive a hearing, some sympathy."

He rose to his feet. "I feel I have said both too little and too much. Our patients need more understanding than most so I hope you will write *nothing* that makes it harder for them to be understood. But now I really must get on with my duties. Let me show you out."

We walked back through the house, and I caught tantalising glimpses of rooms that I must have seen before in a totally different guise. But it would be wrong to linger. The doctor had recruited my sympathy and I felt a trace of guilt for having lured him beyond his professional instincts. We parted warily on the front staircase, but I tried to reassure him that my intentions were good.

"Goodness does not always reflect intentions. But thank you if that is so."

As I walked down the steps to the gravel drive, I could feel eyes on me. It could have been the medical staff looking through the French windows; or some of the patients, perhaps even Billy; or, as I looked ahead, perhaps the eyes of the cottage were on me. I felt I had a legitimate reason to visit the cottage, possibly even a duty, given that Mrs Hardinge was aware of my interest.

Millie let me in. She was waiting, with the door open. "Bring him through, Mildred." So I followed the direction of the voice.

Mrs Hardinge was sitting in the armchair with a shawl around her shoulders. "I knew you would want to visit there," she stated. "I understand your trade, your need to pry. I will curse you if you bring bad consequences upon us."

"Why would I do that? I mean well. I would not harm you, or Iris. Where is she, by the way?"

She stared at me, still assessing the amount of trust she could place in me. It would not be much. "We have suffered. The family has suffered. Iris perhaps most of all. She has days when she is best not showing herself to others. She finds consolation only in the wetness of her pillow."

I nodded, as if understanding. I did try to, of course, but it was hard. "What makes her like that?"

"What? Many things. Just think. Her husband, my son, feeling the need to be patriotic. Our country needed officers but it was cruel to send him to war when everything was so new. He and Iris might have been good for each other, given the chance. But there was no chance. Just fate. And no peace in peacetime, not for Iris."

"So she wasn't able to put it aside?"

"It? The war, I suppose you mean the war. It left too many dead, and it left the living aware that they were dying."

"But the living are not yet dead. And there is much to enjoy in life."

"We all suffer from the terminal disease that we know as life. Terminal – that's the word people use nowadays. It is used all the time on my hospital board."

I looked around at a sound behind me. Iris was standing in the doorway, her face as white as her bedsheets.

"I see you have dressed, Iris. That is good. Will you join us?"

"I thought I heard your voice," she said to me. "Were you not even going to see me?"

"How could he, Iris? You were in bed."

"Do you think that would stop him? He's used to putting his foot in the door. Finding his way inside. Getting his way."

I had no idea what to say, so I said nothing. I simply smiled, with a grin on my face that might have seemed like a taunt. To my surprise she smiled too.

"Very well," she said. "I will join you. Millie, can we have tea?"

She sat down at the table as if nursing a hangover but making a determined effort to shake off the blackness of her mood. "I can remember, you know. I can remember those days before the fighting started. It was almost – almost happiness. I wonder if we have photographs of you?"

"I think not," said Mrs Hardinge. "But we can look. Sometimes you find it a comfort to look at photographs."

Millie set down the tea tray on the table, then took a photograph album out of the chest of drawers, setting it before Iris as if laying the table for dinner. Iris opened it to the first page.

"I always liked this one," said Iris. "Mr Hardinge looks so distinguished." She pushed it towards me to look at. George Hardinge gazed at me in black and white, perhaps looking more colourful than he ever had in life. He looked the city banker that he was, with his dark suit and a top hat tucked between his forearm and waist: a man used to dining well but unused to coping with adversity.

"He looks handsome, doesn't he, Ma'am?" asked Iris. For some reason my agreement came first.

"Ah, you think so too, Mr Shepherd? That is something. He always strove to be good to you. I could never understand why, at least not then."

"Oh yes, Thomas," taunted Iris, "you were the apple of his eye. For two weeks anyway."

"Two weeks is more than he gave to his own son," said Mrs Hardinge with some bitterness.

"Yes, Ma'am, there he is. My Teddy, your Edward." Iris held the photograph for us to see; Teddy was upright and smart in his army uniform, peaked cap in his hand, swagger stick under his arm.

"Also handsome," I said. "I remember him well."

"Then you have an advantage over me," said Iris. "I hardly remember him at all."

Mrs Hardinge gave every sign, in the moistness of her eyes, that her son was still in her memories.

"A bullet between the eyes," Iris said. "We were given a report. His commanding officer. The surgeon. Died in an instant. Nothing to be done. Except he had done his duty. And people said that was a comfort. Though I'm not sure to whom."

"To me. And the photograph shows him before there was ever any sign of a bullet heading his way. Look at his smile."

"He looks satisfied with his lot. On his wedding day."

"Thinking of Rosie, I expect."

There was a sharp intake of breath from the woman in the armchair who seemed to shrivel deeper into the fabric. "Women are cruel to women. It is true but hard to understand."

"Perhaps because there were no men around – to be cruel to. They had all disappeared."

"That is what it was like, my dear. The men went off to war and left us to our own amusements. They can hardly complain now that we discovered distractions like voting."

"Perhaps I will – vote soon. Now they think me old enough. Though what for – I'm not really sure."

"So we can choose our government. I'm not sure who was more surprised, the men or the women. Will it make a difference?"

"Perhaps we will not – rush to war so eagerly."

"It will still be the men who do the fighting. The women will still send them off with guns in their hands."

I sat there between them, invisible to them, or so it seemed to me. They shot words as bullets across the trenches in between them, and it became hard to distinguish one from the other. They spoke, not necessarily what they believed, but simply to counter the position taken by the other. Perhaps everyday proximity made them used to each other, so that they hardly noticed the potshots they fired. A silence fell, a lull in the sniping, suddenly broken by the thud of the album, pushed off the table with some force by Iris.

Clearly I would not see Iris again that day. Her footsteps were heavy on the stairs. Mrs Hardinge shook her head and motioned to Millie not to follow. I picked the album off the floor and put the two photos of the Hardinge men on top.

"May I keep these for a while? It might be best to keep them out of Iris's sight anyway."

"If you wish."

"For sentimental reasons."

"We must say goodbye, Mr Shepherd. You bring feeling into our lives. I suspect we can only deal with life without feeling. It is the way the war taught us to be."

"We cannot live without feeling," I ventured.

"We have managed," she said. "You can bury emotion, put it out of sight. You might not enjoy life but you can live it."

I shook my head. I had no inclination to argue against such hardened defences. I wondered if I would see them again; and, walking to the station, with the thought of Iris in my mind, I felt a deep sadness. But I knew that my sadness was shallow compared to that felt by her, and this brought a visible shadow of pity into the face that I saw reflected in the window of the train as it pulled out of Luckhurst station.

•

A week passed. I showed Bert a feature I had written about the hospital and he liked it but insisted that I should check it with those most involved.

"Dr Vaughan?"

"And Mrs Hardinge."

There was no avoiding it, not if I wanted to be paid, and I had not managed to place many stories for a few weeks. I had been too caught up in the 'silly story of the baby bones' as I put it to Bert, wanting to be absolved from following it any further.

"It's not silly," he said. "I still think there's something there. You should follow it through."

I was in two minds. I feared seeing Iris again; she was unpredictable and I could not bear her rejection so it would be better to avoid even the possibility. On the other hand I longed to see her, she remained in my thoughts through every day, in my dreams through every night. Like a game of Dare, I decided to at least put myself in her vicinity and to let fate play its part.

So I engineered another appointment to see Dr Vaughan. *Over the top*, I told myself grimly. But the only likely conflict, as it turned out, was over who would pour the tea. I backed down immediately; he was on his own ground. Then I sat back as he read the article typed on the *Messenger*'s thin paper. "May I?" he asked, holding up a pen. "There are one or two inaccuracies."

He wrote his corrections with his fountain pen and handed the pages back to me. "You have done a decent job," he said. "Will anyone be interested enough to read it?"

"I think so."

"Well, they will not think too badly of us then. They might be surprised by your description of our patient. You seem to understand him."

I had recognised Billy Tree but I wasn't sure if he had recognised me. But knowing him from an earlier time made the change in him all the more unsettling. So I found it easier to write the article with Billy as its central example.

"I met him in the woods. I felt sorry for him even though I felt he might attack me."

"No, I think not. Billy is not violent. We worry only that he might damage himself. He suffered terribly in the war then we put him together again. He had returned home and was recovering when he was in a train crash. The very worst thing for him, he found himself in the mud of a railway cutting, being lifted from the wreckage. So the nightmares returned."

"What were they?"

"Not for your story. But his repeated nightmare is of digging bodies from the mud. It never stops, there is always another one."

We sat in silence, thinking of Billy's trauma. It was all too easy to link such a nightmare to the sights he would have seen in the war. And perhaps afterwards too, in the train crash, in the woods.

"One thing I meant to ask you. Have you heard anything of a baby's body discovered in the woods?"

"That old story."

"You know it then?"

"I know the police investigated and found that there was nothing suspicious, no one to suspect."

"No connection to the hospital then?"

"What? Of course not. Whatever are you thinking?"

"Just asking."

For the second time we had had a cordial meeting that ended on a sour note. He had risen to his feet, ready to show me out.

"You know, Mr Shepherd, there are hidden things in people's lives. They bury secrets deep inside their minds. There are memories below the surface. Bringing them into the light is my job – not digging for the bones of a long-dead child."

I thanked him but smiled to myself that he had in fact told more of the story. If this was a murder, or something innocent, it was a tale from some time earlier.

I braced myself for the second part of that day's mission. I really didn't want to face Mrs Hardinge but my steps made for the cottage. As I drew closer, though, I saw Iris waving at me from the edge of the woods. She was smiling, her wave almost jaunty, so I headed towards her. She took me by the arm, as if we might go for a Sunday afternoon stroll on this working weekday. I felt confused and flustered in her presence and, there was no hiding it from myself, I was pleased to see her again.

"Ma'am is inside. Did you want to see her?" She laughed, knowing my feelings. "I thought not. But I did wonder if you wanted – to see me again. Or was that it, our afternoon fling?"

"Iris, how can you even ask? You know I would want to see you. But you behaved strangely."

"You must not mind me, Tom. I have funny ways – but I cannot change them. You have to take me as I am. And there are compensations." She smiled at me, a conspirator. "We should go away. Take a little trip. Just a couple of days. Let's call it research for my next book. We can be alone and not worry who might walk in."

There were so many questions in my mind but I didn't want to ask them in case the answer raised an obstacle. It was simpler to kiss her in the grey shade of the trees, knowing that we were alone here and that there was the prospect of being with her soon in even greater seclusion. There was something, though, about these woods that worried my mind with the thought of unwanted discovery.

"I must go but we will do what you say."

'Think of it as part of my recuperation. You can help me, doctor."

"Don't. You'll put me out of humour, this talk of doctors. I have had my fill of them for today."

"Then this is my prescription for you. Next week – Monday, meet me at the station."

"I could bring the car."

"Still best to meet at the station. You cannot turn up at the cottage – not with the car. I can carry my case – to the station – that far."

We arranged a time to meet in the mid-morning, a time that had no need to take account of train timetables. I looked hard at her, scrutinising her to see if there was any hesitation. "You are sure? You have no doubts?"

"Silly boy – what do you mean? Moral doubts? Am I worried – about the state of my soul?"

"Who knows? Sometimes you try to do good but it can turn out bad."

"So let's not worry. That will be good for both of us."

6

BRAZEN

That Monday I took the train from London to Tunbridge Wells to visit the *Messenger* first, then to collect a car from the garage. Bert was in his office, already wreathed in smoke.

"On the job, Tom?"

"Still on the case," I replied, tapping my little suitcase on the side. "Things are happening."

"A little bit of sleuthing, eh. I knew you would find something. Where are you off to?"

"Luckhurst first. Then I think I'm going to head for the coast."

"Really? Well, I look forward to reading the results. And you know we scrutinise your expenses."

"No need to worry, Bert. It won't show. But I'll need a car."

I offered him a cigarette, knowing the way to Bert's confidence; inevitably he took it, hardly noticing that he did so. But he started to write the chitty for the garage. He handed it to me: "I trust yer. Don't know why."

It was a good day for a drive. The sun was out in a clear blue sky and the roads had few cars on them. I had the roof of the car down and the wind streamed over the greased top of my hair. I pictured Iris, imagined her sitting in the passenger seat with her hair blowing around her face. I soon arrived at Luckhurst station, at least fifteen minutes before the appointed time.

Iris was already there, waiting. "You're keen," I said.

"Aren't you?" I would have kissed her, by way of answer,

but this was too public a place. I glanced around, looking down the village high street. To my embarrassment, I saw Millie watching us from the butcher's shop across the street. I whispered the news to Iris.

"So what? She can go home and talk about sausages."

"I'd rather she didn't. I don't want people talking."

Iris called out to Millie, as if to show she really did not care. "Millie dear. Tom is giving me a lift. I realised there's no train to where I want to go."

With that she waved and put her small suitcase in the back seat of the car. "Oh look – side by side – those bags are friends already."

We drove off; I could not wait to be out of sight of the village and its residents. Over the rattle of the engine, Iris shouted: "All this subterfuge is silly. There's nothing wrong with what we're doing."

I wasn't so sure. I did wonder if we could trust Millie's discretion. "Will she say anything to Mrs Hardinge, do you think?"

"Good Lord, no. Not if she wants anything like a quiet life."

We drove along, not talking much; you had to shout to be heard, but Iris was in good spirits with her long scarf fluttering behind her in the wind. I kept looking sideways at her, basking in the fact that she was next to me, looking beautiful. Iris's clothes were so different from when I had first known her. The long white dresses of that Edwardian age had been replaced by clothes simpler and more colourful. A silver satin dress that touched her knees, with the silk patterned scarf and a blue cap that clung to her head over her ears. I could only gaze in admiration, in adoration, and feel myself a little shabby by comparison.

But I would do, I told myself. I was twenty-four but knew from my job that I could look older. It's just a matter of clothes. Wear a suit, white shirt and tie, top it off with a hat, and people would think you a proper grown-up. This mattered to me. Iris, though, was in her early thirties, but dressed so well, looked so elegant, that she passed for any age but never old. I hoped people would call us a well-matched couple. That also mattered to me.

After an hour we stopped in Lewes. It was a town with bookshops and Iris liked that, stopping to look in the windows. It was also a town with pubs and one of them, unusually, could provide a ham or cheese sandwich as well as beer. I ordered myself a pint of the local ale.

"Not for me," said Iris. "It makes me feel nauseous. I once tried it – and didn't like it. A lemonade will do."

I wondered whether I should ask her now about this mystery of the buried baby. Bert's voice was in my ear, asking. But it might just put the kibosh on my plans with Iris and I didn't want anything to get in the way. *Perhaps later.*

"You're not saying much," said Iris.

"Just enjoying being with you. But tell me then, what did you say to Ma'am about where you were going?"

"I always go away for a few days every month. I walk – then write about the walk. At the end of a year, you have a book."

"Really? I didn't know. So you're a proper writer."

"Except when I'm being improper."

I laughed and squeezed her hand. She went on: "I am writing a novel. I'm always writing novels. Who knows, one day I might even finish one. If I find Mrs Woolf has not beaten me to it."

"I wonder sometimes if I might do that too. Write a book, I mean."

"Why not? I think we can – we can all write. Whether there are enough readers to go around – that is the question. What will you write?"

"That's the problem. I don't know. I might need to get all this journalism out of my system. It's not proper writing, it's just tittle-tattle I've been doing. I might have had enough of that. But I have to earn a living."

"Most of my writing is about walking. I like going on walks by myself then writing about where I've been. One of my books was in the window of that shop. *Woodland Walks in Kent and Sussex*. I was going to point it out. Then I thought you might laugh."

"Why would I do that?"

"Because *I* would. It's not real writing. I'd like to see my name on a book that takes a bit of effort. I can toss these off like a – like a man."

"It's more than I've ever done. You should be proud."

"*Country Walks in Kent*. That was my first. Then the one in the shop window. Followed by *Coastal Walks in Sussex*. You see how I am spreading my influence. I could walk the country – and then the world. Each year I meet my publisher in Maidstone – they pay a pittance – but I understand. There's no money in it. We agree the next subject – I do the walks, one a month. Then write up my notes into an essay. They add maps. Some people like the books."

"That's terrific. You really should be proud."

"Huh, I'm not. I'm sure you have more readers – for your stories in the papers."

"My stories are used to wrap up the fish and chips. There's no real value in them."

"Why stick to it then? All these false stories in the papers. The ridiculous Zinoviev letter."

"Not me."

"Turning German bodies into soap."

"Not me either. They say John Buchan."

"*He* can't write either."

I knew I would never win any argument about writing with Iris. I knew I'ld probably never win any argument on any subject with her. We'd finished our sandwiches so we could move on and I was keen to do so.

Less than an hour later we were in Brighton. I parked the car round the back of the seafront hotel I'd identified. Walking into the Albion House, I tried to look nonchalant, despite the dryness in my mouth. I had never done anything like this before and I was sure it showed. The curtain ring on my finger, bought in a moment of timid bravado, slid around uncomfortably.

Iris, on the other hand, seemed in her element, as if she did this regularly. Perhaps she did. There was an ease to her conversation with the receptionist that I could never manage.

"Could someone carry my suitcase up? It's not too heavy."

"Of course, madam. Let me check you in first. Your name, sir?"

"Smith," I said. Next to me Iris started giggling. The receptionist saw me fiddling with my ring.

"There's a jeweller down the road, sir, that might be able to help. If it doesn't quite fit."

"Oh yes, let's," said Iris. "We can look at their curtain material."

I ignored her. Iris had these ways, I was beginning to recognise them; it amused her to embarrass people around her.

"Did you have to?" I asked, when the receptionist went in the office to get a form.

"It's harmless," she said. "He knows the game. I should think everyone here is playing it."

The receptionist and Iris had both called out my 'ring'. So now signing false names didn't bother me, I could be as brazen as the ring. "It's all right," I said. "I can manage the bags myself."

So I unlocked room No. 3 on the first floor. There was not much to inspect in the room: a double bed, a table and chair, a wardrobe. Clean sheets. A sink. I needed nothing more but worried that Iris might have higher expectations.

"It will do. For what we have in mind," she said. My mouth got drier still. "I wonder if Teddy used to come to this sort of place. With that girl Rosie, for example?"

She surprised me with that. I had not really thought much about either Teddy or Rosie for a while. It was a reminder that I was supposed to be following a story that might have their involvement in some way I did not yet understand. I was certain that the baby's bones were linked to the Hardinges, but at this moment, with Iris before me, removing her hat and shaking her hair, I had no wish to be distracted. And, it became clear, she was in no mood for unpacking her bag.

When we made love it made Iris laugh and cry. I wasn't sure that I could cope with either reaction. The thought flashed through my mind, as if seen through leaves, *we are making the spider*, and a deep orgasmic sigh burst from so deep inside me *Oh Ro...* that I struggled to stifle the rolling consonant, swallowing it inside the O of my mouth.

"You're getting better," Iris said, lying back with her arm as a pillow. "Which is just as well."

I looked at her sideways, not knowing what to think. This seemed a little like a threat. In the sack, was I being threatened with the sack? It made me lean towards her and kiss with what even I realised was too much desperation.

"I want you. I love you," I said, unfamiliar words to come to life outside my head. "I love all of you."

"Really? I don't know if I can – give my all to you. There is early death in your face – and I cannot risk that again."

She stared at me, so hard I blushed and turned away. "You say some strange things at times."

"At times? Times like these? Do these times come here often?"

I was at the window, looking at the pier opposite. "Shall we go on the pier?"

"Why not?" she said with scarcely a trace of enthusiasm. "We have two days after all. We must see the sights of Brighton."

Her sudden laughter made me laugh. The uneasiness passed between us as a kiss, then I watched her put her clothes back on.

"I haven't brought enough clothes," she said, unlocking her case and hanging a couple of dresses on the hangers in the wardrobe. "I didn't think I'd need them. Will I? Just two days. Then my walking clothes. Not quite the style for Brighton."

I was tempted to undress her again but we needed to get out, if only to mark time between lovemaking. There was the frantic air of the pier, the swinging around on fairground horses, the farthings in slot machines, the forced shrieks to merge in with the crowd, toffee apples to make fingers sticky enough to lick. We walked on the clinking pebbles of the beach, sat in abandoned deckchairs before the attendant came around, chucked stones into the placid sea. Held hands. Iris was pushing me in unaccustomed directions. I gazed at her but kept half an eye on everyone else, not wanting to be observed, apprehensive for no good reason that I might bump into someone I knew. But what would it matter? I was with a beautiful woman, someone to be proud of.

She was running over the stones, on the upper level of the beach where the tide didn't reach. I called out after her but she didn't stop. All I could do was run in her trail but she was fast and I was dressed in my suit and best shoes. It took a while to catch up.

"Let's go in these gardens," she said, as if nothing out of the ordinary had happened. When we sat down on the bench, with the municipal flower beds all around us, we must have been a picture of respectability until Iris leant over and kissed me. In my head I could hear my mother tutting.

"You don't like me doing that."

"I do. But not here. Not in public."

There were tears in Iris's eyes so I offered my handkerchief. I made sure it was clean first. She took it but didn't really use it. I have to admit that in the softening rays of the sun, the glistening tears on her cheeks made Iris seem even more beautiful and I suspected she knew this. I put my arm around her, chastely, comfortingly, and after a while we walked on until we found a place to eat. Fish and chips. I hardly knew what we were eating and I couldn't wait to get back to our hotel room as the sun was sinking to the horizon. All I really remember was the smirk on the receptionist's face as he gave me the key.

Afterwards, lying in bed under a white sheet, we fell into a conversation that was closer to natural. Perhaps we were getting used to each other; or perhaps I was getting used to her. My hands ranged over her skin, feeling again the creasing of the stretch marks.

"So how come?" I asked, my fingers gliding over the surface of the issue. "Do you want to tell?"

She shook her head and I feared for worse.

"We know each other now. Quite well," I stroked her

stomach, my finger in her belly button. "Something happened. You should tell me."

"Are you writing a story?" she asked. There was a hint of anger. "Will this make the front pages?"

"Oh Iris, of course not. Nothing goes any further."

Eventually she spoke quietly. "I had Teddy's baby. But it didn't live. Not for long anyway."

I didn't know what to say so I said nothing, comforting her with closeness as best I could. We lay in the gathering darkness, aware of streetlights along the promenade; I could see her face, glistening again, and I wiped her cheeks with my thumbs, kissed her hand as I raised it to my lips. "I'm glad you told me," I said. "It makes no difference to us."

"No?"

"No. Of course not. It was a long time ago."

"It doesn't seem so. And Ma'am remembers. Constantly."

"That can't be easy. What does she say?"

"We hardly talk. When we do it's only to taunt each other with mortality." She paused, as if weighing up whether to say her next words. "'Webster was much possessed by death, he saw the skull beneath the skin.' That's what I read the other day – in Mr Eliot's book of poetry. You could substitute Ma'am for Webster – though it would ruin the metre."

I had no wish to ask what she meant. I realised that her reading of books was much greater than mine; I could do no more than admire before giving in to puzzlement and, I hoped, as she leant into me, her head on my chest, to sleep. The night-time passed and I slept little. Iris was restless too but eventually she settled. I watched shadows on the ceiling from the one or two lights outside that remained on that night, and I listened to the sounds of people reeling back to homes and rooms after a night of drinking until the dawn came with the clinking of milk bottles in the road below.

At home, in mum's flat, daylight would be grey and ushered in by a low burbling from the deep throats of pigeons. Here, lying in bed, trying not to wake Iris, I listened to the harsh cries of seagulls, like public bar drunks arguing with each other or with the world in general. It revived the memory of waking as a boy at Hardinge Hall, with the competing songs of the woodland birds, another age, another place. The shadowy figure of Teddy disappearing into the trees, a man on a mission; a boy at the window watching the man's furtive movements to spy, to learn, to understand the ways of the world, to keep secrets.

Trying not to wake her, yet willing her to wake, I was taken back to that boy, so hesitant yet so eager. As I felt my body come alive, I turned over, changing position to stir Iris gently.

"I wondered when you were going to wake up," whispered Iris, still drowsy from a dream, sliding towards me like a caterpillar. For me, lying beside her, marvelling at her, she seemed to open up a treasure chest of comparisons, that I sifted through, picking up one or two to test them, holding up to the light to see a gleam, yet finding that none matched the wondrous reality of her presence. The eyes inches from my eyes, the nose, the cheeks, the mouth. Melting. The undulations of this new-found world. We had a leisurely awakening before the smell of bacon made me feel hungry.

"What shall we do today?" I asked as I buttered some toast to go with my cup of tea. I was making conversation to break the awkward silence of the breakfast room, a place where eyes seldom met across the tables, perhaps out of guilt or simply because there was nothing left to say. My attempt at being as bold as Iris was undermined by her giggle. "More of the same?" she wondered.

"You know we have to leave the room during the day," I couldn't stop myself laughing too. "So where shall we go?"

"Well, Ma'am thinks I've gone on one of my walks, so we might take a stroll along the seafront – arm in arm like a married couple. As we are, of course," she spoke to the room, and there was a stirring of sugar into teacups. I was getting used to this; I was on Iris's side of any argument that she might start. But there was none, only a clearing of throats, a rustling of newspapers.

"I wonder if they've got *your* newspaper, Tom?"

It was already warm outside. Iris had put on a cotton dress with red and yellow diagonal stripes. I would not lose sight of her. Whereas I had not come prepared; all I could do was leave off my tie and hold my jacket over my shoulder.

"You could leave it, you know."

"It's got things in it I need. My wallet."

A wind blew in from the sea, bringing some relief as we made our way down the promenade towards Hove, and the morning passed pleasantly enough, stopping for an ice cream, then for a beer at opening time, grazing food from stalls. "What we did on our holidays," we smiled at each other with a growing easiness.

"How far are we going?"

"We can turn back here – that's far enough."

"It's very hot."

"Then we must have too many clothes on."

"Shameless hussy."

"I know. Let's go."

"We can't, it's too early. The hotel will still be cleaning rooms."

We walked into town, looking at shops, but there was nothing to interest either of us. Victorian furniture and knick-knacks in antique shops aroused the most interest but only because we could remember some of the items from our childhoods. "I always hated this stuff," said Iris. "And now I'm living among it anyway."

The cinema lights seemed to wink at us. The film was not one I recognised, nor one that I would remember. It was a romance in flickering black and white images, with posed expressions unlike those on any faces I knew. But I was looking at Iris in the silver light and that was enough. I was pleased to see her smiling. We all have such an impetus towards the pursuit of happiness. No one seeks misery in their life. But we like to see happiness in the lives of others too. This struck me as I sat with Iris in the cinema watching this film that, frankly, was silly. Still you couldn't help wishing it would all turn out for the best.

Coming out blinking, the streets looked washed out, like blankets soaked too long and left to dry in the May sunshine. We slipped into our next refuge, a café for a cup of tea. Iris was not easy. Her mood had changed and she started being self-deprecating about herself, saying she was highly strung, whatever that meant.

"It doesn't mean much at all," I answered. It was true, though I would not say, that I never quite knew what she would do or say next. But I yearned for her to be happy, I wanted to make her happy. If I managed that, I would be happy too. So it was upsetting to feel Iris sobbing as she sat across the table from me. I could feel the quivers in her body.

"Are you all right?"

"It will pass. These things come and go. Like the weather."

I reached across the table to hold her hand. The man on

the next table raised his newspaper pointedly, as if to shield himself. Lindbergh was on the front page. It seemed that flying airplanes was our new obsession, as if we wanted to rise above any troubles down below on the ground.

"I would like to fly one day," said Iris. "Soon – before everyone's doing it."

"I have the feeling," I said, "that the world's on the brink of something. Flying's just one sign. Who knows what? But the war seems like it settled nothing; it just allowed the worst people to regroup."

"Of what? On the brink of what?"

"Something more likely bad than good. The Fascists, the Russians."

"Really? Should we run away? To a South Sea island?" She was recovering; her sense of humour returning.

"It's not so much the place as the time. It feels like a bad time ahead. It's only being with you that keeps it away."

"We could put off the bad times. Make them go away by fucking."

The word in her mouth and her accent came as a shock. I had been brought up to avoid what my mother called bad language.

"See? You shouldn't. You are bad."

"I try."

So we went back to our clean room at the hotel and we made love, for that was how I thought of it. I didn't want to think of the act in crude terms that coarsened it. Yet she excited me with her unexpected acts and words; I had never known anyone like this; and she was not like the girl in a pure white dress, demure in my memory. I made love with an abandon I had never experienced before, my urgent hands squeezing her skin where I could feel its plumpness, taste its sweetness as ripe fruit, gorging myself on her even as I felt emotions surging from deep inside. While Iris was impassive on the surface, her eyes closed, in the grip of a profound hunger that could not be expressed in words. But perhaps we were doing as she said, perhaps we were putting off the inevitable, keeping away bad times, at least till another day and that might be a better day.

I mouthed Iris's bad word to myself, with a secret smile as I turned away, not wishing to share it because it might be misunderstood, slipping out of the sheets. When I returned to the bed a couple of minutes later Iris was already deep in sleep. It was only seven o'clock.

She slept as if she had not slept for weeks, and perhaps she had not. Perhaps she had waited and wanted too much for this to be happening. Whereas I was fitful, not wishing to toss and turn and startle her from a slumber that was therapeutic. For there was a stirring inside me of an emotion that I felt growing, and I wondered if when grown it might be described as love. I lay there in the thickening darkness, my open eyes full of wonder for the shapeliness of her body, for the slender slope of her neck, for the cupped curves of her breast. Once when she turned in her sleep I held my breath, fearful that she might wake and with her waking break my own wakeful dream.

People pretend, because we're English, that we have no sex lives. In that case I wonder at all the children – where do they come from? Such mysteries might be instilled by Christianity but I had no faith in its ministry or ministers. My days and nights with Iris were my sex education, my sex life, my spiritual life. She opened up everything to me, beginning with my eyes – she was so beautiful – then absorbing every sense.

The window looked out onto the seafront. Restless I moved between the bedside and the window sill. Early next morning, grey clouds and the absence of wind turned the sea into mercury. A silver light shone on every surface, reflected off the sea. As the dawn slipped through the lace curtains puffing inwards on the gentlest breeze, I continued to stare at the beauty of her sleeping face. Her breath almost whistled, a barely audible sound that I listened to with the hope that it might always be like this. Because I had a sudden fear that this might be the climax, there might never again be anything to match these heights, and perhaps the decline might begin with her surfacing from sleep. The morning light made the faint down on her cheeks glow. I knew at that moment that love might last longer than happiness.

Iris stirred and her eyes opened to find me looking at her. I could do nothing but smile; there were no words. She rested her head on my chest and our hands stroked each other with greater tenderness than they had ever known.

"What is the time?" The words came to my ears from a distant place, shaking me from the dream that had finally come with sleep.

"It's late." I picked up my watch without looking at it. "We'd better get up."

"Why?"

"Because the chambermaid will want to do her job."

"She could work around us."

Our laughter might stop the chambermaid coming in before we were ready. And Iris was right, it was too early, not nearly time to get up. "It's only half five," I said, taking another look at my watch.

Later I found the breakfast room a bit of an ordeal again. Everyone was so careful with the cutlery, fearful to make a sound – except Iris, she did not mind, she spoke at normal volume as if to challenge the other couples. "Let us go then, you and I – I long to read that again. I will do so as soon as I return to my own bedside table."

She was speaking loudly in the knowledge that our words were being listened to pruriently. "Soon," said Iris, "like other journalists – you will need to make your excuses and leave." We giggled, Iris with an air of defiance, me from embarrassment. "Our laughter tinkles among the teacups...Mr Eliot again, I'm afraid. But he has words for many situations and he would find a humour in this."

An hour later, having breakfasted and paid, we got into the car. Looking at the map I found the route to drop Iris off at the place where she would stay, to change into her hiking clothes and set out on the next walk for her book, before I headed back to Tunbridge Wells in the car, half happy, half sad, strangely relieved to be alone again.

7

PAPERS

Back in London, the city had an air of rushing by, all haste and bustle, after the sea breeze of Brighton where time had blown past more gently. Walking down the Strand, there were couples heading towards an evening's entertainment at the theatres and restaurants. Some people were still slipping out of offices even though it was well past six. A feeling of relief passed through me again, that I didn't have to work in an office, I had no need to be confined by its set times. And neither did my mum.

I found her in her usual spot in Kingsway. Nellie Shepherd, my mum, worked on the streets: she sold evening newspapers at the bus-stop near Holborn. It was a job she'd been doing for a year or two now. As she hadn't noticed me yet, I stood on the corner of Great Queen Street observing her. I could hear her reedy voice calling out the names of the papers; every so often someone stopped to buy. *She has a nice smile*, I thought. Part of me was making compensations for her beginning to look a little elderly.

With the sun going down, London started to feel different. The shadow of nightlife was approaching and I was never sure if I liked that. With my mum there in front of me I found it almost embarrassing to see people behaving as if they would not be seen. People carried on in public, young men and women growing up after the cataclysm, and feeling no need for pre-war propriety. Or so I imagined the time before the war. Nowadays people in London kissed in doorways as if they were private rooms. I felt a blush as I thought of Iris in our private room, knowing that it was no subject for my mother.

At my back was the Freemason's Hall, a place of some mystery to me that, one day, I wanted to write a story about. Surely there must be some strange goings-on there among the circles of rolled-up trouser legs. No one spoke about these things, no one admitted to being a Mason, at least not to me, yet we all suspected that they ran the country. *One day*, I told myself. The thought made me look at my mum with even greater pity and affection.

Let me explain. My mum is an old lady of 47. I know that's not much of an age but she looks much older. I can remember her being younger and prettier, but her youth and looks were scrubbed out of her by a daily cleaning job. She had carried the mops and brushes and dusters from room to room in the bank everyday, using them with less and less effectiveness until she had to give the job up. The truth was, her knees were giving up, rubbed raw by kneeling on floors to clean. It turned into something worse than rawness, with arthritis in her knees and hips. You could hear her bones creaking at times as she moved around the flat. One day, we both knew, she would be crippled by the pain. She had good days and bad days, and like all of us she probably dreamed she would find a fortune down the back of the armchair.

But now she needed to work. She had struggled since the war, never having enough money, and I supported her with the wages I earned. Still she needed to work; it made her feel better about herself, it gave her some respect. The cleaning job was too much, though, twenty-five years bleached away, leaving her washed-out and aching. So I found her this job selling newspapers through a contact of mine in the union. The best part of it was that she could sit on a stool to hand out the papers and take in the coppers, so her knees didn't get quite such a battering.

When I could, I dropped past at the end of her shift, so we could walk home together, just five minutes away. Tonight the crowds had thinned out, it was seven o'clock and the streets were already quiet. Mum was handing over the unsold papers to her mate Len.

"Are you ready, then?" I asked.

"That you, Tommy? There's a good boy." She stuffed a paper in her bag to read later or just to use around the house. As a journalist I should have been proud of the many uses of a paper: firestarter, chip carrier, wet floor drier, shoe inner, general padding. "Anything by you in here today?" she asked. I shook my head.

I had found it hard adjusting to being back at home after my days with Iris. Everything in the flat seemed worn-out, from the oil cloth on the table to the chipped enamel in the sink. We sat drinking tea before mum set to getting some dinner ready. It would be bread and dripping and not much else; I didn't mind, I felt the scarcity more for her sake.

"What happened, mum? We never used to struggle quite as much as this."

"Sorry, Tommy. I didn't know if you was gonna be in. I'd 'a got something if I'd known."

This was true but I wanted to pursue the question a bit more. I had my reporter's mind on because I'd been thinking about the story that day – the story that perhaps never was.

"It's true, though. Before I was really earning, you seemed to get by better. How come? How come it's worse now? I'm giving you what I can."

She looked at me. Exhaustion spoke. "Your father used to provide a bit."

"My father? What's he got to do with it all of a sudden? He's long gone, never was around."

"That's right. He couldn't help dyin', comes t'us all. But there was, like, a bit of a pension till that ran out."

"That's news to me."

"Thought you was into the news."

"Very funny. Peculiar and ha-ha. Why'd you never tell me?"

"Why'd you never ask?"

It was true. I hadn't asked. There were things I just didn't like to ask about in case I found out something I'd rather not know. I had never asked much about my dad, who he was, as I'd never met him and never needed to know. Mum had never encouraged me to ask either. There was probably part of me that felt ashamed, without knowing why. If not now, when would I ever ask?

"You never talk about it. How I came to be here. Should you tell me more?"

"Not much to tell. Much as it pains me to say, I hardly knew your father. So I can't tell you much about him."

This was not easy for her, or for me. But perhaps there was something to explain: "How did it happen?"

"It happened," she said. "You happened. And that was good. I never regretted having you, never for one moment."

"And how did he die, this unknown man? Were you going to marry him?"

"Who knows? Perhaps one day. But probably not. That wouldn't happen."

"Not the marrying kind?"

"He died."

"And you? Why did you never get married after?"

"Obvious, ain't it? None of the men could marry me after that. They didn't want to marry me and a young boy in the family too. And no chance now. The war just took away most of the men, most of the husbands, the fathers. But at least now I'm not so unusual. It's normal to be a widow and it's true mine died in the war – if I say so."

"If you say so?"

"People go along with what you tell 'em. They're not really that bothered by what really happened. It's good to know no more than you need to know."

She got up to take away the empty cups and plates, putting them in the scullery "I'll wash them up in the morning," she said. "You've worn me out."

Mum went off to bed; exhausted, it seemed. I was different, unable to face sleep for a long while yet. There were so many things to think about. Actually there were two: Mum and Iris. They both worried me. I tried thinking about a third thing to distract myself, though the baby's bones in a woodland grave seemed strangely close to the other subjects. Now that I knew Iris had lost a child, the bones of the baby in the wood seemed to stand for any lost child as well as that very particular child. The thought would not let me go that the baby's bones were those of Iris's child. But if so, why? Why had it been buried; literally buried out of sight?

And if so, this would almost certainly not be a story I could write for the *Messenger*. I didn't want to lose the future by being too honest towards the past.

8

SECRET

We hadn't arranged anything after Brighton. Iris had gone off on her walk and I'd driven away. I had hardly dared tempt fate by suggesting anything as a next meeting. Stupidly I hesitated to seem keen, fearing that callow eagerness would frighten her off or expose me to contempt. So I said nothing about the future, and neither did she. It was better to seem blasé than committed.

The truth was – and I could hear her pitying laugh as I thought this – I was in love with Iris. In love but not daring to declare that to her in case she felt I was a foolish boy. She was older than me; that age difference had always been part of our relationship from our first meeting when I was just a nine-year-old boy. The eight years' gap was less important now than it had been then, but I still felt she had to take the lead. I would seem ridiculous if *I* did. Which of course made me seem even more of a boy than our relationship suggested. My mind was in confusion and I didn't know if it was love or embarrassment. I feared that reality would slap me in the face one day soon.

Days passed. No word came from Iris. I hoped for a letter and no letter came. *She doesn't have my address. But she can contact me at the Messenger.* With each passing day I grew more anxious and I started thinking about making another trip to Luckhurst. I persuaded myself that I really needed to tie up the loose ends of the story, even though I feared those loose ends might make a noose.

A week with no word from Iris convinced me I should catch

the train next day to Kent. I would just have to call on her and hope to catch her at a right moment. Of course I could have written but I imagined that would raise Mrs Hardinge's suspicion even more than a visit. And thinking about the permanence of written words, I did not know what I could say. I knew I was being irrational but I could not help it; she was making me slightly mad.

When her letter arrived early next morning I trembled. So she did have my address; I must have given it to her after all. But was she writing, taking that formal approach, because it was easier to break the relationship at a distance? Words on paper might be easier to express; they might also cut me more. *Did she want to cut me?* I hesitated to open the envelope, dreading to find out.

"Good news?" asked my mum, seeing the smile on my face.

I needed to savour the news without being scrutinised, so I simply nodded to her and rushed out the door with a 'won't be long' thrown over my shoulder. I found a seat on the wall in Short's Gardens and read Iris's letter:

Dear Tom
Well, I fear you have not used me well. It seems you have abandoned me, like the wronged woman in a cheap film. You had your way and discarded me.

However I give you the benefit of the doubt. I see your puppyish eyes in my mind and suspect that it is not cruelty but naivety that causes this silence. I will make it easier for you because I have become surprisingly fond of you.

I will come to London on Saturday. A weekend in London is required and I will make the arrangements. I long to have a jolly time so you must put yourself into that frame of mind.

You need make no arrangements – leave that to me, I know it embarrasses you. We will stay somewhere nice so be prepared.

Let me know by return and meet me at noon on Saturday at Charing Cross.

With love

Iris.

I read it and read it again. I pored over it. I gazed at her signature and the two words above it with some wonder. This was an affair that was becoming a love affair, and I could hardly believe my fortune. I read the letter again and knew that I must reply quickly, to leave no doubt. *But what to say?* My emotions were too full for words to contain them. I bought a postcard from the tobacconist and wrote: *Thank you – T*. Enough for her to understand; little enough for her to excuse or explain in whatever way she wished to Mrs Hardinge. Thinking of Iris, I licked the stamp.

By now I was used to time passing slowly. And time passed very slowly from Tuesday to Wednesday to Thursday, overcast days dragging the hours behind them like a heavy weight. Work was a relief, having a couple of stories to write that took very little concentration – fortunately as I had little concentration to give. At least Friday brought a sense of impending arrival as well as dazzling sunshine even in our gloomy room. The oilcloth on the table gleamed; the window panes showed off the smears of old rags. Walking from scullery to living room and back, busying myself by making tea, I had to tell mum I was going away for the weekend and I tried to say as little as possible: when it came to my mum, I was not a good liar.

"So it's a girl, is it?" she said, blowing on her tea and making my face flush red with sudden heat. "About time." She knew better than to say more and embarrass me further.

Next morning, dressed up in my suit, I shuffled out with my small, battered suitcase, too early by far. There were still two hours to wait for Iris's train to arrive. I walked down the Strand towards Charing Cross, passing the Savoy on my left. It made me uncomfortable, so much glamour and silver and glitter on display just five minutes from my mum's poky, dark flat. To kill some time I went into the National Gallery and pretended to look at paintings by old masters. I was surprised at the number of naked women in the pictures; most of them were not proportioned at all like Iris. She was much more beautiful, I could imagine her as I sat on a bench looking at what claimed to be a goddess. Not to my eyes. People wandered past in pairs, exchanging the occasional word, perhaps about art; more likely, I thought, about the time. *What time is it? How much longer?*

I made my way to the railway station on the other side of Trafalgar Square. The clock said five to twelve, so I was early but not too early. I searched the Arrivals board to see which platform her train would pull into.

"No point looking up there," she said. "I'm here."

I could say nothing. I hated public displays of emotion but I simply enfolded her in my arms before kissing her.

"You said people should never do that," she smiled, straightening her red cloche hat after our embrace.

"I'm pleased to see you," I said, perhaps the most honest thing I had ever said to her.

"Good. Good, we can have fun then. So let's get started. We can walk from here, no need for a taxi."

I had given no thought to where we might go after meeting. I simply accepted; Iris was in charge, and we walked out of the station into the Strand, with me carrying both suitcases; her willing bearer.

"I hope you don't mind," she said. "I've booked us into the Savoy. I thought you should learn how to do these things properly."

"The Savoy? That's a bit out of my range."

"I know. But I'll take care of it. I had a bit of a windfall."

She walked along in front; I followed in her slipstream, feeling a little too sweaty on this hot day.

"Never mind," she called back, as cool as Iris could be, "it will be comfortable inside."

It was impossible to say more before we arrived at the Savoy. I had enough wits about me to hand over the task of bag-carrying to the bellboy at the door, though I was flummoxed about tipping him. *Now? Later? How much?* But Iris was already announcing us at the desk. I gave the boy sixpence and he looked unsure rather than grateful, not quite able to disguise his disdain for the poor quality of one of the cases.

"We'll have lunch first," she was saying. "While you ready the room. We are early."

The receptionist here was as obsequious as the one in Brighton had been obstreperous. He snapped his fingers and we were shown through to a sparkling room for lunch. As we walked between tables we could observe our progress in mirrors on the walls, with chandeliers gleaming above us.

"Isn't it lovely?" Iris spoke over her shoulder to me. Her excitement was obvious and that pleased me, reassured me that I might not be as out of my depth as I had imagined. Suddenly I felt that the age difference had melted away, mainly because Iris now seemed so much younger, like the young girl I had first met in Hardinge Hall, with the same hint of nervous desperation.

"We'll have a good time," she offered as a promise. "But you have to be good. No sulking."

"What do you mean?"

"You must do whatever I say – and first we will have some wine."

I lifted my hands as if surrendering. *Whatever you say.* But I needed to ask a sensible question before becoming embarrassed by not asking.

"How are we going to pay for this? It's beyond my means."

"I told you – not to worry – I had a windfall. My dividend came through from the Trust – so there, my treat. But you promised not to sulk."

"I'm not sulking, I'm just not comfortable about you paying for everything."

"I know, poor boy – look, take this." She slipped an envelope towards me across the white linen tablecloth. "It's hateful – I know – but it will be easier – for everyone – if you pay for things."

I looked inside the envelope and saw the pound notes, crisp and new; more than I would earn in a week. I left them in the envelope, too embarrassed to count.

"You can be my kept man for the day – you will grow into the role. And then you won't like me when I go back to my usual – when I'm poor as a church mouse once again."

I closed my eyes and shook my head. This was difficult. But I opened my eyes to see Iris's eyes staring at me, startled, glistening, the welling of tears threatening the mascara on her lashes. I dared not risk a scene.

"I might prefer you as a church mouse," I said. "Let's not talk about it any more."

She was instantly brighter, relieved enough to smile. "Oh good," she said, and flashed her smile at the flunky she addressed as '*sommelier*'. He would, she insisted, suggest the wine for them to drink. I was pleased not to have to choose. I let Iris choose the food for me too, dutifully eating whatever was placed in front of me, but too distracted by Iris's presence and by our conversation to really notice.

In all innocence I asked that most dim-witted of questions: "Have you been here before?"

"Of course, silly. Teddy brought me here when we were engaged – I think he did it to show off."

"So are you showing off to me?"

"Of course not – you don't need that. And clearly you are not impressed as I was."

"Wealth doesn't impress me. I think that's why I like you so much. You don't really have any. This is just pretending."

She pursed her lips, shrugged her shoulders and gave a smile that looked conspiratorial as the waiter spooned a bread roll onto her plate. I weighed up what I might dare ask while the waiter provided this interlude.

"Why did you marry Teddy? It seemed to me that you didn't really like each other."

"No, we didn't – no fear. But we had to – families, you know. There was so much friction at home. Mother drove me up the wall – desperate to marry me off. They were in financial trouble – and the only thing I could do for them was to get married. Preferably to someone wealthy."

"So you married him for his money."

"For my family's sake because they needed the money."

I shook my head but she laughed. "Of course that little ploy didn't work – we didn't realise that the Hardinges wanted Teddy to marry me for my family's wealth. Hopeless – they should just have got auditors in and declared both families bankrupt. Bankrupt of feelings more than money – completely without understanding. The families deserved each other."

She paused; I wondered if she was upset but she seemed more relaxed than she had been. She found the story amusing, she was enjoying the tale she was telling, and I knew it must be true.

"You see George's bank was failing – and daddy's business was failing too. But the facades were deceiving. Stout British gentlemen and upright British businesses – solid bank built on coal, what could be stronger? And a department store in a well-to-do country town, what could be cosier? But neither was doing well – and then the war. George gave so much to the government for the war effort – all the reserves were run down. It was a relief to hand the hall over to become a hospital – no need to pretend we could maintain it. Ma'am was distraught, of course, but satisfied to keep the house in Chelsea. She liked the house but hated London – never went out."

I had imagined only a tiny part of this. I knew there had been financial difficulties, hence the need to live in the cottage. But I hadn't anticipated the extent of the fall.

"After George's death it was inevitable that the businesses would collapse. They dragged each other down – instead of lifting each other up. Clung to each other as we fell off the cliff – too much for my ma and pa. They slunk away – escaped to New Zealand after the war. I haven't seen them since."

It hadn't occurred to me before; Iris's absent parents. My understanding of her and her situation was shaped so strongly by the Hardinges, I had almost imagined her as an orphan who had been adopted.

"So you see, all that money was just a mirage. What was left from the fire sales of the businesses was put into a Trust – stocks and shares that I can't touch for another couple of years. Just an annual dividend – that's hardly anything – enough for a stay at the Savoy."

I found myself with a spoon in hand eating strawberries.

The food had passed unnoticed; along the way, as a side dish to Iris's story, we had eaten main courses.

"But did Teddy know? When he married you, did he know what was going on?"

"Oh, of course – he didn't really want to marry me. Poor dear, he didn't much like me – and I didn't much like him."

"Why not?"

"He wasn't up to much – to be frank, he was a little stupid. But there were not great brains on either side of the family. Not enough brains to run a business or two. We put them together – we? I was just a girl. We united our incompetence as families. What's mine was his, what's his was mine – disastrous. Teddy was never cut out for much. Had he survived longer in the war he might have risen to the incompetence of a general. But only because those in front had already been killed."

"But before it came to war," I asked. "What had he done? Had he tried to help? I thought he had been groomed to take over his father's business."

"Good God, no. He was hopeless at that – he could hardly add up. So they tried him at *my* father's business. But at Fakenham's my father had to check his every move. Until he was entrusted with nothing – not even selling ladies underwear – though he knew more about that subject than most."

Iris spluttered with laughter into her coffee. She had been seeming lighter with every revelation as if casting off the weight of her history. She might just float away with a dreamy look on her face.

"So what would have happened if he had survived the war? If Mr Hardinge hadn't killed himself?"

"Teddy only ever wanted to be a country gentleman. He might have managed it then – but it would not do for now. The world has changed."

"Has it?"

"We don't allow that kind of idleness any more."

"I see it all the time."

"It leads to self-absorption – a sense of entitlement. We expect more these days."

"Not that I've seen."

"You, Tom, are an example. You have no truck with privilege – I think you like me despite my background. Certainly not because of it. The newspapers – you know them – would call you a new man. You show the world we have created – and that makes you a good man, a man for these times."

I opened the envelope and set grubby pound notes on the plate to pay the bill. We all start with good intentions but life muddies what we mean by good. We end up doing what serves our own interest, which might not be so good.

And so, not long afterwards, in our room upstairs that represented some luxury to which I did not feel entitled, I found myself inside Iris and I wondered, even in that moment, what she would think of me afterwards? Would she thank me for doing good? It didn't feel that way to me as I slid sideways off her, still distracted, not really present in this manicured room.

"A cold coming we had of it," Iris breathed out, lying back onto the pillow.

"I'm sorry."

"You were supposed to be fun – you promised. Now look at you."

I felt shrivelled before her gaze, and I pulled the sheet over us to hide the evidence of my body. We lay there, exhausted but without any physical reason for exhaustion. It became difficult to say anything so we lapsed into uneasy silence that dozed off into slumber. The sleep must have refreshed us both. Restored to wakefulness I could see nothing but good in her beautiful vulnerability, in the surprising jaggedness of her emotions contained inside the smoothness of her body.

"Iris, I love you," I said, and brushed away her riposte of 'silly'. We made love again and lay there in an easier companionship of white linen, enjoying the ability to stretch out to the full width of the bed.

"Come on," she said eventually, as evening shadows fell through the frame of the window. "We should go out – you promised me a good time."

"Did I?" I raised a quizzical eye brow. "I thought you promised me."

"For each other – all for one and one for all – together. And nonsense like that. I want to hear music."

I could tell she meant it so I would do my best to meet her wishes. Yet I felt inadequate to provide what she wished. My entertainment horizon was set at an evening in a pub, perhaps a picturehouse, but I knew little beyond that.

Iris took down a dress from the wardrobe rail. It was shimmering with sequins; definitely not a picturehouse dress. I watched her holding it up against her body in the mirror before she went to the bathroom. The water gushed steamily into the bath. It was something else to share. Afterwards the white towels were fluffy and soft as cotton wool. I sat on the bed wrapped in a towel and watched Iris dry herself, then put on silk underwear followed by the silvery dress. As she dressed she started to sing to herself, as if unaware of my presence, so I watched, a spectator at the show.

Iris was singing '*Ain't we got fun?*' She was singing and dancing like a flapper. It made me smile and she was animated by her performance. It seemed she knew every word and she swayed and kicked her heels sideways as if in the limelight. But then her movements slowed and she just sang, but the singer slowed down like a record at the wrong speed. *In the morning in the evening, ain't we got fun.*

She had a voice that made you listen. *In the meantime, in between time, ain't we got fun.* So I listened with a heart growing heavier with the slow burden of her singing, as she dragged the words out, a monotone with emotion absent yet heart-breaking through its absence. When she got to *the rich get rich and the poor get...children* she juddered to a halt and there were tears in her eyes.

"What is it? You can tell me."

"I can't have children." She sobbed and the sobs convulsed her body. I held her tight and said the only words it seemed possible to say: "It doesn't matter."

"It matters to me. Even if not to you."

The tears passed. I decided it would be wrong to ask more. Too many questions might tip her over the edge; and I felt for her, I had no wish to cause her any distress. It made me almost manically jolly, in a way that seemed unnatural to me, but I felt the need, at that moment, to pretend.

Inside I was heavy-hearted. In thinking about the future, in considering the possibility of marrying Iris, I had thought about children. Our children. The bright eyes of a future we would share together by creating together. This possibility seemed to have been snatched away, like a wallet lifted by a pickpocket.

"You gave me this money," I said. "We should go out and spend it."

She managed a wan smile. "Ain't we got fun," she breathed the words, a whisper that made me cling even more tightly to her.

"We have a chance," I said. "We give each other life."

"I'm not sure – there's a shadow over you. I've spent years shirking away from death."

"Iris, you're life itself. No more nonsense. You told me we were going to have fun. So let's."

There were cabs waiting outside the Savoy; the flunky with the top hat whistled and a taxi pulled forward, its door magically opened for us. "Where to?" the driver asked, just as I asked Iris the same question.

"Jazz club," she spoke, as if there could only be one.

"Which? Kit Kat? They're strict about members."

We both looked blank. "I'll take you to Benny's," he said. "You'll like it."

We drove through the streets under a darkening evening sky, but the lights from the West End buildings were getting brighter every minute. I had hardly ever seen London like this, from the back of a taxi. We passed what my mum always called Lousy Island at the top of Shaftesbury Avenue, a place where the dossers were gathering for the night. We hardly gave them a thought; Iris was preoccupied with her own concerns, I was bound up with worry about Iris. Fragile as she was, would she cope with the evening? She took a compact out of her bag to dust her cheeks with powder, applied some more lipstick, dabbed on rouge as the cab swayed around corners.

Inside the club in Mayfair, she was fully revived. There was music and there were drinks. When it came to drinking, I was not particular; I just went with the flow. If I was in a Trumans pub I drank Trumans beer. But this was something different for me. I was puzzled by so much choice so I just had the same as Iris. I wasn't really sure what a cocktail was and the name Brooklyn Bridger didn't enlighten me. It tasted nice enough.

"What's in it?" I asked.

"A secret. Once you've had a couple you forget to wonder."

A trio was playing, and the pianist was good. I recognised *'Blue Skies'* even though the tune was buried deep in the improvised notes. He raised his hat at the applause, then went into *'After you've gone'*, hunched over the keyboard.

"This is more like it," Iris whispered in my ear, singing *'and left me crying'*, gently brushing her lips against my cheek, *'there's no denying'*. Her black-ringed eyes stared at me, pityingly it seemed, while her mouth mimed *'You'll feel blue, you'll feel sad, you'll miss the dearest pal you've ever had'*.

The barman was right. After the second and the third cocktail, I stopped wondering what the drink might be. Iris wanted to dance; I couldn't deny her, though I hardly knew what to do with my hands and legs, and my hips were unmoving. I enjoyed watching Iris dance; she had an ease and a grace that amazed me.

We danced a lot. Iris danced a lot and I enjoyed watching her. In between dances we drank; the drinks were seductively easy. I was just sober enough to notice that midnight had passed; Iris was reluctant to leave, I was now eager to go. Having persuaded her up the steep steps from the basement, the chillier air of the August evening hit us, and Iris swayed, leaning against me for support.

"You're drunk," I told her, laughing because I knew I was drunk too.

"Let's just walk – walk it off – a bit," her bare footsteps slurring down the road, holding her shoes by their straps in her hand. We crossed Park Lane and went into Hyde Park. It looked dark and forbidding to me but Iris insisted: "It's lovely – no one will see us."

Iris clung to my arm, hardly able to walk, so we stopped at the first bench we saw in the light that filtered through from the streets outside. The bench was welcome to me at least; having sat down I wasn't sure if I would manage to get up again. But Iris was soon on her feet, plunging into the bushes behind the bench. I heard her retching but I left her to it, sitting on the bench, while behind me in the darkness she brought up a mess of cocktails. It wasn't me being callous, just that I was in too bad a way myself to help.

After a while, she sat down next to me on the bench, resting her head on my shoulder. She shivered a little but burrowed deeper into my jacket for warmth. The summer night was still, not a breeze to stir the bushes around us. I looked up and could see stars even though there was a glow from the city lights above the rooftops beyond the trees. We both dropped off to sleep, Iris stretching out along the bench, resting her head on my thighs. We must have slept, even if it was just a stupor, because the next thing I knew there was a grey light across the sky and the birds were singing all around us.

I felt terrible. My temples were throbbing; there was a dull pain behind my eyes. At least I knew what was wrong, and every stirring of muscles in my body reminded me of the alcohol I had drunk.

"I had a lovely dream," said Iris. "I was still dancing."

She looked none the worse for wear, as if sleeping out in the park was a regular way for her to pass the night. My head thumped, resenting her instant wakefulness. She stretched and stood up, raising both arms, fingers flexing towards the sky.

We flagged down a cab in Park Lane, the last of the night brigade or the first of the morning.

"Looks like a good night," the cabbie said, managing to be both grumpy and cheery.

"It was fun," Iris insisted and slumped against me in an almost instant slumber for the ten minutes of the journey, before I shook her awake so that we could make a reasonably dignified return to our room in the Savoy.

9

SHADOW

Nellie had been doing the washing. It was one of my reasons for living at home; I got my washing done for me. Mum had been arms-deep in hot water in the laundry room at the end of the balcony, a place equipped with big sinks and a mangle and washing lines just around the corner. When she came in, her arms were an angry-looking pink; pink shading to red over her hands and up to her elbows.

I was at the kitchen table typing on the machine. It was still a novelty for me to have my own typewriter at home. Mum's friend Gert came in with her.

"Why ain't yer got a girlfriend yet, Tommy? About time y' settled down an', got married."

"Leave him alone, Gert. In his own good time. I've a feeling he's sorted – just won't tell me."

"Come on, Tommy, tell us."

"No, nothing to say on that front." Head down at the typewriter, trying to look industrious but not sure if Gert's generation understood the possibility of 'working at home'.

Gert's voice was sibilant, at times difficult to understand, and her mouth even in silence moved as if it were chewing. I knew she was not well-fitted with dentures. I found it easier to ignore the words that came out of her mouth than the false teeth that only just stayed in. Gert's daughter Edna came in, a woman just a couple of years older than me, someone I looked upon as more like a sister than a neighbour.

"You wasalways a flyboy, Tom." said Gert.

Edna went into the scullery to make a pot of tea; she was used to helping herself in our house. It was as easy for me to talk to her as it was to say nothing. Silences between us never embarrassed me as they did with other girls, and Edna was always a good listener, to silence and the stories that might emerge from it.

But it wasn't a good situation to be sitting at my typewriter working on the story of the baby bones. By now I thought I had enough of the truth to write something for some of the papers, not just the *Messenger*, but it was not coming easily. I was being held back by my scruples. I found it easy enough to shut out chatter between my mum and her friends but the needs of the *Daily Mail* were more intrusive. I found it hard to contemplate ever writing a story that would be published while keeping my conscience clear. I kept trying to find an angle. The only one that started to make sense was to make it about families: the secret heartaches of ordinary families. But I wasn't sure if this family qualified as 'ordinary'.

I stopped typing, not knowing what to write. Instead I flicked through the paper for inspiration, unsurprisingly finding none. I was often amazed by the subjects discussed in respectable papers. Some of these stories would have been frowned on in my cub reporter days. Now you could read the lines, not just between them, to find the sordid if that took your fancy. That morning I had bought the *Daily Mail* to see if one of my stories was in it, and I felt grubby as I turned the pages.

"Do you read the papers, Edna?" I asked as she stirred the tea in the pot.

"No, not much, no. Never much in 'em."

"What do you want to see in them?"

She thought, still stirring. "Stuff about people not like me."

"Really? Why's that?"

"I get the ordinary stuff closer to home, just listenin' to them two. Sometimes they do stories about people damaged in the war, blokes like Billy. That can be interestin'. So what you workin' on there? What's the pictures?"

I had placed a couple of photographs face down on the oil cloth that covered the kitchen table. I turned them over so Edna could see. The first one was George Hardinge, the second his son Teddy. They were the pictures I had borrowed from the cottage, thinking they might come in useful, if only to remind me what they had looked like now that memories were being covered over by the dust of time.

"Who's that? I feel like I know 'im. Is it you, Tom?" Edna joked. "Looks just like you. You in your suit."

"What's that?" my mum asked, so I had to hold up the picture. She looked closer, then looked away. "Why yer got that? Gotta sort out the washing," she called behind her as she went out the door.

I had to explain who he was to Edna. "This man ran a bank. When I started working he was my boss. I used to be the messenger boy at the bank he owned. And mum used to do the cleaning there."

Edna showed some interest so I explained he had a big house in Kent, and that I had gone there as a boy for a holiday.

"Really? Why's that?"

All I could do was shrug. It was so far in the past now and he was no longer alive; his death a bit of a mystery, a taboo subject. The house he owned had been turned into a hospital. I said where it was and that I had visited it.

"That's where Billy is – it's the hospital where he's looked after for shell shock."

So it was Billy Tree I had seen the other week in the woods. I would wait for the right moment to tell her; I didn't want to let on that he had been in a bad way, though Edna must know. He had been away for years, never seeming any nearer to recovery.

"Billy does all right down there," Edna said. "Considering. Poor bloke. Better off in the country, too noisy for 'im in London. Gets set off by the backfirin' of a car, thinks he's been shot at."

"Don't think 'e'll evergetbetter," said Gert from the side of the room. I had forgotten that she was there, and now the words rolled around her mouth, struggling to get out past her slippery dentures.

"Stop it, mum," said Edna. "It's not fair."

'Not sayin' nothin' y' never'erd before.' Gert was what the social recorders of the day would immediately label working class. I felt a need to reclaim my label in that world as my job and my friendships kept sliding me off elsewhere.

"When are you going down to see Billy next, Edna?"

"Due to go at the weekend, Tom."

I hardly paused before offering to go down with her. I made the vague promise that I would see what I could do to help. "Anyway, it'll be good to see Billy. Haven't seen him for years."

Mum came back, with yesterday's dried wash in her arms. Her hands looked even pinker against the white sheets that now looked as white as her face.

"All right, Nell?" Gert asked.

"All right, gel," mum replied but not in a way to convince.

I had no idea what I might be able to do for Billy, except find out more about his situation. If it came to it, I could ask questions of the doctors. Edna might feel reluctant to do that; I wouldn't be.

Edna seemed grateful; her mother Gert a bit resentful. "Itdontbotherme" she chewed on the words inside her mouth, swallowing them so we hardly heard. Aware of her mother's truculence, Edna made a point of saying: "Glad you're comin', Tom. They'll listen to you. You, your different. Your bettern the likes'o'me."

I brushed away Edna's comment, not wanting to claim any special virtue. After all, I knew that a large part of my reason for going was to have a new excuse to visit the house and perhaps bump into Iris. I liked the idea of taking her by surprise, just turning up on the doorstep. After visiting Billy, of course, after doing my duty.

"You know what, I might have seen Billy the other week. Think he might have run away from me. Hope I don't have that effect again."

"Don't suppose you will. You'll be with me so he'll trust yer. He's up and down. One minute he's all right, then he's not, up and down, like...never mind, he'll get over it again, always does."

"Not easy for you, though. You stick by him."

"Billy got me straight. I was in badways, bad compny. Not that he was in a good way after the war. But bless'im, he married me. No one else would. So I stuck by'im now he's goin' thruthings."

It was settled then. I abandoned my attempt to write; that day it would not come, I felt I still didn't have the complete picture. The headline would still be "Mystery grave in the woods" without a proper explanation of the mystery – so the story had not moved forward enough. No good for the *Messenger*, nor any other paper come to that.

Instead I wrote a letter to Iris that said nothing much more than 'I love you'. I was just feeling the need to put it down on paper – where Iris might not be able to brush it away as easily as the spoken word. I no longer felt such a need for secrecy, figuring that Mrs Hardinge would have to be told sometime soon so it would be better to start sowing the seeds of suspicion.

I decided to go out to post the letter then walk on to the law courts to see what was happening, perhaps to sniff out a story I could file. All human life was there. And human life was full of stories waiting for readers, but first they needed a writer. By the end of the day I had written a couple so I would get paid – enough for a day out in the countryside at the weekend, enough for a drink or two in the Cheshire Cheese. I knew I had to keep showing my face there; otherwise I might fade from sight like the Cheshire Cat, not even leaving a smile behind.

At the end of the evening, I had a short, unsteady walk home from Fleet Street. Walking away from the newspapers, passing by the courts of law, I knew, feared even, that I had travelled out of the origins where Edna and my mother remained.

I loved the white precious-metal light of the gas lamps. It gave a silver sheen to roads and pavements wet with rain, but failed to lighten the shadows just out of its reach, in the nooks and doorways of Aldwych.

I walked along the pavement purposefully, following the shadow that stretched out before me under the light of the street lamp. Turning the corner from Drury Lane into mum's courtyard I now saw the shadow alongside me on the wall. *Me and my shadow*, I hummed the song to myself, not wanting to show that I felt threatened by these streets where I had grown up.

10

PICTURES

"How are you today, Billy boy?" asked Edna. Billy hardly registered that he had seen her. He looked suspiciously at me.

"Remember we saw each other in the woods, Billy? I was just having a walk. Then you took a run."

I hated myself for the patronising tone that seemed to come out all too naturally. *He's ill not simple.* Talking to Edna on the train coming down had made me nervous about saying the right things to Billy – actually, nervous about saying the wrong things. We had sat in the carriage side by side, keeping voices low because there were other people in the carriage. Edna had explained: "Me and Billy got married after the war. It was good of him, I needed him more'n he needed me. He was all right then, good as gold, working. But sometimes he woke in the night. His nightmares were terrible, they scared me, but he'd be all right in the morning. I supposed there was all these old soldiers having nightmares all over the place. Billy weren't alone."

Now Billy sat upright on the chair in front of me, clearly not at ease. His hands trembled, at times his whole body seemed to shake. Edna reached across and held his quivering hand but he snatched it away and rubbed his ear as if he wanted to dislodge the contents inside his head.

We were sitting in the family room where visitors met patients, and I had a sudden memory of glasses being raised at a long-ago occasion in my childhood. *Clink, chink, glass on glass.* Looking through the French windows onto the lawn too – this stirred a memory.

When we'd arrived Edna had announced herself: "Mrs Tree to see her husband. With a friend." I'd told her not to mention my name just in case it aroused suspicions that I was back as a journalist to write another story. Anyway it was the weekend staff: no one recognised me, and I recognised no one from previous visits.

"Remember we saw each other in the woods, Billy? I was just having a walk. Then you took a run." The words were out, several minutes ago, hanging in the air between us unanswered. I wished I could call them back, like whistling for a dog; but like a dog the words had gone off on their own.

"He likes the woods" smiled Edna, picking up on what I'd said. "Don't you, Billy? 'S funny how trees matter to him, like his name made it so. Billy Tree. He'd been sent away so I'd come down to see him. When I got here he was nowhere t' be seen. 'Out in the woods,' they said, pointing. So I took a walk with one of the doctors to find him. I walked along keeping an eye on the ground so's I didn't fall but the doctor knew better, and he looked up, spotted Billy perched on a branch."

"*Billy, get down out of that tree,*' shouted the doc in an angry voice, but chuckling as he did. So that was how I knew he was a Tree."

I was slow to realise that this was Edna's joke so my laugh seemed a bit mad when it came too late. Billy said nothing, there was no flicker of a smile on his face, only those round white eyes staring at a far-off point in the distance.

"Noise," said Billy, rubbing his ears again. "Why's it s-s-so noisy?"

"It's all the people, Bill. Visitors."

"Why ain't they s-salutin'?"

"No need, Billy. Not in here, it's not the army."

Billy' stare seemed to go through us to the other side of the room and probably through the thick walls to the staircase beyond. I imagined Iris, a young girl in a white dress, standing at the top of the stairs, returning this intrusive stare.

I have to go down there, I can take you. Or you can take me. That's what I'd said back in London. But now I didn't know if Edna welcomed me being here or not: I hadn't asked, just assumed it would be doing good. *Would it?* My mind was wandering, already not really wanting to be locked into this conversation that was no conversation. Billy started scrubbing at his face with his hands as if he was trying to rub something out.

"Why don't you show them pictures, Tom? Billy likes looking at pictures."

I'd shown Edna the photographs while sitting in the railway carriage. She'd seen them before and I'd brought them mainly with the thought that I would return them to the cottage – they were my excuse for calling.

"He likes looking at pictures, don't you, Billy?" Edna repeated, so there was no chance of ignoring the request. I took the photographs out of the envelope that was in my jacket pocket.

I looked at the picture of George Hardinge before putting it down on the table in front of Billy. "This," I said, "is the man that used to own this house. See. He owned a bank but not any more."

Billy shook his head, or perhaps it was just that his head shook. He looked at the photo and seemed to take an interest in it, even picking it up to hold it closer. I became nervous in case he decided to damage the photo but the act of holding it and looking at it seemed to calm him.

"Just there," he said, pointing at the wall on his left. I looked at the photo again, taking it back.

"You're right. Well done, Billy. See, Edna, the picture was taken here, that wall in the background."

Edna and I clucked at each other, a pair of happy hens, eager to praise Billy for his powers of observation. So I looked down at the second photo, the one of Teddy in his army uniform, with his wavy hair and his cap held in his hand. His eyes had gazed straight into the camera at a photographer's studio and now at me from the print, displaying a sense of pride in the patriotic role he played.

"This man, Billy," I started. "Well, I knew him too. He was the son of the first man and this is a picture of him in his army uniform. He was a nice man too."

I held the picture out in front of me, ready to answer any questions Billy might have. But not ready for Billy's instant, violent reaction. He stared and started shaking, hands on the table edge causing it to shudder, uttering a scream from deep inside his throat, his arms jerking out of control. I was scared he might be having a fit and reached out to touch his arm with a steadying hand, but his shaking carried on.

"It's the captain. No face."

I could make out the screamed words and sensed the eyes of everyone in the room on Billy and me. Edna had jumped up in concern and put her arms around his shoulders. Nurses came, male assistants in white tunics, clamping Billy's arms to his side, then walking him, half-carrying him out of the room. Edna followed but I decided to stay where I was, guilty that I had instigated such a commotion. The room calmed down, people looking sidelong at me. *It could have been us.*

I sat there for fifteen minutes in a state of shock. Then Edna returned and beckoned me. She led me up the staircase, these familiar steps, and into a bedroom whose window looked over the lawn. Billy was lying flat on his back on the bed, covered with a white sheet, sedated into a kind of sleep. None of the furniture had any memories for me but this room, and particularly the view through the windows, made me a child again.

"I'm sorry, Edna," I said. "I didn't mean that to happen."

"Course you didn't. The doctor's gonna talk to us." She nodded at the tall, gaunt figure coming through the door. He pulled up a chair so that we were sitting facing each other at the side of the bed.

"What you saw is not unusual with this condition," he explained, a voice drained of emotion, simply reporting. "You must not worry too much. Episodes like this might lead to improvement eventually. Think of it as lancing a boil in the mind. There are memories, poisonous ones, festering inside. It's for the best to let them out. What caused him to react like that? Did you say something?"

Edna looked at me, so I told him about the photo. "Show me," the doctor asked.

"Who is this?" I explained who Teddy was, the son of the previous owner of this building. A man who had been a captain when he was shot in the trenches, killed in action.

"I suspect this is the man whose death Billy saw. He talks about it when he can but it leaves him stressed. We try to let him talk about it in a quiet situation, if he can. But most of the time he can't."

"Teddy – the captain – was killed by a sniper's bullet, or so I'm told."

"Billy was with him when it happened. Right in front of him. That would traumatise anyone. But he needs to face it."

"That can't be easy. Thousands of men would have seen similar things."

"They are the wounded with no visible wounds. But they must face their problem. There is no cure possible by hiding from it. They have to face it in a manly way, to speak it, remember it."

"Is this shell shock?"

"We don't call it that. Though of course it is. Whatever caused this might not have been a shell though. But there is stress caused by combat. This man imagines his face wounded, hit by a bullet, so he hides it constantly behind his fingers. He saw something so horrific in battle that he cannot scrub it from his mind back in this life. All these men have variations of that story. But there are many stories, even if it is just one thing that triggers the reaction."

We all turned towards Billy as he had started to speak loudly and fluently enough despite stutters, his eyes wide-open but giving no real sense of consciousness. "I w-w-w once sailed the landship and p-p-people ran away from me, r-ran away from my metal armour shell, as the land plunged down then lifted up to the smoky-grey sky with the booming guns exploding around us." Having spoken these words, as if reciting a message in a stage play, Billy closed his eyes again and his head that had been raised now sank back onto the pillow.

"He was one of the first to be assigned to the tanks but it didn't turn out well for him. They had to transfer him to lighter duties. Apparently he was good at running, so they made him a messenger. He ran messages through the trenches. That was what he was doing when the captain was shot."

"No wonder he's a wreck," I said, placing my hand on Edna's who sat impassively next to me. "Will he ever get better?"

"He has all these symptoms. He tells me so and I have no reason to disbelieve him. You can see it in his eyes, his hands are constantly in a tremble. He rubs his ears to get the sound out, and covers his face whether because he imagines a wound or because he cannot bear to look at the world. If he can talk, he becomes quieter, calmer. But a sudden noise might break him out of that in a trice."

"So has he lost his wits?"

"In a way. But has he lost his reason? Perhaps he has too much of it? The weight of his reason makes him extremely sensitive to the suffering inflicted on himself and the others. He's at his best when he can look after one of the other men. Then he becomes a good man and you wish you could preserve that moment."

It seemed possible, it even seemed something to hope for, as we watched Billy's now easy breathing in the bed. Edna wanted to stay there in case he woke up; she pulled her chair closer and held his hand. But I felt restless, in need of some fresh air, a change of scene.

"Edna, we've a few hours before the train. I'm going to have a walk around. I'll be back in time to take us to the train."

I stood at the window, as I had done years before, watching the woods, wondering who or what they might be hiding. Then I walked down the staircase that no longer seemed as grand as it had done in my memory.

11

HIDE

I took a walk in the east woods that skirted the hall. I also felt obliged to go to the cottage as that had been my real reason for coming but I was in no state to see Iris. She would demand too much of me, wanting to know what I had been doing. And I was in no mood to explain. I wanted others to explain to me. How can life be so difficult for some? There was a deep unfairness that concerned me; it always had but at that moment the feeling was especially strong.

I hoped a short walk in the woods would calm me down. It did, at least a little, enough to raise my courage to walk up the path to the cottage and to knock on the door. I was relieved to receive no answer. I now had a couple of hours to kill, so I headed off into the west woods, expecting to find solitude among the dense trees. In my memory I thought of them as the Wild Wood, a place with a shiver of danger, a feeling forever conjured up by the effect of the children's book on my imagination.

The wood was much denser and darker than the one on the other side but, seen through adult eyes, it was full of interest rather than foreboding. Again I wished I had a better knowledge of the natural world so that I could identify the birds, animals, plants and trees. But I did have some of that childish feeling of acting out an adventure, reconnecting with the feelings of that nine-year-old through whose eyes I had first seen this wood. I listened to the underfoot sounds of twigs snapping and the swishing of leaves that had fallen early; then I decided to avoid all sound, to creep silently through the woods like an Indian tracker.

So I came upon the hide. I remembered it immediately from its shape and its position in a small clearing among the trees. It soon became clear, though, as I drew nearer, that the hide was much changed from the place I had once sat in as a quiet refuge for reading. It wore an abandoned air. Its dereliction became more visible as I saw that the timber on the external wall facing me was charred. Black timber around the edges, where the wall had joined the roof, told a story. I imagined the flames that had destroyed most of the hide. Had the fire just spared this one wall or was there more intact? I walked alongside the burnt timbers and turned the corner.

I was surprised by the sight. By then I expected to find nothing left of the interior. But I had not expected to find Mrs Hardinge sitting there on a seat improvised from a log.

"Are you all right?"

"Of course. I come here for peace and quiet. It seems I am foiled in that purpose."

Clearly she would like to be left alone but I now found it awkward to withdraw. I had to attempt a conversation.

"How did this happen?" I asked, opening my hands towards the absence of the former building.

"It was a long time ago. Set on fire. Upsetting as it is, I regard fire as God's chosen weapon of revenge."

"A spiteful God then."

"He can be. Why shouldn't he be? We know his expectations of us."

"But this was deliberate. Not an act of God."

"Oh yes, I think so. Someone had a grudge. Edward was most upset. I did not even know that he knew this place. People always surprise me – even those I think I know best. I know he used it for no good purpose but – but it sometimes consoles me to remember him. So that he is not forgotten."

"I know he is not," I said. "I had an example today."

She looked at me, weighing me up. She pointed to the second log that had been set there as a seat among the trees. I thought she would ask me about the example but her thoughts sent her in another direction.

"What's the good of remembering all the bad things that have happened? Can you tell me?" Her stare made me uncomfortable; she was trying to see inside me to a deeper place than I was willing to go. "On the whole I'm happier not remembering. This is a melancholy place but sometimes that suits my mood. We should remember the fallen but not the parts of their lives that made them fall. Leave the dead in peace."

"Are you happy?"

"That is an impossible question. And, I think, not one for you to ask. I'm not even sure I ask myself that question. I survive. There is no point expecting more."

"Don't we all expect more? "

"We might hope that experience teaches us not to expect."

"You could do something to make life better. If not for you, then for someone else, don't you think?"

"Not really. That sounds like a recipe for disappointment to me."

"No, you have to do something. Otherwise this is all a terrible waste."

"Oh, it is. A terrible waste."

We made an odd couple, a strange sight if anyone had come upon us. But the woods were deep. Surrounded by trees, it seemed we were in a secluded place where no one else would venture and where unexpected words might be said. There was no sound apart from the occasional chirp from a bird and the buzzing of insects. And the swishing of her fan as she kept flies and heat at bay.

I was conscious, in Mrs Hardinge's presence, that I was pushed again towards the status of a boy. But this made me more determined to resist. Once, many years ago, she might have driven me towards my natural tongue, to 'talk common' as she would see it, to drop my aitches and ditch my word endings. Now I tried to speak as she would think 'proper', a sign of a standard achieved, a bar jumped. Because I knew she would value me less, hear me less, if my accent lost her respect.

"I called at the cottage," I explained. "But there was no answer. So I came here."

"I do not imagine for an instant that you were there looking for me. Iris is away on one of her book-writing walks."

"Of course. She has to do that. She has her own life."

"I know about your relationship with Iris. Of course I do. How could I not? The cottage is too small for secrets. But knowledge does not mean approval." She wafted her fan, reinforcing her thoughts. "People know what is right or wrong but they choose badly. *You* know. They could be good but they decide not to be. They don't have the backbone."

"Sounds like hypocrisy to me. You apply standards to others not to yourself."

"You misunderstand me then. I apply those standards even more to myself. It makes me hard to live with, I know that. Hard for me to live with myself too. It has left me grasping for happiness at times but it falls through my fingers."

"Perhaps it is time for greater candour. Can we be honest with each other? I always feel you have so many secrets that you're unwilling to admit."

"Secrets seldom last. But I always think it best if they emerge when they no longer matter."

There were many questions I had in my head, and now it seemed I might be able to ask them.

"I always think of Rosie when I think of this place. What happened to Rosie? Did she have a baby?"

I felt as if I had kicked down the door of the hide, but she hardly blinked before replying.

"Not that I knew. And I think I would know. She was only a barmaid, of no importance. In the end Edward could keep no secrets from me. No, that girl went away, I assume to get married to someone of her own standing. Perhaps she did one last malicious act before she went. This place. I always suspected her, I think she had that vindictiveness in her. Edward thought so too. For him it might have been the final straw, the one that drove him off to war. This place, he loved it but I didn't know until it burned down. For that I cannot forgive her."

"Your son meant so much to you?"

"Of course. Exasperating as he was. He was precious to me."

"More than Muriel?"

"Oh, by far. Muriel is always an afterthought. Edward's death squeezed the last few sour drops of love from my heart."

"And your husband?"

"We were a partnership. We set it up to manage our life. It was an arrangement like a business. Marriage has to be like that. I always thought so. It was what we wanted for Edward and Iris."

We sat in silence. I pondered how much I could ask, and I felt she was weighing up how much she might answer. I suspected the scales might be tipping in favour of honesty, confirmed when she broke the silence.

"Men want women to be rational. They can't abide the emotion otherwise. That is no bad thing. What is called insanity in women is regarded as leadership in men. And emotion is considered unmanly. It comes with a skirt and a hankie to dab at the tears. That is the way the world is."

"There is something, isn't there? Something you haven't spoken about. So much seems to be hidden. Isn't it better to talk about it?"

"You have been talking to the doctors at the hospital, I see. The talking cure, they say, even while the men are screaming out of control."

I nodded, agreeing, encouraging. Then the words came out in a torrent. She told me about Iris's difficult pregnancy, her son away at the war, herself needing to be more caring and maternal than she would have wanted, the birth of a deformed baby, the black mental depression that came after birth.

I looked at her. I recognised the silk dress, still in that style from before the war, perhaps worn specially for this occasion of remembering. I recognised her clothing but her whole demeanour was not what I was used to from her, nor what she was used to from herself. But she continued nevertheless.

"Iris went doolally. It was unbearable. My son fighting for his country, his wife not able to face her responsibilities. The baby was never meant to be. A boy they said, but born blind and deaf. He would not have had a life. And he didn't have one. He soon died."

"This was Iris? She never said."

"Why would she? It's not something to be proud of."

"No shame either. There's a lot of people damaged by the war that never held a rifle."

"She's neurotic, of course. Most of the time she seems normal. Doctors gave it fancy names, connecting it to childbirth. Past-partum this, puerperal that. But in the end it was as simple as insanity. Neurotic to be kind. She still is though she hides it. It bursts out every now and then."

"What do you do?"

"I can do nothing. When she is mad she is mad. We make her rest, keep her out of company. In time she reverts to something manageable."

"She copes well," I said. "She has had so much to contend with."

"Haven't we all? She hardly cared when her husband died. But then they did not love each other."

"I love her." I felt that I had spoken significant words but she ignored them; perhaps registering them but thinking them unimportant, like a request for sugar in tea, made without words or fuss.

"It was no bad thing when the baby died. Iris could not cope, she rejected the child. Doctors gave him no chance. It was no surprise when he simply stopped breathing. Better for everyone. I shed no tears, it was relief. But Edward took it hard, as did George. With Iris it did not seem to register, she just shrank into herself."

"The baby died. But where is he buried?" There was a long silence; she studied the ground at her feet. "So we get to the point that brought you to us. I should deny you the satisfaction. But I won't."

"I ask as Iris's friend. As a friend of this family, not as a journalist."

"It was very private. No fuss. That was Iris's decision, and we backed her on that. Our lawyers took care of everything."

Another silence rested between us. If I allowed it to rest, more words would emerge before long; that much seemed clear to me, even if I had no idea what those words might be.

"Iris took the child and buried it in the woods. She had help, of course, she knew how to get her way. She marked the grave with a wooden stick. She left flowers every so often but I think that was to pretend to me that she cared. The boy, had he lived, would now be twelve but seeing nothing, hearing nothing, thinking nothing. It was better that he simply disappeared, a wartime aberration."

"So did anyone ask? Doctor, police, priest? Was no one interested in how she felt?"

"At the time it was impossible. Questions would have pushed her over the edge and we needed to maintain appearances. People respected a tragedy and they averted their eyes. So we left it unsaid. Forgotten in time. That was always the plan, to forget, to forget that anything had even happened."

"So that's what you did. You forgot, a deliberate forgetting."

"Until the animals scratched at the ground and exposed the past. You were the past too, and here was your cue to re-enter the present."

"It was strange for me. To be honest I had not kept strong memories of the time I spent here – at least not until I returned, and then memories came back. Mr Hardinge had always been good to me."

"George took a shine to you. I never understood. You weren't mine. But he loved your eagerness, so he said, the cheekiness in your smile. I never did, but you know that. I was hard on you. I don't regret that, it did you good."

"He looked after me. He gave me the job at the bank, that got me started. And I was very sad, that day he died. He said goodbye in a way that meant something, I could tell afterwards. He was a good man, I wished I could have done more."

"Make no mistake. George was no saint. None of us are. George was less saintly than most though that would not have been apparent to a boy. But I repeat, none of us were saints."

"I was young. But sometimes you understand a person's real worth better as a child. There is a childish instinct that helps."

"Oh no. You should put aside such instincts. Let me do so for you."

She paused, gathering herself, and there was part of me that now wanted to shout 'stop'. I felt a curious need to protect the memory of this man, but she was now beyond such attempts at protection. She waved her fan from side to side in front of her face, warding off the heat of embarrassment.

"George had affairs, many of them. They became apparent, at least to me. I knew him too well. But secrecy was ingrained in us."

"That was what people of your class did. It could not have been a surprise. Even though it still surprises me now."

"Our class? The thoughts of Marx always seemed nonsense to me. We simply lived the lives we were accustomed to."

"Affairs that betrayed loyalties? Kept within the family."

"I felt I had permission to retaliate, to follow an instinct without humiliating him by indiscretion. So I could match his affairs. God knows, with him away all week, I had the opportunity. I made use of that opportunity."

"There's no need for confession."

"No need but I must. I wish to. And you have become the person to tell, the one who must be the keeper of our knowledge. The connection between then and now."

I looked at her and murmured "Why me?" She looked into my eyes and we held each other's gaze.

"I liked Rupert more than George, at least in that way. But we reached a point where I had to seduce my husband to cover my traces. Otherwise questions about immaculate conception might arise. I was not ready to be the Virgin Mary. I wanted Muriel to be brought up as one of the family."

"Muriel?"

"Of course. Muriel became our daughter, as Edward was our son. Rupert slipped back into the bosom of his family. His wife had an advantage there. A large woman."

"You kept it secret?"

"George never knew. Or he turned a blind eye so that he could be free to do as he wished. But really I think he never suspected. Yet he never quite took to Muriel, as if he knew deep down she was not his."

"And Muriel?"

"There came a time when I had to tell. She was becoming close to a young man and I had to do something. Only I knew that Arthur was out of the question, I could not allow it. She could not marry her brother, for that is what he was. A half-brother, but never acknowledged."

"That was a terrible thing. And a terrible deception."

"You can deceive for good reasons. Muriel hardly spoke to me again, she hated me for making her love match impossible. Now she's lost to me. George was gone, there was no confession needed to him. Which spared him the need to reciprocate. So Muriel went away, married, had children. I have never seen my grandchildren."

"Perhaps if you had not deceived her?"

"There was no real deception. It was done for her sake. It is possible to deceive people for good reasons. I have said that, I believe that."

"But there might be bad consequences."

"Oh, life can have bad consequences. But you take what you are given. Deception can do you good. You ought to know."

She looked at me in a knowing way that puzzled me. She

was aware of my affair with Iris, it had become apparent, but I had no wish to discuss that with her. I felt a greater need than ever to liberate Iris from these clutches. Suddenly I saw Iris as the beautiful princess in need of rescue.

"Life is not a fairy tale," she said, anticipating my thought.

"You see, you tried to do something good. You succeeded."

"Out of self-interest. I am not against doing good – that is why I support the hospital. I just do not think you need to seek it out as a way of life. You have to look after yourself first, otherwise you cannot look after anyone else."

I knew I would never persuade her to think otherwise. There was little connection between us. Like all of us she was made what she is by what she was brought up to be. Things become set, like jelly, like stone, from our earliest years. We are the same but different, hard or soft but made from the same elements. But at least I now felt I could argue with her. That had not been an option in those days before the war when we had first met. There had been an expectation of deference then.

"What happened to Rupert?"

"Another casualty of war. The week before Edward, and George, of course. I think George must have realised from the tears I shed. Unusual for the senior officers to cop it but that was Rupert, he forced himself forward, against his instincts. He was a shy man but he had the garrulity that can come with shyness. I was always afraid he might blurt something out at the wrong moment. Only death could silence him with any certainty. In that sense his death was a relief. It removed the possibility of an indiscretion let loose in company."

"Do you think of him?"

She sighed; there might even have been the glimmer of a tear in her eye.

"Memory is like a disease. It can linger beyond your wishes, never allowing you to be at ease again."

"And George?"

"As I say, we were a partnership. George was not the most attractive of men, he was never good in company. Money was his best asset and he no doubt used it. He paid to satisfy his needs. That was acceptable to me and to most of those he dealt with. A transaction, just like his work at the bank. But no receipts given. Part of the job, as it were. One or two cases became trickier when the transaction was less clear-cut but settlement was possible, obligations recognised."

She locked her eyes onto mine, as if challenging me to disagree; her eyes seemed to speak 'I know' in the intensity of their gaze.

What did she know? There was more, I was sure, but my appetite for revelations was exhausted. The sun was sinking below the trees and the shadows were thickening. We both rose to our feet, and I gave her my arm to take as we made our way through the wood in the direction of the cottage. "Shivelight," she murmured to me, pointing at the slants of dying sunlight pushing through the canopy of leaves. "Beautiful word, isn't it?" We picked our way carefully through the undergrowth, trying to find what might pass for a path through the woods.

"I will say nothing about any of this," I said, as careful as my soft tread.

"I knew you would not. You could not."

"There is something I would like to do. It will not bring secrets into the open but it will help to bury them properly. I would like to speak to the lawyers, to take care of some of the unfinished business. I hope you will trust me."

"I am left with very little choice in that. I am in your hands but I think you now have nothing to gain from anything other than discretion. I will write to Mr Thomas so that you can visit him soon. Here is his card. Now *he* is a good man."

We said goodbye at the edge of the lawn; she returned to the cottage, I walked to the hall where Edna was waiting. Billy was still asleep and it was time for us to catch the train back to London.

12

LAW

Back in London next week I felt closer to understanding. It was a family mystery, buried out of sight with no real conviction, as if expecting to be discovered. But with very little sense of guilt: secrecy was their due. They felt entitled to a complicity of silence along with a place in society. Iris was the complicating factor. I loved her and could not do anything that would harm her.

I sat at the kitchen table with the typewriter in front of me. Could I write about this? Could I then sell the story? It would feel like a betrayal. But even if I couldn't sell the story I still felt obliged to complete it. What passes for professional pride dictated that; and the knowledge that Bert would expect to hear something. I tapped away at the typewriter but the words hid between the keys.

I needed to round the story out, and that meant seeing the family lawyer, Bryan Thomas. I was surprised how easily I made the appointment for the next day. It seemed he was expecting me and no doubt Mrs Hardinge had moved quickly. Perhaps I should have been faster off the mark, to get in there before a warning could be given.

The lawyer's office was just off the Strand in the Adelphi buildings. I walked up the stairs to the offices on the first floor, following the 'Thomas Brothers' board that had been slatted into the list of companies on the entrance wall. I walked straight in to the offices; there was no waiting area so I told the woman at the first desk that Mr Thomas was expecting me.

A shock of white hair gave him the initial appearance of an elderly man, but the smoothness of his pink skin made me think that he was at least twenty years younger than first appearances suggested. He offered me a cigarette from the silver box on the desk.

"How is your mum?"

"She's OK. Why'd you ask?"

"She's a lovely lady."

"So you know her?"

"I know Nellie, yes."

"How come?"

"Oh, another time. Long story. Let's get on, this is costing me money."

He rose from the desk as the tea was brought in by the woman from the front desk. Taking off his jacket revealed the blue braces underneath. He poured the tea into china cups.

"Mrs Hardinge has asked me to tell you whatever you want to know. But I'm a lawyer, so you won't expect me to tell you everything."

"How come you are their lawyer?"

He sat down in his wooden chair and stirred his tea. He looked at me in a way that seemed friendly enough.

"My own good fortune," he smiled. "I was starting out at a country solicitors. I'd been articled there. We were local and we looked after the Hardinges' legal needs, the family stuff not the company affairs. That was my training – it was all straightforward and they came to trust me. Then the war came." The thought of war seemed to demand an extra stir of the tea in his cup. "I got rejected for the army – unfit. Knowing the law came in handy. I'd feel guilty but it's the reason why I'm still alive. I could do more good by working, that's what I told myself. It wasn't a war to believe in. The only reason to be grateful for this," he rubbed his hand across his white hair, "was it made me look old. Kept away the white feather harpies."

"So were you young?"

"Old enough to do the work I had to do. At first it all seemed very straightforward, before the war, but then it became really quite complicated. There were a few deaths and the making of wills never quite kept pace, so there were things to sort out. The property too, the hall itself, and the financial problems started to get worse. But there I was at Mullings, I'd been the junior lawyer and now I was a senior but it never felt close to me. Mullings had become a dying practice after the war and I needed to get out, go to London, find my own way."

"But the Hardinges, the ones who were left, they were down in Kent?"

"They stayed with me, as clients, I stayed with them. Although the Hardinges couldn't pay their way properly any more, I stuck by them. Gratitude, in a funny way, the paying of dues as they'd helped to train me."

He leant back in his chair and drank a swig of tea. Then he went on.

"So I came up to London and set up in partnership with my brother, here in this building. He'd done his bit in the war and now needed to do something again. I was moving towards industrial cases, labour disputes, that kind of thing interested me. My brother did matrimonial and divorce. John Thomas of Thomas Brothers. It was a shared joke for years. Then we went our separate ways, it no longer fitted."

"So here you are, a London lawyer with some famous clients, taking on some cases that are noticed in the newspapers. The *Daily Mail* calls you an agitator. And none of that work seems to fit with the Hardinges. So – why?"

"As I said, I liked them. I felt I owed them something. I felt sorry for them because they'd lost so many people and so much money. I was just a young lawyer, and I felt sorry for Iris in particular. She was vulnerable and I didn't want her to face public scrutiny. Another casualty of the war."

I looked at him, and he returned my stare.

"It's this I wanted to talk about. Mrs Hardinge has told me about the baby dying. She told me you made the arrangements."

"Arrangements? Not sure what she means."

"I'm sure you do. And I'm sure she told you to answer any questions – I'm not going to do anything with the answers."

"The honourable journalist. There's a turn-up for the books."

"A friend of the family. I just want to help. Like you, I want to help Iris in particular. I just think it will be better to face the truth."

"To be honest, there's not much to face. The baby died, it was inevitable and natural. It was the war and people were concerned for the living – the ones who were away fighting – knowing that they might soon be dying. A baby like that one had no chance. So we kept it quiet, in the family. No record, no grave – there are ways." I closed my notebook to encourage him to be more forthcoming. "This was an England where money bought privileges. But it would have been a distraction, making it public, a distraction from the war effort as the family saw it. The baby's father was on the front line in France."

"He must have been upset?"

"Of course, but babies die. Even the upper classes suffer from mortality. We did nothing wrong from the point of view of being human. In fact I'm proud of it. It didn't really matter that the death was not officially registered."

"It's irregular, isn't it?"

"Perhaps, but who cares? No harm has been done to anyone. Far from it."

"You're a lawyer who has broken the law."

"No need for your newspaper morality. I don't believe you see it like that – you're better than that."

"It should – at the very least – give you pause. You have taken advantage of privileges that others would not enjoy."

"Oh really, Tom. Don't be so pompous. I hope things have changed, I hate all that now. But this is a sleeping dog, and we should let it lie. I don't know if that's a good thing to say, or the right thing, or even the legal thing, but it seems what we have to do. What we have to do is seldom a choice between good and bad. If Iris wanted something I would help.'

"She wants this. It will help to bring the episode to an end."

"If you say so, I believe you. Now you just need to believe yourself."

He drained his tea cup. There was an air of dismissal in the way he did it, and I had no wish to extend the conversation now. He opened the desk drawer and took out an envelope.

"Mrs Hardinge asked me to give you this letter before you left. She knew you were coming here but didn't have your home address. Quicker anyway, I daresay, as we were due to meet."

Curious as I was to find out what she had written to me, I wanted to do my reading without being under scrutiny. We shook hands and said goodbye in a cordial enough way. Then I walked down the stairs, not quite trusting the clanging doors of the lift, and headed to Embankment Gardens. Finding a bench there, I opened the letter.

"*Dear Thomas*

I no longer worry if I puzzle people. If I cannot follow my own instincts at my age, when can I?

I have decided that I must do more to remember those who have departed. My inclination had been to forget them because remembering only brought back grief. But you see, you have changed me. Talking to you and remembering made me feel more at ease than for many years.

I recognise that I have a family and that I must remember them, especially Edward. There is also a daughter who is lost to me, also to my regret and my grief. Another member of this family is in his grave but needs to be honoured more than he has been. I must regard you as family too, so that you will not be lost as Muriel is. You have shown me kindness, more perhaps than I deserved.

My decision that follows this change of heart is that I will go to pay my respects at Edward's grave. I will visit the cemetery in Flanders in August. The cemetery in Poperinge is big, I am told, with hundreds of gravestones. Perhaps Edward never wanted to stand out. He certainly lacked the chance to – too short a life – so now I will remember him properly, as well as others who fell with him. Mildred will come with me – she tells me that Rodgers is buried in the same mournful place.

I have made arrangements to go in the last week of August – the same month that British troops set off for their unfortunate expedition all those years ago. Iris says she will not come, she wishes to stay at home. I give you this information because I no longer wish to keep you apart.

With sincere wishes
Catherine Hardinge"

A tugboat floated past, carrying its cargo of coal. It sounded its horn as if to honour the dead. My eyes followed its slow passage up the river.

13

REMEMBER

The war memorial in Luckhurst was like many of the others that had been erected in English villages. A tall cross reached upwards from a stone plinth on whose sides were chiselled the names of the dead. I looked down the list and found Teddy's name alongside 'Corporal J.R.Rodgers' in the next column. There was a simplicity about it that I liked, an absence in the stonework of mawkish religious symbols, no doves, no hearts, no flowers, no angels.

I had suggested to Iris that we meet here. I cared less now about being seen in the village but I was not comfortable seeing Iris at the cottage with Mrs Hardinge around. Two was better than three: smaller conversations led to bigger consequences.

I had written to Iris and suggested that I would come to see her the following Wednesday. 'I hope that this will be a time when we can have a private conversation.' I was aware of sounding pompous and I didn't know if I would find the right time or the courage.

All I knew was that I was in love with Iris and I could not stop; but that my natural feelings were making me behave unnaturally. Loving her had become part of what I was. I wanted to ask her to marry me but I was not certain of her reply, I dreaded the wrong reply. In a romance we would smile and live happily ever after but life's not a romance. Bad things happen and we try to make good things out of them. But there's always a tide, up and down, and I just hoped I could catch it on the rise.

Iris approached me as I stood by the memorial. I was wearing a hat, feeling this was an 'occasion'. At the very least I would be able to take it off as a mark of respect. I raised it towards her but there was a hesitancy in Iris's walk, as if she didn't quite want to arrive.

"My goodness, your letter sounded portentous. 'A private conversation' – seems a bit of a to-do – just to say goodbye."

"Goodbye?" She surprised me. "Of course not. Far from it."

"Really? Well, that's a relief."

She had surprised me again. I should have made the most of this surprise but I wanted first to get the full story out into the open – at least between us. I had searched again for the birth record of a baby but could find nothing. Did this baby ever exist? It was as if he'd been written out of history. We will not forget him, the armistice poem insisted. This baby is one of the fallen to be remembered as much as his father: I almost wanted to shout it.

The memorial backed me up. The words were clear in their tombstone lettering: "We shall remember them" "Those who fell in the Great War 1914–1918 from this part of Kent". There were names in two columns listed alphabetically. There at the foot of the first column was Captain E.G. Hardinge followed by Reverend G.A. Jones.

Lately I'd been doing a lot of remembering. Whether it was getting older or the lagged effect of the war and all the remembrance it engendered.

"That caused a row," said Iris. "Really it did – listing them in alphabetical order. All the local Tories – lots of them. They couldn't stand it. When it was unveiled there was a frosty silence – not because of the Last Post – not out of respect for the dead. Just an inward seething – that the Alphabeticals had won."

"As opposed to?"

"Let's call them the Rankists. Ma'am was furious that Teddy was not top of the tree – leading from the front."

"Why should he?"

"Why indeed? But he was the senior ranked soldier on the list. So the argument went."

I suggested we take a walk. Keen to waste no more time I asked her about her pregnancy and the baby. She answered quickly to say that her pregnancy had been difficult from start to finish. She had an air of wanting to get this done.

"I always knew there was something wrong. The body was screaming inside me. Its screams stabbed their way – inside my head until all I could hear was screaming. Then he was born – and now everyone could hear the screaming. And they insisted – they made me hold it. It was an it. They told me it was a boy – but it wasn't."

"What was your baby called, Iris?"

"I never called it anything. It didn't live long enough for a christening – and we never announced its birth. It was like a shameful secret. George hated much of that."

"Why George?"

"He wanted to believe. He always wanted to. In this God he prayed to – with such little effect – obviously. Poor George – I liked him – he was kind to me – we would have called him George. But not this deformity – it would have been an insult. The baby – the thing – never acquired a name."

"Did you have no feelings for the baby?"

"Of course, I did – that's why I could never regret its death. It had no life."

"But you held him. He was yours."

"Mine but…It was agony. Torture. It could not even look at me. Its only working part was its mouth – and it used its mouth to scream. Then I couldn't stand it any more. Its screaming was driving me mad. The nurse had gone out of the room. I picked him up and held him – but he screamed louder. I shook him – not hard – just to say – please be quiet. So he went quiet – and I hugged him – and said thank you. I hugged him tight for the first time – then I laid him down in his cot. But I knew he was dead."

"So...Mrs H, Bryan Thomas, the vicar. It was all a conspiracy to keep it quiet."

Iris shook her head, but not in denial, more to quibble about words. "Conspirators – hardly up to that. We got all the paperwork to make it official but were told we would never have to show it. The police turned a blind eye. Paperwork was our fall-back, in case – our get out of jail card. Reverend Jones saw to the religious necessities – didn't matter to me but to our parents. Dr Brown saw to the medical side. Albert the gardener did the digging – not too well, it seems – but he was getting old, even then. Now they've all gone, all passed away."

"Apart from you. And Mrs Hardinge. And Millie."

"Millie never knew. At the time she was grieving herself. Her poor Jack caught a bullet – and Millie was away for a long time. She came back because there was nowhere else for her, what could she do? We were her family."

We had walked into the east woods, finding some shade under a leafy tree. I had hardly noticed where we were heading but suddenly I realised we were close to the tree where the baby had been buried. Iris could no longer suppress the tears. They burst out of her, like rain down tree bark in a storm, her face creased with emotion. Trying to suppress the tears she shook even harder, her whole body convulsing with the failed effort to be calm. She sobbed and shivered inside my arms.

I hadn't proposed and now I couldn't. Other emotions had

intervened to make it seem the wrong question at that time. But at least I felt strengthened in my position. We were a couple, sharing everything, and we would find the right time together soon.

"Don't abandon me. Come and stay – when Ma'am and Millie are away."

It was arranged.

A thought formed in my mind and I scribbled at it on the train back to London. My only doubt was Iris's reaction but I felt so strongly that it was the right thing to do. I had spent so much time looking at those carved gravestones and monuments. The only one lacking a memorial was this sad abandoned bag of bones who had been the child of the woman I loved. The woman who I knew needed to face this part of her past. I worked out, as the train rattled along, jogging my hand frequently, the wording for a stone memorial.

IN MEMORY
OF THE UNNAMED CHILD
A life not lived,
one of many.

It would be a present for Iris, not given until completed. First I must ask her to marry me. Then the stone tablet would be easier to share. I asked myself: has anyone ever imagined a stranger engagement gift? It would seem strange but I could not shake off the thought that it was right.

Coming out of the railway station, I turned right and headed down the Strand. I was in a hurry, one of the crowd walking fast, heading for an evening out or eager to get home as quickly as possible. It was a shock when I bumped into a man with pure white hair; we recognised each other before the opportunity for irritation flared up.

"Where are you off to?" Bryan Thomas asked.

"Home. I've Just been to see Iris."

"So you have your story."

"Yes. But I can't write it."

"Of course you can't. Too much damage to the living."

"The limits of journalism."

"But you can do more. You are a writer. And an investigator."

"Not good in either role. I need to think what I can do with myself."

Bryan looked at me. "Come and see me. Let's think about it. You could report from the courts, send people our way."

"And still write my stories?"

"Need to think about that."

"Let's think on."

I had a lot to ponder as I crossed the Strand towards Covent Garden and home.

14

READING

Mystery in the Kent woods
Police have denied any knowledge of human remains discovered in woods near the village of Luckhurst. "There is nothing to investigate," claimed Chief Superintendent T.J.Lewis. Yet locals are adamant that the bones of a baby were uncovered recently, only to disappear without explanation.

The woods surround the house once known as Hardinge Hall, now the King George V Military Hospital. The Hospital's inmates are survivors from the Great War still being treated for the consequences of their service.

These words took me an hour to write, and they resulted from months of trying to discover the facts, any facts, and then realising that the facts I knew could never be revealed. I was finding it impossible to write the story. It would not flow but still I felt obliged to try to write something that I could show to Bert Sermon to justify the time I had spent on the story. I knew he would reject it: I wanted him to reject it.

From the kitchen table drawer I lifted out the Derwent pencils. So familiar from my childhood but now hardly ever used. I wondered about drawing instead of writing but most of the pencils needed sharpening.

It was a bad time to try to write as Iris was due on the 11.30 train so it was hard for me to concentrate. She had written to tell me she was coming to London. She said she had something to show but would have only a couple of hours.

I was puzzled, anxious, fearing a further revelation that might endanger my plans for us. I walked to Charing Cross station with a sense of foreboding instead of excitement. Always with Iris I felt that the next time I saw her might be the last time.

She walked down the platform with a steady step, and there was something in her bearing that added to my fears and had me wondering. *Did she have the air of someone about to break off a relationship?* She had a business-like air about her, but there was a lightness too. She was unlike her normal self but I was never sure what Iris's normal self really was. I looked at her, with a desperate feeling, knowing that I loved her, whatever passed for normality.

She smiled and said "It's good to see you." I embraced her with relief.

"How long have you got? Where shall we go?" I asked. "The Savoy's off the agenda."

"Only for special occasions. Save it for best."

Neither of us had any money but we knew that and were comfortable with that knowledge. Lyons Corner House seemed like the best option. We could fade into the bustling anonymity of the place and not be noticed.

"The food doesn't matter," said Iris. "We just need to talk."

I always find it hard to talk when the prospect of a 'need to talk' is ahead of me. We walked up Charing Cross Road hardly knowing what to say to each other, knowing that we could not broach the subject of Iris's mission. Crossing through the Oxford Street traffic, I took her arm; it came naturally, I just wanted to look after her.

Inside Lyons Corner House Iris became more nervous as we sat down and faced each other across the tea cups. She picked up the spoon and put it down again.

"What is it then?" I asked. "You might as well get it out, the suspense is killing me."

"Don't worry – it's nothing."

"Then why the mystery?"

"It's a bit awkward, that's all. Family things I think you should know."

"Everything to do with you is a bit of a mystery. I don't know why, you just need to be straight."

"That's it – I want you to know. It's not about me. But about the people around me – parents."

"Your parents? You've never talked about them. What happened to your mum and dad?"

"Not much. Nothing much ever happened to them."

"They went to New Zealand – so you said."

"Oh no. I didn't want you to know – they popped off within weeks of each other. Like children who'd caught a disease, and the disease was death. Even if it was diagnosed as 'heart'."

I looked at her until she could not ignore my curiosity prodding her to say more.

"It was in the war. Things were going badly. There was – there were – deaths. It affected them. Everything got too much for them. The war – the business – nothing was easy."

"Teddy? His dad?"

"No. They missed that. Not by much but – it was something. They went first."

"I'm sorry."

"No need. We weren't close."

"You can never say that about parents."

"They just gave up. We give up too easily."

Iris talked about careless people, as if quoting from a book. I had no firm idea what this meant. People who didn't have any worries or people who had no compassion? Perhaps both. But

I felt people did care, in both senses. We all have worries, we all think of others.

"I'm sure your parents cared. Perhaps that's why they died."

"You never met them."

"I met people like them. Mr and Mrs Hardinge."

"They were careless too — they hardly realised what they had lost."

"I still see some good in them. I think they tried to do their best."

"Not good enough, though. It's what I wanted to show you — just so you have no illusions."

She took a letter from her handbag, handed it to me in its envelope.

"This was delivered to me — on the day George died — the day we heard about Teddy. I've never shown it to anyone else."

Suddenly it became clear that everything so far had been a preamble. This letter was the point of the meeting. I opened it with some trepidation. I saw that it was written on the notepaper of the Newcastle & Durham Bank. Turning the page I saw that the letter was signed 'George Hardinge'. The handwriting was familiar; I had read it often at the bank.

"Dear Iris
It is not my intention to burden you further but with you I have at least the hope of understanding.

I have just heard that my son is lost. My future was invested in him. A son has a special relationship with a father, stronger perhaps than that between husband and wife. I do not mean to belittle your own grief but Teddy's death has left me without hope for the future and now I find I cannot face that future.

The hope of your forgiveness — or at least understanding

— is the last hope that remains. Everything else is gone and I cannot face it any more. The Bank will die as surely as I will. Nothing can save us, nothing can stop that coming to pass.

It comes down to this, I cannot face Catherine's judgement because I know it will be harsh. You will be more forgiving, such is my hope if not expectation when I have so few beliefs left. Perhaps my last belief is that time will judge me more kindly than present times are disposed to do.

So, dear Iris, think as well of me as your heart allows."

I read the letter a second time, raising my eyes to look at Iris between the words and sentences that read like those of a guilty man before a judge, making a final plea for mercy. And as I read, as I saw the fear in Iris's eyes, I felt an irresistible compassion for this man who in desperation had entrusted his last thoughts to a young woman he hardly knew.

"I needed to share this," Iris said, her voice without expression. "It has been a burden."

I reached across the table and put my hand on hers.

"More tea?" asked the waitress. It was incongruous enough to make me laugh; I couldn't help it. 'Of course', I nodded to the waitress, even as Iris started to smile.

"It's not funny," she said.

"No, you're right. But sometimes you have to."

We were quiet while a fresh pot of tea was placed in front of us. It gave me time to think but I hardly knew what to think. Were there consequences for me and Iris in this? Unspecific fears raced through my brain, failing to form into definite concerns.

"So does this change anything?" I asked.

"It changes me," Iris replied. "At least that's my hope. I have kept this secret — it has been ten years — just one more secret among many. I wanted to share it – and you are the only person I felt I could share it with."

"Thank you. Mrs Hardinge knows nothing of this?"

"No. George was right. Why would he not tell her but tell me? Of course she would be harsh. But she was always able to cling to the possibility of an accidental death. She would judge a self-inflicted death as cowardice – and she only wanted heroes in her family."

"It was good of you. Good to do that."

"Good? Oh Tom, I am not *good*. I kept it secret in case – one day – I might need to use it. I thought it might be useful."

"In what way?"

"It might be something to use – a card to play – or so I thought. Something held by me – something to counter what Ma'am held on me. Each of us having a trump in our hand. But she didn't know that I held this one."

"If she doesn't know, how can it be useful?"

"She will find out – if she ever tries to do me down. I will use it then. The coroner's verdict on George's death was open. An accident? Possibly. Or even robbery and murder. No wallet was found on him."

"Really? Do you think that's possible?"

"Of course not – I knew – I had the letter. But none of us ever believed there was anything criminal. It was just a smokescreen to protect Ma'am's reputation – her feelings – her place in society. She could live more easily with any death but suicide."

The waitress was giving us strange looks. No doubt she wondered what we were discussing so intently and wanted us to surrender the table to better customers. I paid and we left the corner house to emerge into Tottenham Court Road, relieved to be swallowed up into the tide of strangers outside.

Again it was hard to know what to say but Iris seemed relaxed, as if a bad headache had suddenly cleared. She clung tightly to my arm and we sauntered cheerfully enough towards the British Museum. Without words we were absorbed into each other's feelings and I felt a contentment. I could sense the same in Iris, and the somewhat puzzling absence of tears.

"You don't seem too upset," I observed.

"Well, I'm not. I've had ten years of being prepared – and now it's just relief."

Before I realised we turned into Drury Lane. This was too close to home, and I would normally avoid walking this way with Iris. I became uncomfortable in these too-familiar surroundings, anxious about meeting people who knew me, who would wonder about Iris. Iris whom I kept as my own secret, not ashamed of her, perhaps ashamed more by what she might make of me in my own surroundings. I suddenly understood that Iris had steered us this way until now it was too late to turn back. Iris always liked a dare, a moth playing with flame.

There was an inevitability about the meeting. I saw my mum walking towards us down Drury Lane, with a shopping bag in her hand. She was wearing the pinafore she wore most days and, even in this hot weather, those thick stockings.

"Hello. Who's this?"

There was no avoiding it. "Mum, this is Iris."

"Are you Tommy's girl? You're lovely. I knew you would be."

"You know," said Iris, "he's told me so little about you."

"Why should he? Not much to tell."

"Oh, I'm sure there is. Let's have a cup of tea. I'm gasping."

So we went into the tea shop we were standing outside. I was surprised how well they got on together. At the very least mum and Iris shared the capacity to drink endless cups of tea.

We even shared some cakes, just to mark the occasion as Iris put it. A half hour slipped by before I had to say, looking at my watch, that Iris needed to catch a train.

So I ushered her out and took her to the station.

"You see," said Iris, "that worked out well – didn't it?"

On the way through Covent Garden with its discarded vegetable leaves, and then in Charing Cross station among the drifting clouds of steam, Iris confirmed to me what I already knew: Mrs Hardinge and Millie would be away the following weekend. We hugged each other tightly. So I would go down to the cottage to stay. I waved Iris goodbye, perhaps for the first time with some certainty that there would be another time together.

•

I went home. It was time to put the story to bed. I was getting irritated with journalism but a bit scared at such a thought. What would I do, if not earn my money in this way? Thinking more about it, I had a growing resistance to seeking news and presenting it in a way that no longer seemed fair to those involved. Behind news, and all its leanings towards drama, were stories of people, and people could be looked at and described from many different angles. I wanted to stand back and find more interesting news of people – then tell it in ways that weren't journalism.

The past has its secrets and sometimes it reveals them. When it does, they can be stranger than fiction. There were two ways of telling this story. The first was the way I had been trained. Write it under a headline like 'Mystery of the baby's bones in Kent wood.' Could I write this story? I could but did I want to? Could I live with the repercussions it would bring for people I knew and, in a sense, loved. I was not just thinking of Iris now, not just the living but the dead.

I had to write it, if only to dispose of it. So I sat at the table and clattered away at the typewriter.

"What you workin' at, Tommy?"

"Just that news story. Have a read. It's no good. You might be the only one ever to read it."

I pulled the paper out of the machine, the bell dinging as I did so, and handed my words over for reading. My mum sat down. As she read I started to feel nervous. She looked at me over the top of the foolscap paper, and I thought she must be judging me.

"I know that place, don't I? Ain't that where you went as a littl'un?" I nodded. "That place would tell a story, I imagine."

"Not to me. It seems it keeps its secrets."

"I know."

"How'd'you know?"

"Well, I did work for them for years."

Of course she had. I knew but was always inclined to forget. To be honest, I felt a little bit ashamed that my mum had been a skivy to this man who had been my first boss – and, as I remembered him saying, my benefactor.

"What was he like? Mr George Hardinge? From your point of view did he treat you well?"

"He was a good man, I always thought. And, at times, like a father to you."

She looked at me in a way that seemed to say 'don't you dare'.

This time I dared.

"Mum, you've never said anything and now I really want to know. Who was my father?"

She turned her eyes down again, as if proofreading the story. The pause got longer, stretched till I thought it would snap. Eventually she put down the paper and spoke.

"I've never felt comfortable even thinkin' about tellin' you. It was something that happened. And we never married. Was never a question even. I had to keep quiet for your sake."

"So you still leave me guessing."

"Your father was someone I knew I could never marry."

"This man forced himself on you. And I'm the result?"

"No, no, Tommy, it wasn't like that."

"That's what you seem to be saying."

"No, I didn't. He was alright. I liked him. He was a nice enough man."

"Why didn't you tell me?"

"I was never brave enough. Hoped he'd tell you, but he never did."

"So?"

She got up and walked into her bedroom, returning with a letter.

"He left a letter. I could never find the right time to give it to you. But it might as well be now – after all this."

This was a letter day, but I didn't want to call it red. I expected no consolation from this second letter from the past. The letter was written in black ink in handwriting that immediately seemed freshly familiar, on paper with the heading of Hardinge Hall.

To Master Thomas Shepherd
At the right time

Dear Tommy
I always feel I am one small misstep from my own demise. So I am writing to set the record straight.

If you are reading this letter, you will have received it from your mother. I am sure you love your mother. In my way I have loved her too. And I hope she had some feelings for me. You are the evidence for that.

She will explain more, now that I have said the main thing. You are my son.

That might be a shock – I'm sure it will. I have stayed as close as I could without risking the exposure that could spoil everything. The collapse of my life would have done you no favours. I have tried to provide for you and your mother. It might not have been enough but credit me for trying.

I have watched you grow up. A fine boy soon to be a fine man. You are a source of pride to your mother and I know you have always been close, and will stay so. It always pained me to see you, to be near you, and not be able to acknowledge you fully, not even in that time when you became part of our family in this house.

That time has long gone. By the time you read this I might also be gone but at least, I console myself, my going will not have been a great cause of distress to you.

I wish you a happy life
Your father
George Hardinge

I was numbed by the letter. Now that I knew I felt that I had always known in some deep recess of my heart. I remembered moments, fleeting moments, when he had smiled and shown affection. Then, as we always did, we had moved in different directions, resuming the courses of life that had been set by – what? Was it tradition, social practice, shame, embarrassment or just an unwillingness to take responsibility? I felt myself getting angrier as the knowledge sank in, as I felt deprived of so much that I could not yet fully fathom.

The worst thought then flashed like a scudding cloud

across my mind. *Iris.* What would this mean for Iris and me? A dark thought of incest rose but a further moment's thought dismissed it. There were precedents, including those dredged from my school history lessons. Henry VIII's Spanish wife had first been his brother's. But this made me realise all the more clearly that if Iris was a connection between us, her husband and I shared a family relationship. I had acquired and lost a brother in the same discovery.

"I'm glad it's out at last, Tommy. It's been hard."

I could not be angry with her, not with my own mother. She had been the main one to suffer. My birth had blighted her life. But she had stood by me, had brought me up with love – so how could I feel any less love towards her now?

She put a cup of tea in front of me. We place so much faith in the restorative power of tea. I thought of drinking tea with Iris earlier in the day, and it made me smile. This discovery would change nothing. And mum, suddenly released from years of concealment, seemed willing to say more.

"He was a good sort really. For a year we were close, till you came along. But he did his duty by you. He couldn't own up but he did his bit, with money and that."

"Really?"

"It's how we got by. We kept this flat, we always had food. You got an education and a job – he saw to that. He got you the job at the bank then arranged for you to be an apprentice on the newspaper. Funny how the newspaper led to this."

"Funny indeed. Did you – did you get on? Did you like each other?"

"Georgie, that's what he liked me to call 'im. So I did. For a year we was together just about every night of the week, the flat in his office. Bought me clothes, I kept them there. Then in the mornin' it was my shift startin' by making the bed, cleaning the room, then working my way through the offices, mop and bucket, till Ellen and I joined up halfway down."

I would need time to adjust, to rewrite my own life story, to start a new one. To sweep things away, scrub things down, to give everything a polish. The thought of Iris gave me every incentive to do so.

15

FLAMES

We were in Iris's narrow bed, my hand resting on her breast, when I finally asked: "Will you marry me?"

I had been enjoying the closeness of her, the sweet smell of her *eau de cologne*, the taste of her on my lips, the shining patina of perspiration on her shoulders. My nervousness might have made my question inaudible in the dryness of my mouth. Perhaps I had just whispered the question, perhaps she had not even heard it. I repeated it, louder: "Iris. Will you marry me?"

She laughed. She looked at me to see if I was laughing. My face remained serious, probably anxious.

"Oh dear."

I leant on my elbow, staring into her face. "I mean it."

"What does it mean, though? Will we have to change – from fucking to making love?"

"I hope so."

I took this as acceptance though I would press her later to be clear. We made love. It seemed the thing to do. Now more than ever I enjoyed her being so close, our two bodies as one. Lips joined, chest to chest, the film between her skin and mine, the faint sound of squelching, the sound that made us both laugh, the laughter that brought us even closer together. Lying there, fingers entwined, my main cause for anxiety behind me yet smiling at me, it became easier to talk from sheer relief.

Then I noticed her tears. With Iris they could come with the suddenness of a spring shower. The tears came in a flood but they seemed necessary. I kissed her eyelids to release them further, not to stop them. I was learning how to deal with Iris; there was no point in trying to turn back the emotion at its height, just roll with it, wait for it to pass.

It was easy to be together; words no longer seemed to matter quite as much. She hadn't yet said 'Yes', not in so many words. Not that Yes amounted to many. But we understood each other better, despite the presence or absence of words. She became quiet again, the tears dried.

"How about it then?" I asked, pushing aside the sheet to see her face better.

"You are serious? Oh, I know you are. You are a serious man – too much so at times. You make me cry."

"Only when you need to."

"Will you make me laugh?"

"I keep trying. Will you marry me?"

"If you mean it," she replied. "Yes." And we both laughed.

Now we could talk about all those things that were shared, that had once threatened to separate us. The two letters. She had taken my news – the news of my newly discovered father – with very little surprise. "Oh, isn't it funny?" she had said. "Will you tell Ma'am?"

"I will not. How could I?"

"I would love to see her face. Except I'm pretty sure she knows."

"She knows? How?"

"We all did. We all suspected. Why would he invite you down to stay for two weeks? You, the child of the office cleaner. As I said, careless people."

"Everyone knew? Everyone but me? Everyone but the one who ought to know."

"Come on Tom, don't get aerated. In this family – and now you're one of it – we have secrets, and we keep them."

I was annoyed but I didn't dare show it. I was certainly not going to risk breaking my so recent engagement, if that is what it was. "What a mess," I breathed out, contenting myself with the mildest show of emotion.

"You'll get used to it. We all live with the lies of the past. It's what the English are really good at. That's what we mean by good – it's nothing to do with morality."

Now I wanted to know more. We had never spoken much of our first meetings, so many years ago, when age had seemed such a gulf between us, me a boy, she soon to be a bride, and there seeming to be no possible connection between us. She laughed, and I could understand why, when I said I had loved her even then. That I had felt she liked me at least; a liking that seemed daring when Mrs Hardinge was so set against me.

"She saw you – still does – as a taunt," she said. "This ragamuffin who showed up for a fortnight. For no good reason – for no good reason that she could understand anyway. Unless – and she wondered – she must have wondered. So she disliked you from the start. Then it became worse. Others liked you – Teddy liked you. You became the messenger – between what was good in him and what was bad. She knew about that too – it was stronger than suspicion in Teddy's case."

"I know she knew about Rosie. Not that she'd ever call her by name."

"And she suspected you too. She suspected who you were – but no one ever said. George denied anything wrong. He would. He had to. Otherwise his home life would become even more insufferable. But she didn't know your mother. So she didn't – couldn't – confront her. That would have been beneath her. *She* would have been beneath her. She found comfort in that at least – and suspicions left to fester became a comfort too. They fed her rancour – and she thrived on it – in her own mind. It gave more purpose to her life – to poison the lives of others."

"She's never been too bad with me. Despite everything. After all I was there in her own home and she never kicked me out – even if she suspected who I was, and that couldn't have been easy for her."

"Don't fool yourself. That fortnight you were irrelevant really. *You* hardly crossed her mind. George and Ma'am wanted one thing – one thing only – it's what united them. And so I ended up marrying Teddy – that's what they wanted. Not sure I did but – I had no choice. Not at that time, not at that age."

"I could see that. It upset me. All I could do was go deeper into the woods to escape, deeper into the book he gave me to read."

"I remember you always reading. What was the book?"

I found myself talking about *The Wind in the Willows*. How did that come about on this day of all days? But I had always remembered that book with such vividness, thought of its characters with such affection. That time was gone but in my memory it was within touching, feeling distance.

"My dear Mole," she laughed. "I'd rather you were one of the Magi – more romantic." She lifted up a pamphlet of poetry on her bedside table, showed me the title *Journey of the Magi*.

We decided to get up. A walk in the woods would seem like a celebration, a connection between present and past. After all the woods had brought us together all those years ago.

"Only if you look at them from the inside. From the outside they were a barrier. The wild woods. Come on, we might find the weasels and stoats have taken over."

We dressed but only lightly. In those former days, the days before the war, the lack of formal wear would have been frowned on. This world now wears its seriousness more casually. But we knew the woods would be empty, we would not encounter anyone else, and we felt free to wander without the ties and laces and buttons that might once have constrained us. Even so we would not have offended the sensibilities of a gentleman water rat. *Vagabonds*, he'ld have said. It was simply a time to feel liberated from so many worries, the anxieties of uncertainty, time to reach out to the future that we could share.

Of course there was the reality of the tree and, *did I imagine it?*, the different colour of the earth beneath it. Yes, I did imagine it but there was no denying that this had been the burial ground of Iris's baby and I felt the shadow passing and a ghostly rustling in the canopy of leaves above us. It seemed the right time to mention my plan for a memorial stone.

"Just a simple one. Perhaps for the church graveyard. For your baby and for all the babies deprived of life by the war."

Iris nodded, saying nothing. I could not tell if her silence was acquiescence or just a numbness of emotions. We had experienced the highs and lows in the last few hours, and it was best to walk on. I took her hand and we walked back in the direction of the lawn fronting the hospital. There we saw a group of convalescent soldiers taking a circular walk around the perimeter, each with a hand on the shoulder of the man in front.

"One of them's Billy," I said. "I'd rather he didn't see me. He might be upset."

Iris was still not speaking. I was relieved to enter the front door of the cottage and find ourselves inside, its air made cool by the stone walls. I went to make a cup of tea – that was my mother's training. And gradually the coldness that had seeped into us started to thaw and by the evening, with the sun sinking behind the trees, we were sitting like a married couple, comfortable with each other. I found things to eat, bread and ham and butter, and some ginger beer, and I felt like Mole at a picnic.

With the deepening shadows smudging the corners of the room, we chatted easily in the twilight. The time passed, gliding smoothly by. The only dilemma was whether we dared that night to sleep in the double bed. We decided against. It just seemed sacrilegious; we might arouse too much of the past.

But perhaps it meant that we slept more lightly than we might otherwise have done. Every time one of us turned over, it seemed a big disruption. But neither of us wanted to be disentangled from the other. I looked at her and knew that I loved her. I kissed her eyelids and said *Goodnight* once more. I must have drifted into sleep and dreams. But my dream was as deep as my sleep was shallow. I was running away from danger with the noise of bells loud in my ears, running fast but desperate to be faster, plunging into the darkness of churning sea then treading water gulping and spluttering and drowning and tossed between waves with the ship's bell clanging ever louder and more urgently with a white light sweeping across the surface *justabouttobeengulfed…*

I woke with some relief to find Iris sleeping peacefully alongside me. My wide-open eyes stared into the darkness that was unexpectedly bright. *Surely it could not be daylight already?* The windows were rattling in their frames as if a storm was about to break, and then I heard the clanging of bells. Real bells not dream bells. I slipped out of bed to see what might be happening.

I went to the window, pulling aside the curtains. I saw the lawn cast in an orange glow that was puzzling until my eyes shifted right towards silhouetted figures huddled in groups or running here and there. The cause for their obvious panic became clear when my eyes reached Hardinge Hall itself. There it was, but not like itself. The house was on fire, flames were soaring above the roof tiles into the deep blue of the night sky, spreading an orange smear that obliterated the stars.

I recognised the need to help so I quickly put on some clothes. Iris was sleeping, exhausted and now able to stretch out without my presence restricting any movements in her dreams. I shook her awake. The clanging of the fire bells should have woken her but her sleep was deep. She murmured drowsily. "The hall's on fire," I shouted, running down the stairs.

Outside, Hardinge Hall was ablaze and it seemed to me it was already beyond saving. I had to see if I could help so I ran towards the roaring brightness of the fire. The closer I approached, pushing against a hot curtain of air, the greater the heat from the flames that were leaping up from the roof. As I ran across the lawn towards the house I wondered what might have caused this. I had reported on many fires and I knew the likely causes. It had started perhaps with a spark from a struck match, or from the contact of a bedsheet with a gas mantle, or the running of flame down the fuse of a faulty wire beneath the floor boards. An accident. Or perhaps the act of someone who was bored or vengeful or simply curious.

I looked on, impotent with astonishment, with fury. The fire had taken hold too long ago and too rapidly to reverse its blazing progress. The clamour of fire bells offered a prospect of respite but the clear sight of the hall engulfed in flames extinguished the fleeting ringing of hope. Yet I ran, to see what might be done, to help and to not be called a coward.

When I drew closer I saw the white nightgowns of patients like agitated ghosts and there in the middle of them was Billy, a figure of detached calm in a tableau of Biblical panic. Our eyes met and, so it seemed to me, he smiled.

"Scared out of their wits," shouted the fireman. "Move them away."

Billy didn't want to be moved. He had his mind set on rescue, there was a determination in his movements, his body bent to that purpose as he headed into the inferno. "No," I shouted after him. I should have run to stop him. But Billy was fast; there was no one faster. "No, no, come back."

He came back, bringing with him a limping, hysterical man from the roaring flames, his white cotton shirt charred black by the fire that Billy had beaten out, his own hair singed by the sparks that floated off the burning curtains. Others took over the task of beating down the fire on the man's body.

Looking upward I saw a face at the window where once I had looked out as a boy. A face was pressed to the glass, a mouth shaped into an O. You could see but not hear the panic that emerged from deep inside.

And when my eyes lowered again, I watched a figure plunge back into the burning building, too hot and forbidding for any of us who stood in mute horror, appalled at the destruction of fire and distraught by our own shortfall of courage. The figure, I knew it must be Billy, pushed his way inside, knowing there were more men in there, too disabled or too frightened to make their own exits, and as we watched him we knew this was now the end as a mighty crack and then an explosion, followed by a fireball of blinding light brought the upper storey crashing down into the lower floor. A sudden eruption of flames set off billowing clouds of smoke, flashes of colours as different materials caught alight and intensified the incandescence.

I touched the low brick wall that ran across the lawn and had to snatch away my hand. I felt my skin blistering as I touched the surface. The firemen were pointing their hoses at the blaze but, it seemed to me, with no great expectation of dampening the fire. Looking around at those who had escaped, shivering in their nightshirts despite the heat, we were all paralysed by what we saw, feverish with the waves of hot air and emotion. When another section of the house collapsed, wood and brick and plaster from above landed with a huge puffing of dust, and I thought it must reduce the flames, but seconds later the licks of fire rose from the rubble, as if renewed by fresh energy, leaving the acrid stench of burning and the piercing screams of those just-rescued, covering the silence of those trapped in the conflagration.

The fire had become a pyre. There was a pungency in the air. I wondered if it was the smell of roasting flesh.

"Is anyone still inside?" I asked the fire chief, but he strode past me without answering. Now I was in the middle of a group of half a dozen men wrapped in blankets. I didn't recognise them.

"Did you see Billy?" I asked. "Did any of you see Billy?"

No one answered, each in his own trembling world, the place that had been their home disappearing to a shimmering shell. The firemen persevered with their water hoses, creating streams of steam to mingle with the black smoke. A doctor was there, doing what he could to comfort the men in blankets.

"Do you know if Billy Tree got out?" I asked him.

"No idea. See for yourself. These are the ones I know about."

"He's not here."

"If he's not here now, he's a goner. He could have gone back. Some of them did. We brought them out and they rushed back in. For them it was home – and they didn't want to leave home."

I turned around and there was Iris among the shocked ranks of onlookers. Her face was streaked with soot and tears, and I realised that mine must be the same. Her eyes seemed to shine white in the artificial darkness of her face. She said nothing, what could anyone say? I felt foolish for talking to myself: "Billy went back in. He had no chance."

My words were overheard by the man in the dark police uniform. "He couldn't bear to leave it."

"He was trying to save the others," I shouted.

"A brave man. No coward he."

"You could've said that to him when he could hear it." My anger was stoked by the sight before us and the memories it contained. Memories of Billy in white hurtling into the fiery furnace that for years had been his home. *We will remember.* Billy had performed his last act of wartime service, he had died a hero, at least in my eyes.

I drew Iris to me. As I did so there was the loudest explosion yet, a thunderous crack that sent the remains of the upper storey crashing to ground level. Billy had perished, along with others, men tested in war who had come back, but come back damaged.

"Once I lived there," said Iris to me. Her statement was true – indeed I could have said the same – but it was still surprising. Because now the grand house that had been Hardinge Hall was laid low, reduced to crackling campfires among the rubble and ashes. The men in blankets were being led away towards ambulances. It was a time to weep, and we wept, the tears trickling down faces grimed by smoke.

The night passed, we hardly moved, staring into the ruin. In the morning, with the sky's greyness tinged with the smouldering from below, there was still a glow in the rubble, the embers now with nothing left to ignite. I became aware that many more people were now moving around while we stood stationary: doctors and nurses dealing with the injured, firemen dampening down the fire that had almost spent itself. There was a sour smell in the air, a pricking at our eyes, as we huddled now at the edge of the woods under the fringing shelter of the trees.

"What a sight these trees have seen," Iris said. "Silly, I know, but…"

"They won't have a tale to tell. Tomorrow morning they'll just look the same, as though nothing happened."

"Perhaps nothing did."

As the heat from the fire subsided, we began to feel the chill of the new dawn, drawing even closer for comfort, but unwilling to retreat into the haven of the cottage. We sat on the bench outside the window, among the flowers of the garden, among the hollyhocks and buddleias and anemones, and I remembered not the details but the feelings from earlier times when I had sat there.

"Nothing more to be done," I whispered to Iris. "Shall we go in?"

She shook her head. "Don't know what Ma'am will think — when she sees it."

"She'll think it's a punishment for an evil done. An act of revenge. But we'll never agree what was being punished — or who."

Iris had her eyes closed. Her face was so dirty, I needed to clean it — it seemed the kindly thing to do. I took the handkerchief from my pocket and dipped it in the rainwater barrel, then wiped the grime from around her eyes and ears and mouth. Her skin glowed a little, not from the now-distant fire but from the sun rising before us. I don't know who said it, Iris or me, or whether we just passed the thought between us. *Memories don't go up in flames. Houses do. We can rebuild houses, memories stay alive. We will remember.*

We were not ready to go inside the cottage; at least that was the cue I took from Iris. We rose from the bench and walked back into the woods, hand in hand. As we walked we went deeper into the trees and the past. The further we walked the further from the harsh sounds of that night, and the sweeter the sounds of the birds singing.

Now we could share the past, and the present and the future. We had something before us both in the darkness of these trees and in the morning light streaming through their leaves.

All this had started as a story that I wanted to write for the newspaper. It was my job. Then I discovered I could not tell the story in that way. It was my life. Telling that story would betray people I loved and the memories I had of them, the good messages they continued to bring from the past.

The story still mattered but it had reshaped itself. It needed to be told, if only for my sake. I agonised over it. I picked it up, I put it down. Years passed.

In the end I wrote it. Reader, you are holding it.

•••

JOHN SIMMONS is an independent writer and consultant. He was a director of Newell and Sorrell from 1984 until the merger with Interbrand in 1997. He headed many large brand programmes with companies as diverse as Waterstone's, Royal Mail, Air Products and the National Theatre. He established Interbrand's verbal identity team before he left in 2003. Since then he has continued to work with the widest range of companies and organisations on branding, consultancy and writing projects.

John has run "Writing for design" workshops for D&AD and the School of Life. He also runs "Dark Angels" workshops, residential courses in remote retreats, which aim to promote more creative writing for business www.dark-angels.org. uk. He has written a number of books on the relationship between language and identity, including "The Dark Angels Trilogy" – *We, Me, Them & It*, *The Invisible Grail* and *Dark Angels*. These books are now published in updated editions by Urbane. His books helped establish the practice of tone of voice as a vital element of branding.

He's a founder director of 26, the not-for-profit group that champions the cause of better language in business, and has been writer-in-residence for Unilever and King's Cross tube station. In 2011 he was awarded an Honorary Fellowship by the University of Falmouth in recognition of 'outstanding contribution to the creative sector'. John is on the Campaign Council for Writers' Centre Norwich as Norwich becomes the first English City of Literature.

Other books are *26 Ways of Looking at a Blackberry*, about the creative power of constraints, and *Room 121: A Masterclass in Business Writing*, co-written with Jamie Jauncey as an exchange over 52 weeks. In June 2011 John's first work of fiction, *The Angel of the Stories*, was published by Dark Angels Press, with illustrations by the artist Anita Klein.

He initiated and participated in the writing of a Dark Angels collective novel *Keeping Mum* with fifteen writers – the novel was published by Unbound in 2014. In 2015 he published the novel *Leaves* with Urbane Publications, followed by historical novel *Spanish Crossings* in 2017.

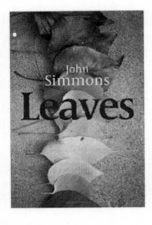

LEAVES
by John Simmons
ISBN: 9781909273771
£8.99 • pbk • 224pp

'John Simmons is the best writer you think you haven't read. In fact he is one of the architects of the language of our daily lives. With his novel Leaves the secret is now out.'
Caroline McCormick, former Director, PEN International

Ophelia Street, 1970. A street like any other, a community that lives and breathes together as people struggle with their commitments and pursue their dreams. It is a world we recognise, a world where class and gender divide, where set roles are acknowledged. But what happens when individuals step outside those roles, when they secretly covet, express desire, pursue ambitions even harm and destroy? An observer in the midst of Ophelia Street watches, writes, imagines, remembers, charting the lives and loves of his neighbours over the course of four seasons. And we see the flimsily disguised underbelly of urban life revealed in all its challenging glory. As the leaves turn from vibrant green to vivid gold, so lives turn and change too, laying bare the truth of the community. Perhaps, ultimately, we all exist on Ophelia Street.

SPANISH CROSSINGS
by John Simmons

ISBN: 9781911583806
£8.99 • pbk • 360pp

'From the very first words this is a beautifully written novel.'
Vesna Goldsworthy, author Gorsky, professor of creative
writing, UEA

Spanish Crossings is an epic tale of love, politics and conflict,
with the yearning but elusive possibility of redemption. A
woman's life has been cast in shadow by her connection to the
Spanish Civil War. We meet Lorna in Spain, 1937 as she falls
in love with Harry, a member of the International Brigade who
had been at Guernica when it was bombed. Harry is then killed
in the fighting and Lorna fears she might have lost her best
chance of happiness. Can she fill the void created by Harry's
death by helping the child refugees of the conflict? She finds
a particular connection to one boy, Pepe, and as he grows up
below the radar of the authorities in England their lives become
increasingly intertwined. But can Lorna rely on Pepe as he
remains deeply pulled towards the homeland and family that
have been placed beyond his reach? Coming through the war,
then the post-war rebuilding, Lorna and Pepe's relationship will
be tested by their tragic and emotive history.

Urbane Publications is dedicated to
developing new author voices, and publishing
fiction and non-fiction that challenges,
thrills and fascinates.
From page-turning novels to innovative
reference books, our goal is to publish what
YOU want to read.

Find out more at
urbanepublications.com